Bone Dust

By

Rick Maier

This book is a work of fiction. Places, events, and situations in this story are purely fictional. Any resemblance to actual persons, living or dead, is coincidental.

ISBN: 1-4107-3152-9 (e-book)
ISBN: 1-4107-3151-0 (Paperback)

Library of Congress Control Number: 2003091904

This book is printed on acid free paper.

Printed in the United States of America
Bloomington, IN

www.rickmaier.com

1stBooks - rev. 04/29/03

Dedication

To Matthew, Madison, and Morgan, my wonderful children who endured all the time I spent on this work. The three Ms provided me with lots of material and inspiration.

Author's Note

I started writing *Bone Dust* in 1997 when a mid-life urge to publish converged with a desire to share some of my wonderful experiences working and living in Macon, Georgia. A PBS documentary on the 1918 influenza pandemic provided the needed framework for the story.

The events of September 11, 2001 had an eerie similarity to some of the events in my manuscript. Following 9/11, I modified some of the thoughts and reactions of the characters, but other similarities to dates and events are purely coincidental.

RM

The youthful vigor that fills his bones will lie with him in the dust.

Job 20:11

Chapter 1

Foreboding Chants

Saturday, September 12

"Daddy, where are all the dead guys?"

Five-year-old Amy Spiker stood next to her Dad on top of the Great Temple Mound. The earthen pyramid stood guard over the city below just as it had for centuries before the Europeans discovered Georgia. The chants from within the mound rose skyward unnoticed.

"You said we would see people bones!" she said, apparently disappointed that skeletal remains weren't lying about on the grass plateau like seashells on the beach.

"So you want to see dead guy bones, do you?" Mike Spiker asked, playing along. Amy must have recalled something about the excavation of Indian remains in the documentary film they had just seen at the visitor center.

Just the mention of bones evoked an image that Mike had been carrying on the edge of his consciousness for years now. The heavy gray soot from the collapsed towers had rolled down the Manhattan streets like an avalanche, a mixture of pulverized metal, glass, plastic…and bones, human flesh and bones. Mike snapped back from the nightmarish memories at the sound of his daughter's voice.

"Well, where are they, Daddy?" Amy cocked her head and placed her hands squarely on her hips.

"It's been so long since Indians lived here, their bones have turned to dust. When the Indians did live here, they buried their dead in the Funeral Mound over there," he said, pointing a few hundred feet in the distance.

Trying hard to hold her attention, Mike pointed further away toward the city of Macon. "And over there is the hospital where you were born. There's the coliseum where we go to see the circus. And…" Mike looked down and Amy was admiring the way her Mom had painted her fingernails.

"Oh well, spotting landmarks from high ground must be a guy thing," Mike mumbled to himself, continuing to study the countryside like a sailor from a crow's nest.

Standing here, it was easy to understand why the Indians built their city at this bend in the Ocmulgee River—great hunting, fishing, farming, and a wonderful lookout. A short distance away, the Macon skyline appeared as blocks of brick buildings topped with steeples and towers amidst a grid of wide, sun-lightened asphalt boulevards. Beyond the city in every direction lay a sea of rolling hills covered thickly with pines.

Ocmulgee National Monument held a mystical grip on Mike. It fulfilled some romantic connection to human life in its most honest and simple form. It was a comfortable, natural place, like returning home after several days of being out of town.

Each time he climbed up the big mound he could sense a connection with the ancients. They weren't really voices, but a kind of rhythmic chant. Even if Mike could describe the sounds, he would never tell anyone about them. What would people think of a corporate executive who heard the voices of dead Indians?

Standing very still, Mike breathed in the chant that swelled up from deep in the earth and across the centuries. But today's expressions were nothing like the mellow choir voices from rain dances or tribal celebrations in the past. This was different—like screams of agony or torture.

Mike often wondered about the demise of the Mississippian tribes who remained peaceful even in the face of bullying from Spanish and English explorers. The Indians lacked the immunities of their European counterparts who had for centuries been exposed to the germs and viruses carried by their livestock and domesticated animals.

Mike shivered despite the warm Georgia air.

Tearing his attention away from the wails of the earth, Mike found Amy busy provoking a colony of fire ants by kicking the edges of their sandy mound. "Amy, don't get too close to those ants."

Mike hoped that Amy would stay occupied so that he could get back to the ancient cries, but she was headed his way. The connection was broken.

"Daddy, where are we going to eat lunch? Can we go to the bagel store?"

Mike flinched a little when the kids spoke of bagels and other things considered Yankee. The Deep South is the land of grits and sweet tea, not bagels and cappuccino, he figured. Being a Marylander allowed Mike to enjoy the best things, Confederate and Union, but he made every effort to fit into the adopted Southern culture he had learned to love.

"Sure, baby, we can go anywhere you want. It's your date." Mike smiled at his daughter, but couldn't shake a growing uneasiness.

She looked up at him, flashing shiny white teeth and deep dimples. He was struck by how the sun made Amy's blond hair, tanned skin, and light brown eyes glow with slightly different shades of golden amber. His wife Courtney was right. Her little finger was just big enough to wrap Mike completely around it.

"Daddy, I have to go to the potty," Amy reported. "Number one."

"Are you sure you have to go?" Mike asked. "Can you hold it until we get to the bagel store?"

"No, I need to go now," she said drawing out "now" into two syllables.

"Okay, let me hold your hand, baby." Mike grasped Amy's hand tightly as they descended several flights of wooden steps down the side of the mound.

They drove to the visitor center where Mike accompanied Amy to the restroom. She could go by herself, but Mike liked to help her whenever possible because she was too young to understand all the hazards, especially the ones that lurked on seemingly clean surfaces.

"Let me help you wash your hands, sweetheart. I'll show you how doctors scrub their hands really good. They use a lot of soap and elbow grease to get rid of all the germs that we can't even see."

"Are germs greasy, Daddy?" asked Amy as she tried to look at her elbows. Mike chuckled. He quickly changed the subject to avoid what could become a barrage of unanswerable questions.

As they were getting into the car to leave, Mike saw the camera on the seat. Courtney had given him firm instructions to take pictures of the kids and their various outings.

"Amy, we need to go get a picture. Let's go down that path and ask somebody to take a shot of us in front of an Indian mound, okay?"

Without a word Amy ran around the car and down the path. Mike had no problem finding a lady who was happy to snap a close-up of the two of them with the Earth Mound in the background.

As they walked back to the car, Mike couldn't help but glance over his shoulder at the mounds. He squeezed his daughter's hand tightly, smiling down at her as he suppressed another shudder.

+

Driving home on Interstate 75, Amy joined Mike in one of their favorite pass-times—singing old Beatles tunes into make-believe hand mikes:

I'll pretend that I'm kissing the lips I am missing
And hope that my dreams will come true
And then while I'm away I'll write home everyday...

Suddenly, Mike grabbed the wheel with both hands and hit the brakes hard to avoid hitting a car that had pulled in front of them. He looked into the rear-view mirror to check on Amy, but she remained undaunted by his evasive driving maneuvers. He glanced back again to make sure her seat belt was fastened.

Mike let off the accelerator and fell into the slower flow of traffic. Happy and content that their next stop would be the bagel store, Mike and Amy resumed:

And I'll send...
all my loving to you.

While Mike fretted over collapsed towers, plagues, ant attacks, clean hands and close calls, he had no way of knowing that the biggest threat to Amy and everyone else he loved was developing at this very moment, half a world away.

Chapter 2

Lightning Strikes

Saturday, September 5 (Philippines time)

Francisco Maylon watched as his eight-year-old son struggled to lift the pail of grain and pour it into the trough inside the pigpen. The boy's younger brother and sister stood next to him wanting to help, but the pail was too heavy and the trough too high. The kids giggled loudly at the sight of several hungry pigs, anxiously waiting for the little humans to clear out so that they could eat.

Francisco worked every day in the high heat and humidity. The farm was always neat and orderly and he valued every square foot. Although his father had purchased the tractor and some of the other equipment decades before, it was carefully maintained and in like-new condition.

The ten-hectare farm had been in Francisco's family for three generations. The property was located outside Batangas City, a town on the Philippine Island of Luzon, a two-hour drive south of Manila. Over the years, the growth of resorts surrounding the port of Batangas slowly consumed the coconut and banana groves and left sprawling neighborhoods for the people who worked in the nearby hotels.

Though developers had offered Francisco a handsome sum for his property, he never even considered their proposals. He wanted to continue his father and grandfather's proud tradition for as long as the farm could provide a comfortable standard of living for his family.

The seductive prospect of the money and the possibilities it offered did, however, tempt even Francisco on occasion. He sorely missed the peace and quiet of living in what was once a remote, rural area. His new neighbors in the surrounding areas often complained loudly about the sounds and smells of the animals. But the farm provided Francisco and his family with a wholesome family environment. They ate the freshest produce, dairy products, and meat. The kids shared the chores, but Francisco made certain that farm chores did not interfere with their education.

The combination of Chinese, Spanish, Muslim, and American influences made Filipinos a generally industrious and happy people. The closing of U.S. bases at Clark and Subic Bay in the early 1990s made the nation fully independent, but the discovery of an al-Qaida cell in the southern island of Basilan brought American troops back to the region periodically for training missions.

The long-term economic prospects for Francisco's land were strong despite the monsoons and occasional stirrings of the nearby Taal volcano. A strong domestic economy and proximity to Indonesia and Malaysia offered strong growth prospects for his chicken business.

Unique in a land almost completely destroyed during World War II, Francisco and his family lived in a comfortable home nearly 100 years old. Behind the residence were two large poultry houses containing up to 20,000 chickens each. The old structures had been recently outfitted with the latest technology for raising poultry.

Chicks were purchased from a hatchery on one of the southern islands and sold sixteen weeks later to a processor in Manila. In addition to poultry, Francisco raised pigs and a few cows. The eight-hectare field in the back of the property contained a variety of crops to help feed both the livestock and Francisco's family.

+

That evening, a fierce thunderstorm swept over Francisco Maylon's farm. When lightning struck the roof of one of the chicken houses, the wooden structure ignited and the corner of the building was soon engulfed in flames.

Francisco woke up suddenly from the echo of thunder and the drumming of heavy rain. Fearing that one of his buildings had been struck, he dressed quickly and went outside in the pouring rain.

Soon Francisco discovered the burning chicken house and ran back to tell his wife to keep the children at a safe distance while he fought the fire.

Back outside he grabbed a garden hose. After a steady dousing, the water finally extinguished the flames. Francisco's heart stopped pounding only after he realized that the farm would be saved.

His relief would be short-lived.

As he surveyed the damage, he discovered the charred remains of several hundred chickens burned to death in the fire. Hundreds more suffocated when the birds panicked and crowded into the far end of the building, smothering each other. A few birds escaped through a hole in the building caused by the fire. Francisco wearily tacked tarpaper to the scorched wood studs to seal the hole and avert further escapes.

Exhausted, he went to bed for a few hours of rest, with no choice but to wait until morning to continue the repairs.

+

Unbeknownst to Francisco, the latest batch of chicks were infected with a much higher than normal concentration of type-A influenza. As he slept fitfully, a unique set of conditions kindled by the fire enabled the viruses to mutate. It was an extremely unlikely combination that created the tragically ideal situation—the perfect temperature introduced to a large quantity of virus ready to slightly change their composition. Molecules in the virus particles near the intense heat of the fire performed a deadly metamorphosis into a new, virulent strain of influenza. The never before seen virus multiplied into trillions of contagion in less than two hours.

The wet, warm, partially burned remains of the chickens created a perfect incubator for the new virus. In a few hours, multitudes of particles were airborne in search of new cells to infect. The gentle breeze of the warm September evening carried the viruses directly to the nearby pens that held the pigs. If the pens had been much farther away, the virus would have perished in the open air. The pigs, which were sleeping soundly after having been woken up hours earlier by the thunderstorm and fire, felt nothing as an army of microorganisms invaded their bodies.

+

Physically exhausted and emotionally drained from the trauma of the previous evening, Francisco and his family woke up early the next morning anxious to assess the damage and restore order. The putrid smell of smoke and the stench of dead chickens hovered in the damp morning air. The chickens that had escaped from the building during the fire were running wildly around the farm. Francisco began repairs on the building and disposed of the dead birds. As he worked, the airborne viruses from the pigs invaded his body.

The microscopic viruses entered through Francisco's nostrils and successfully navigated their way to his throat where they began the process necessary to imitate the protein in a human cell in order to invade it. In a few hours his throat would become raw as the viruses efficiently cloned themselves and his immune system began destroying healthy throat cells in an attempt to attack the invading enemy. His entire body would soon ache torturously as it became more involved in the internal warfare, and his own cerebral thermostat would elevate his body temperature well above normal, creating an even better incubator for the growing virus. The fever would elevate his blood pressure causing his brain to swell and his eyeballs to ache. He would shiver violently from a rapidly rising fever until he lost consciousness. His lungs would fill with fluid, and each breath would become a major effort in a losing battle. His skin would take on a bluish hue, because his lungs would fail to deliver sufficient oxygen. Then, within hours, as a result of this unusually prolific virus, he would die struggling to breathe through a blood-tinged froth gushing from his nose and mouth.

The new strain of influenza that had developed in the burned chickens and traveled to the pigs was now passing through the air to the rest of the Maylon family. The arrival that day of dozens of family members and neighbors to help Francisco recover from the fire served to rapidly accelerate the spread of the disease to the nearby neighborhoods, the Philippine countryside, and out into the world beyond.

Chapter 3

I Like Mike

Sunday, September 13

Mike Spiker approached mile ten of his twelve-mile Sunday jog. His weary body tried to convince his mind that it was incapable of lifting his leg another time. He had been running for over ninety minutes, stopping every three miles or so to sip water. He pounded out each stride, trying to think about anything except running. Running was something he endured as a means to stall death, not something he enjoyed.

The morning sun hung lazily in the hazy Georgia sky. Despite the early hour, the sixty-eight degree temperature was about as cool as it got this time of year, and it would warm up quickly under the sweltering sun. The humidity was high, producing what the local weatherman called "air you can wear."

A chorus of mowers hummed in unison, leaving behind the scent of fresh-cut grass. Passing cars, barking dogs, and sprinkler systems periodically interrupted the early morning peace and quiet of the countryside. Mike added his own sounds as his shoes pounded the pavement and his lungs gasped rhythmically for air.

As he ran south, the church traffic picked up. The narrow road provided no shoulder, and cars passed him within inches. To stay safe and keep his mind off his pain, Mike made eye contact and waved to as many drivers as he could. He understood what a nuisance joggers were to drivers and how thoughtless many drivers were toward joggers.

A teenage girl chatting obliviously on her cell phone rounded the bend and headed right for him. Mike was a fraction of a second from leaping into the ditch beside the road when the girl finally looked up to see him and zigged out of the way.

"Idiot! Give me a goddamn break!" Mike said under his breath, then immediately stopped short. Not cussing was part of his training in becoming more Southern. It's all right to say hell or bullshit, but not goddamn. Leave the Lord out of it. It was, however, acceptable to use the thinly disguised "dadgum" or "gosh dern" expressions. Southerners cussed with great discretion.

Mike's regular running route provided total submersion into the culture of the Deep South. Magnificent homes graced sprawling estates, some with lush pastures and neatly maintained lakes. Some of the grandest estates remained well-kept secrets nestled far off the road behind thick woods. Beautiful plantation-era houses kept company with new construction, and the "old money" Macon families rubbed elbows, albeit sometimes reluctantly, with foreign-born doctors and other new money moguls.

The origins of Rivoli Drive dated back to the days of the horse and carriage as evidenced by the natural curves and undulations of its path. The near absence of ice or snow, plus a strong indifference toward change, made it unnecessary to spend any money on flatter, wider, straighter throughways.

As is often the case, there were roads along both sides of the railroad tracks to minimize at-grade intersections. Some of the nicest neighborhoods were near the tracks, undaunted by the haunting of the howling horns at night. Impromptu kudzu topiaries populated the areas between the road and rails. The giant green monsters provided an element of whimsy to the destruction they caused by slowly consuming everything in their path.

The thunder of an approaching freight train challenged Mike's competitive nature and beckoned him to race. He maintained a regular cadence as the engine pulled beside him. The deafening roar of the engine and clatter of the wheels on the old tracks made him forget his own pain and panting. The conductor's genuine smile and enthusiastic wave carefully concealed his confidence that the sluggish locomotive would once again win the race.

Giant loblolly pines towered overhead while beneath their needled branches, the sheltered azaleas, crape myrtle, and dogwoods each took their turn to provide a splash of color to the landscape. Magnificent magnolias dripped with Southern charm, and thousands of imported Yoshina cherry trees provided cultural diversity. The sight of the cherry trees, even in their current green fall garb, reminded Mike of dodging the busloads of tourists that came annually to gaze at their delicate blossoms floating through the air like pale pink snowflakes.

One mile to go, Mike turned the corner into his neighborhood. The last mile was always a battle of mind over screaming muscle, so he turned up the pace for a big finish.

Now that it was nearly over, Mike thought about how truly tedious he found running. It kept him in decent shape and allowed him to consume some of the rich, Southern delights he had learned to love. Running was also a good way to reduce stress, not just while he was out on the road, but for the rest of the day as he renewed his energy. Maybe his Dad wouldn't have had a heart attack and died so young if he had jogged a few miles per week.

Mike reflected on the quality of life he enjoyed in the North Macon area compared to Western Maryland where he grew up. It took less than ten minutes to get to work or school, or a wide variety of stores and restaurants. Crime seemed something that happened elsewhere. Atlanta was only an hour to the north and, in less time than it takes to get hungry after a big breakfast, you could be at your choice of the Atlantic Ocean, Gulf of Mexico or in the Appalachian Mountains.

A neighbor waved as she pulled out of her driveway. Mike provided the expected Southern response by smiling, waving, nodding his head, and saying "Hey" even though she couldn't hear him. Mike didn't really make any special effort to speak Southern except that he did quickly learn to say "Hey" in greeting people in the appropriately animated and friendly manner—taking a full second to sing it out enthusiastically.

Only after Mike reached the end of his driveway and began walking did he allow himself to acknowledge the torturous cries of his body. Spasms gripped his leg muscles as his heart attempted to escape his chest with pounding blows from within. He gasped for breath, unable to fulfill his lungs insatiable appetite for air. Sweat stung his eyes as it poured down his forehead in a steady stream. His sense of exhilaration gave way momentarily to the feeling of total exhaustion. Was this what it felt like to die?

+

Halfway around the world, Francisco Maylon too was gasping for breath as his heart frantically beat in his chest. The virus carried out its execution swiftly and without mercy. His muscles convulsed in violent spasms as his feverish body lay wrapped in dripping wet clothing. Had he been capable of a conscious thought at that moment, he would have welcomed death as a venerable friend.

+

Mike's thoughts returned to normal along with his breathing. Quick recovery is one of the many advantages of being fit. He liked running best after it was over, a small price to pay for outrunning mortality. He retrieved the Sunday paper out of the mailbox as he checked his watch—one hour and forty-eight minutes. Not bad for a forty-six-year-old guy.

Hobbling up the driveway and around the rear of the house to the deck, Mike sat in one of the wrought iron chairs and put his feet up on another—his favorite recovery position. Dripping sweat formed round dark circles in the wood decking below his chair. Mike put his head back and stared at the puffy white clouds above. His thoughts turned to work.

+

As general manager, Mike Spiker was in charge of Bio-Lab Research's financial processing operation in Macon. The corporation was headquartered in Wilmington, Delaware and employed people throughout the U.S. who worked in various research, laboratory and administrative positions. Affectionately known as 'BLuR', the company also manufactured and leased animal care equipment at a plant in Richmond, Virginia.

Years earlier, BLuR had decided to centralize all of its financial operations into a single national site in Macon and hired Mike to build and manage the operation of more than 400 employees involved in customer service and back-office administration.

+

Mike cooled off enough to go in the house, but his clothes were still soaked through from perspiration and high humidity. The cool dry air inside felt at first like an icebox. His legs had stiffened up, an expected result of accomplishment, part of the ritual. No pain, no gain.

He entered the house through the kitchen and filled a tall tumbler with ice water from the dispenser on the refrigerator. The TV chattered on as Courtney's blow dryer provided distant background noise along with the whir of the air conditioner waging its relentless battle against the heat. Mike strolled into the great room where his third-grade son, Mark, was lying on the rug in front of the television. His sharp outfit and careful grooming indicated that Courtney had dressed him to go out.

"Did you win the race, Dad?" Mark asked.

"Yeah, I finished first." Mike replied.

"Did anyone else run?"

'No, just me, wise guy."

Mark laughed. "You won because I wasn't running, Dad." Mark laughed again.

"You guys going to church?"

"Yessir. Mom's taking us," replied Mark.

Mike sat on the hearth and stretched out his legs. Amy and her three-year-old sister, Emily, watched TV from the couch where they sat very lady-like, all dressed up in their Sunday best.

"Hey there, ladies! And how are you beautiful women doing this morning?"

"Mornin', Daddy," they said in near unison, too absorbed in TV to engage in idle chatter.

Six-month-old baby Beth would be down the hall in the master bathroom with her mother.

"Daddy, can you give us a horsy ride?" asked Amy.

"Sorry, baby, I'm too sweaty," Mike stood up as he apologized. "But maybe you have time before church for a little *rock and roll*! Get up here, Mark, and join me on stage! Hit it, girls!" He slapped his thighs loudly twice followed by a single clap of the hands. The girls recognized their cue and joined in. *"We will, we will rock you. We will, we will rock you."*

Mike exited the area, kicking his legs and playing air guitar. The kids rocked with laughter as he danced into the kitchen. Once out of view, Mike went about the task of preparing his breakfast, smiling to himself at his great fortune to have children with such a good sense of humor.

Mike's first marriage had ended without children—all the arguing left little time for sex. The years of bachelorhood that followed allowed him to focus on his career. He did, however, feel a slight twinge of guilt at being a "delayed dad"—he would be in his early sixties when Beth was finishing high school. Perhaps that was another reason why he ran and stayed in shape.

Mike flipped on the little TV in the kitchen while he read the paper and ate his breakfast. The local CBS station was broadcasting the *Sunday Mornin'* news. "...and health officials in Manila are alarmed at the extraordinary number of deaths resulting from flu-related complications. Authorities are beginning to take this outbreak very seriously. Scientists here and at the U.S. Centers for Disease Control are diligently searching for the source of the epidemic.

"The government in Manila is asking for help from other nations in protecting the eighty million people who live in the Philippines. They confirm that the disease is highly infectious and people are encouraged to remain at home and away from public places."

Hunched over the dishwasher loading his breakfast dishes, Mike heard Courtney enter the great room, her high heels clopping on the hardwood floor. She struck a momentary pose for his benefit as she paused in the doorway to the kitchen. As she stood there, he imagined her in one of those classy book-like magazines for the ultra-wealthy. The stunningly simple navy dress seductively draped her torso while leaving her lanky limbs exposed. She jutted her hip out slightly to provide an appropriate resting place for the infant that she held lovingly in her arms.

"Hey, dear! Have a good run?" inquired Courtney.

"Yeah, it was exhilarating and excruciating," Mike replied. "You look *very* nice! I didn't know you were going to church."

"Well, we missed last week, and I don't want the kids to miss any more Sunday school. You have your priorities, and I have mine." Courtney's tone was decidedly assertive. "Come on kids, we don't want to be late!" Courtney yelled to the older three children.

They marched single file through the kitchen, bid farewell to their Dad, and went out into the garage.

"See you in a while," Courtney said to Mike as she walked toward him. "I'm taking Mark, Amy, and Emily to my parents after church. You're on your own. Will you be okay?" Courtney kissed him on the lips, lingering teasingly, and followed the children out.

Mike waved as the family SUV pulled out of sight. He whistled as he finished cleaning up the kitchen. He straightened the stack of mail that had accumulated on the kitchen counter and stopped to admire the kids' artwork hanging on the refrigerator that somehow he hadn't noticed before. It wasn't until he had walked back to the master bathroom to take a shower that he caught his reflection in the mirror and realized he was still grinning.

Chapter 4

Never Thank Your Spouse For Sex

Sunday, September 13

As Mike undressed to take a shower, he surveyed the pictures on the dresser that chronicled his recent life. His favorite was a black and white snap shot of Courtney shortly after they met. The absence of color highlighted the strong features that gave Courtney her striking appeal. With her classical nose, high cheekbones, and sharply defined lips, she looked like she had been chiseled rather than conceived.

Courtney Gianatos was born in Mississippi, the daughter of a career Air Force officer who moved his family regularly until settling down at Robins Air Force Base in Georgia. Self-conscious about her last name being so much different than the predominantly Anglo names in her school, her accent was definitely Southern, including local colloquialisms such as "y'all," "fixin' to," and "Coca Cola" for any brand of soft drink.

A mutual friend had introduced Mike to Courtney nearly ten years earlier. Like Mike, she had divorced after a brief marriage that ended without children. Four kids later, she was working on her degree in education at Wesleyan College between managing a household kept in a delightful whirlwind of swimming, soccer, dance, and other kids' activities, as well as her own interests at the church, college, and country club.

Periodically Courtney would run into Jennifer, Mike's IT director at BLuR, at Junior League, Symphony Guild meetings, or at Thursday night women's tennis league at the club. Though they never developed into close friends, they enjoyed one another's company. Jennifer kept Courtney filled in on the latest scoop at BLuR that Mike always seemed to forget to share with her. Such inside information came in handy for the "boss's wife" at frequent corporate functions.

The cool spray from the shower felt wonderful on his aching muscles; Mike's thoughts again drifted to work. Every Monday at 9:00 A.M. Mike and his executive staff of four met to go over the progress of their initiatives and prioritize the current week's issues.

The top leaders consisted of Latrice who led the largest team in operations, Jennifer who directed information technology, Paris in human resources, and Dwight who was the good-natured division controller. Paris liked to eat junk food as much as Latrice liked to work out. Jennifer was as cosmopolitan as Dwight was a good ol' boy. Despite their differences, their complementary skills made them a complete and efficient unit.

+

Carrying a Fincher's Barbecue sack with two "pig" sandwiches, Courtney arrived home around one o'clock after dropping the older kids off at her parents. She put the baby in the high chair and gave her a cup of juice and a bowl full of her favorite cereal.

Mike, sitting at the kitchen table paying bills, acknowledged their arrival with a big smile. "Fantastic! How did you know I had a craving for barbecue?" Mike reached for the familiar brown paper bag with the picture of the happy pig.

"Have you *ever* turned down a barbecue sandwich?" Courtney cocked her head to the side and raised her eyebrow to punctuate her inquiry.

Dependability was but one characteristic that Courtney loved about Mike. He also helped her become more organized and confident. He set an example for the kids by being punctual, cool under pressure, and disciplined. He didn't butt in line, cheat anyone, or take advantage of his position.

"New dress?" Mike asked smiling.

"This old rag? I've worn this plenty of times before!" Courtney responded.

"You mean in public, in front of people? I don't remember ever seeing it before," returned Mike.

"Beth, don't throw those Lucky Charms all over the floor, baby!" Courtney said, changing the subject.

After a few minutes, Courtney took Beth up to the nursery and put her down for a nap, then slipped back downstairs like a schoolgirl sneaking out for a late night rendezvous. Mike watched her anxiously from the kitchen, hoping that things might escalate from that earlier kiss. Sure enough, she was coming his way.

"It's your lucky day, Running Man!" Courtney said to Mike, bringing her lips within an inch of his, brushing her body against his.

"Yeah, well Running Man is about to make Church Lady sing out with a joyful noise!" Mike stood, laughing as he embraced her.

"You know," he continued, reflecting on the rare tranquility of the moment, "we haven't had a chance to be alone like this without the kids since Nevis!" He was referring to their last trip together months ago.

Suddenly, the playful grin drained from Courtney's face. But within a couple of seconds, she recovered and that dreamy, romantic look returned to her eyes. Mike found her reaction curious, but the last thing he wanted to do was interrupt the magic of the moment with some discussion that might go in an unknown direction.

Mike followed Courtney into the walk-in closet and watched intently as she unzipped her dress and allowed it to fall to the floor.

"Wow, you look more beautiful every day," Mike said.

Silently accepting his compliment, Courtney continued to seductively remove her slip, pausing for effect as she reached behind her back to undo her bra. The sight of her long lean limbs, dark skin, and well-toned body never ceased to amaze him.

Mike followed Courtney to the bedroom, his own clothes a pile on the floor.

+

After the final tender throbs and gentle gasps subsided, they lay on their respective sides of the bed, gazing into each other's eyes. Mike gently tickled Courtney's face and body as she lay beside him.

Propping herself up on her side with an elbow, Courtney reached up and tousled Mike's already mussed hair. She wondered if Mike had noticed her reaction earlier when he mentioned Nevis. Maybe she should tell him all about that evening, especially right now while he was lying there beside her so contentedly. But before she could decide, Mike was up and heading into the bathroom.

"Thank you for a great time there, Running Man!" Courtney said as she followed Mike into the walk-in closet.

"You should never thank your spouse for sex, Church Lady. It isn't necessary and it makes me feel cheap," Mike replied kiddingly as he reached for his clothes.

+

Mike went out into the great room where he heard Beth stirring in the nursery. He went upstairs and picked her up, holding her close while she mumbled sounds that surely meant, "Thanks for holding me, Dad" or "You're the best Dad in the whole world." He lifted her effortlessly above his head, ready to give her a torturous raspberry on her stomach when he realized that she needed an immediate diaper change. The diaper had absorbed several times its weight, but wasn't much good at filtering odors. Mike pulled out the wipes and a fresh diaper, and managed the change without making a mess. *It takes a real man to change a baby girl's dirty diaper*, he thought.

Mike gently kissed Beth's delicate cheek and studied her closely as she kicked her legs in the air. She was so innocent. Did she understand who he was and what was going on? He suddenly had an overwhelming urge to hold her close, even if this beautiful creature could produce such a stinking diaper.

+

Later that night, as Mike brushed his teeth before bed, it was approaching noon on Monday in Manila. A young Filipino businessman named Cory Sabugo left work early to go home and prepare for his big trip to the U.S. later that evening. He needed to run a few errands and pack his things, but mostly Cory wanted to spend some extra time with his family, given the outbreak invading the city.

Across all of Manila, people were succumbing to the dreadful sickness. It began like the flu, but quickly worsened into a ghoulish nightmare, often ending in pneumonia and death. It spread fast and hit hard, leading the authorities to suspect a new strain of virus as the cause. But Manila had survived several health crises in the past few decades, and there was no honor in overreacting.

The confirmed presence of al-Qaida forces in the southernmost islands of the Philippines increased the tension felt by thousands of U.S. naval forces who had begun to arrive in the area.

At first Cory wanted to believe that this latest outbreak was just another exotic bug that would quickly run its course. Sensing in his heart that this situation was much more serious, he convinced his family to stay home until the crisis blew over. This did little to lessen his guilt that he would be safe in the U.S. while his family remained essentially in quarantine. Perhaps they would shut down the Manila airport and he would have a virtuous excuse to offer his customers in the US.

As a sales representative for a Manila-based manufacturer of small furniture accessories, Cory was a seasoned traveler to the US. He was prepared for the twenty-three-hour flight to Cincinnati, including a layover in LA, and thirteen-hour time change.

Knowing how oblivious some Americans were to world events, Cory wondered if the Yanks knew of the latest events in Asia. His customer contact in Ohio had mentioned nothing about the epidemic when they exchanged e-mails earlier that day.

He tried not to imagine what would happen if he got sick overseas, or his family got sick while he was gone. Unless it became apparent that Cory or his family was in imminent danger, he still planned to make the trip.

That evening at dinner, Cory gathered his family for one final gut check on whether to cancel his trip. His wife insisted that he proceed with his trip. The kids cinched it when they informed him that they were perfectly able to take care of themselves, plus their need for refills of their favorite music, candy, and other things American should not be denied by some virus.

Chapter 5

The Corbins of Unionville

Saturday afternoon, September 12

She couldn't stand it any longer. "Ma, I gotta have a beer!" Latrice yelled to her mother from across the kitchen. She stood at the sink of her parent's home preparing collard greens for the backyard cookout. Her mother, Muh-Dea, grabbed a beer out of the refrigerator and handed it to her. Latrice took the cold bottle and rolled it slowly across her forehead.

The collard greens were a taxing but important part of the traditional weekend family feast. Unlike lettuce or cabbage, collard greens did not grow in a protective head, so dirt, sand, and bugs clung to their large loose leaves. In this familiar ritual, Latrice first cut each leaf away from the hard center stem, then washed the dark green leaves. She had heard that white folks used a little bleach, which seemed a bit extreme to her. No one ever got sick from eating her greens. She boiled the leaves for about an hour with neck bones, pigtails, and the customary bacon drippings. Each gallon of fresh leaves became a quart of withered greens, seasoned to perfection, and fit for a king.

The seven ladies working in the small, narrow kitchen galley patted the sweat from their brows with crumpled tissues retrieved from sleeves and brassieres, fanning themselves absently as they worked. The old screen door leading to the backyard screeched with the constant comings and goings that ushered the sweltering heat and humidity in as the air conditioning quickly escaped. A big fan next to the door rattled against the linoleum as it attempted futilely to vent the heat and cooking fumes.

Like a hoard of locusts, the aunts, uncles, and cousins descended on the house and yard with a hum of conversation and laughter. The icy beer bottles clanked as family members deposited their coolers in the yard and sat their liquor bottles dressed in brown paper bags on the picnic table near the grill. The aroma of fried okra, macaroni and cheese, black-eyed peas, butter beans, and corn bread hovered enticingly in the heavy afternoon air. As always, Latrice and her parents furnished the meat and other fixin's.

Latrice's father, Kelvin Corbin, stood in the yard tending to the fire as he prepared to cook the ribs. An Atlanta Braves baseball cap shaded his eyes from the sun, and a towel hung around his neck checked his perspiration. The ribs slow-cooked for an hour or so as he tenderly bathed them in a rich crimson sauce. Kelvin's technique involved keeping the fire just hot enough by pouring some beer over the coals every few minutes to douse the flames, then taking a long swig for himself. That was his secret formula—the beer—that ended up mostly consumed by the cook.

Slaving in the kitchen alongside the other women, Latrice helped prepare food and clean up as they went along—a sharp contrast to her usual daily routine of managing a team of more than 200 people in the rapidly growing back office of the BLuR Financial Center. Oddly enough she loved these family gatherings because no one cared or even noticed her makeup or clothes. To her family she would eternally be that skinny "Lil' Treesy."

Similar Corbin family gatherings took place about once a month from March to November, depending on the weather. The festivities began at four on Saturday afternoon under the shade of the giant mimosa trees that sheltered her parents' big backyard. The event generally went on until shortly after midnight, barring any disruption from a violent summer thunderstorm. While the women hovered about the tiny kitchen, the men folk congregated around a massive brick grill in the middle of the yard. The circle of older women and old card-playing men staked out the coveted folding chairs, while the children romped and played.

This entirely black neighborhood known as Unionville consisted of modest homes along tree-lined streets. Schools, shops, and a recreation center created a self-contained community enclosed on all sides by busy highways. But like an inner city, the streets at night turned to drug deals and wars between rival gangs.

The visit of Kelvin's brother Billy, a big electric company executive from Philadelphia, served as the center of this weekend's excitement. A family celebrity, "Billy from Philly," graduated from Fort Valley State University before moving to Philadelphia.

Latrice listened from the sweltering kitchen as the decibel level of the conversation rose with the afternoon heat. The bull session turned more philosophical as the old wrought iron table near the cooker filled up with empty beer and liquor bottles.

"So Billy," asked cousin BayBra, which stood for baby brother, "what's it like livin' up in Philadelphia?"

Billy tugged on his bearded chin. "Philly's like any big city, some bad areas, but a lot of great neighborhoods. I'll tell y'all, I'm not about to leave the good job I've got, but times like this I really miss living in Georgia."

"Think there's any way you could have become such a big time executive if you had stayed in Macon?" asked cousin Clarence. "We don't have a bunch of big fancy bidness offices around here, you know. You haven't forgotten what it's like around here with everything stacked against the black man, have you?"

"You sound like your own worse enemy, boy," Billy said to Clarence. "I'll tell you the truth, there's as much bigotry in the North as in the South, it just takes on a little different angle. It's kind of like they say, Southern white bread lets you get as close as you want as long as you don't get too big, whereas up North, you can get as big as you want as long as you don't get too close."

"I think about you every time the Braves kick the Phillies' ass," Uncle DeMa chided in.

"That'll change next year when we lose two starting pitchers," Clarence said, "but I'm interested in hearing more about whether Billy thinks he could have become a big time executive right here in Macon."

"Can't say. But I know there's plenty of our folks in some mighty high level positions here, and seems they live in any neighborhood they please. Come on, Clarence, aren't you tired of blamin' your own failures on being black? Time to move on."

Knowing that none of the men ever thought to consider that *she* already had more responsibility and earned a higher salary than Uncle Billy from Philly, Latrice stiffened as the conversation continued.

+

Six months ago, a good friend and coworker of Japanese descent had excitedly described the details of a baby shower she was planning at her house.

"I'd love for you to come, but my family looks dimly on minorities," she explained to Latrice.

Latrice laughed at first, thinking the girl was kidding. But this woman wasn't kidding at all. Never had anyone been so openly bigoted and done it with a smile.

Even her own brother Terrence had attacked light-skinned blacks.

"You don't really know what it's like to be black," the darker-skinned Terrence had said, referring to Latrice's caramel colored skin. "Back in the plantation days, you'd be working in the house while I was busting my ass out in the fields picking cotton."

+

Latrice grew up in a stable, loving, two-parent home in a community filled with inspiring mentors and watchful role models. Back then, the elders in the neighborhood acted as guardians over the residents' safety, wielding their influence to enforce acceptable standards of behavior.

Unfortunately, in the years that had passed since Latrice's childhood, crime and decay were now overcoming the forces of good citizens in the neighborhood. Gang graffiti adorned virtually every street corner and the threat of drive-by shootings plagued the once tranquil community. Despite the efforts of police and many outstanding citizens, Unionville was becoming more like a ghetto. Latrice often contemplated moving out of Unionville, but the convenience of having her parents close by held her hostage. As they grew older, she dreamed of buying a house big enough for them to all live together comfortably in a better neighborhood.

Despite all the tension of being among the first group to integrate the Bibb County public schools, Latrice received what would be considered on a national scale to be an average education. Never feeling disadvantaged, Latrice was accepted at the University of Georgia. The two-hours between Macon and Athens provided just the right blend of independence and security. She alternated party weekends in Athens with frequent trips home for some of her mama's home cooking and clean laundry.

During the summer after her freshman year, Latrice met Reginald Rutherford who quickly swept her off her feet. Over the pleas of her father, Latrice dropped out of college, got married, and became pregnant. The happiest summer of her life preceded the series of monumental disappointments that followed.

+

As Latrice helped her mother and aunts clean up after the cookout Saturday night, the new strain of influenza virus that had developed on the Maylon farm the prior week now waged a deadly war in the Philippines. The death toll climbed into the thousands as the disease spread to the densely populated sections of Manila and suburbs. Government efforts to keep the disease from spreading were futile. They suspected that animals were to blame for transmitting the virus and began slaughtering all pigs, chickens, ducks, and geese. Even pet monkeys, dogs, cats, and birds were put to death. But the elimination of these animals had no noticeable effect on the spread of what was now being referred to as a plague. Apparently the disease traveled by the most dangerous manner—through the air, from person to person. The prospect of contraction through inhalation created an uncontrollable scenario and panic ensued.

American CIA agents immediately began working with friendly Filipino operatives inside and around the al-Qaida network in the Philippines to determine the extent of their involvement in the spread of the disease.

+

Latrice and her daughter held hands as they walked home from the cookout. After putting Regina to bed, Latrice flopped down in her favorite chair and turned on CNN for the latest news.

A doctor was being interviewed at the Centers for Disease Control. "…and the flu virus has remained basically unchanged. New viruses like this one in the Philippines often mutate pretty quickly. They are not particularly stable, and when they do mutate, the new strain has the potential to become more or less virulent. It could go either way."

"Has there ever been an epidemic like this before?" asked the host.

"The most deadly epidemic in modern times occurred at the end of the First World War in 1918. It is thought to have started in Kansas, and spread quickly among soldiers who traveled, trained, and lived together in close quarters both in Europe and in the States. Twenty million people died around the world, including 550,000 Americans."

"Did the 1918 flu spread as fast as this one?"

"Maybe not this fast. Normally, influenza takes a few days to develop in people. But this new type in the Philippines spreads in hours. That is going to make developing flu shots more challenging."

"How did the 1918 epidemic end?"

"We're not really sure how it started or ended. It vanished as quickly and mysteriously as it began, probably evolving into a less deadly strain. Or maybe it just ran out of the density of people needed to continue spreading."

"What do you think will happen if the virus in the Philippines mutates?"

"For one thing, those who have been exposed to the current disease and have developed a resistance will no longer be immune to a new strain, so it could kill even more people in a second wave. It could also make a vaccine ineffective in the time it would take to produce and distribute it. The worst case scenario would be for the virus to become "hot", which is military slang for highly infectious and fatal. The best-known hot virus is Ebola, which the CDC follows quite closely, even though it has so far been contained to the central African rain forest."

"Are we dealing with another Ebola?" the reporter followed up.

"It appears, like the Ebola virus, that this new strain also travels by air," continued the researcher, in a matter-of-fact tone. "And there are some similarities in the effects—rapid onset, debilitating headaches, and severe vomiting. At this point we are hopeful that that is where the similarities end. The CDC is watching the situation in Asia closely, and we are all praying that the virus in the Philippines does not turn 'hot.'"

"Finally, Doctor, do you think terrorists are capable of starting an epidemic like this?"

"Yes I think they are capable, and if it's influenza like I think it is, it was a rather creative and effective choice for bio-terrorism. I understand that the al-Qaida cells operating in the Pacific Rim are much more active since the U.S. has disrupted their operations in the Middle East."

The interview ended, none too soon for Latrice. The situation made her uneasy, even if it was on the other side of the world.

Latrice turned off the TV and crawled into bed. Sleep eluded her as disturbing visions of Ebola danced in her head. She hadn't felt this uneasy since September 11, 2001, when a different set of far away events forever rocked that innocent sense of security she felt in her daily routine. If only she had someone to share her bed on nights like this.

Chapter 6

Race Snake

He just disappeared. He didn't call or write or say goodbye. After a few months of marriage, Reggie Rutherford just tired of the routines and responsibilities of being Latrice's husband. He left word that he had gone to Atlanta to take a new job.

Five months later, with still no word from Reggie, Latrice delivered a little girl that she named Regina in honor of good times now long gone. As more time passed, the feeling of betrayal and despair broke Latrice's heart, and the reality of the responsibilities she faced alone threatened to overwhelm her.

After a few months of living with her parents, Latrice found a job at a collection agency in Macon. She quickly discovered a real knack for convincing people to pay their debts and within a few months, she assumed supervisory responsibilities, learning to hire, coach and motivate employees. Her responsibilities skyrocketed. Unfortunately, her income didn't.

Despondent over her failure to secure a raise and ever looking for a bigger challenge, she saw an article in the paper announcing that a major corporation named Bio-Lab Research had chosen Macon to set up a back office operation that promised to create hundreds of new jobs.

Latrice interviewed with the new division's only two employees—General Manager Mike Spiker and Paris Hawkins, the human resources director—in a trailer on the property where the company's new building was under construction.

Latrice needed positive influences like Mike and Paris at this pivotal time in her life, and whether it was chemistry, or the hope for a big opportunity, she felt drawn to them. In a decisive moment that would ultimately open doors to places she never knew existed, she accepted their job offer on the spot.

When Mike hired Latrice Rutherford as the third employee at BLuR, he figured that she would have her hands full creating and managing the collections department. He also assumed she would be the first of several hires at her mid-management level. But Latrice was a quick study, learning the job quickly and demonstrating exceptional leadership abilities. Soon she delegated the daily responsibilities to her team and moved on to develop additional expertise in related areas. She grabbed every additional responsibility that presented itself, and convinced Mike to let her hire people for her team instead of hiring her peers. Within eighteen months Mike promoted her as in-charge of all operations—over the objections of Tom Mumford, Mike's boss at headquarters in Wilmington.

"You mean you're putting a woman who is black and doesn't even have a degree in charge of your operations, Mike?" queried Tom Mumford.

"Latrice keeps taking on more and more responsibility and exceeds every expectation. She's phenomenal. Come on down and meet her."

"You know, Mike, Macon isn't the easiest place to get to and your decisions have to look good on paper to those of us here at headquarters, not just feel good in person. Rutherford doesn't look so hot on paper." Tom paused. "I don't know why we don't just house your operation up here, anyway."

"Well, having worked in Wilmington, I'd say you get about twice the production and quality at about half the cost here in Macon. And it takes less time to get here than it does for you to get to BLuR operations in suburban Dallas or Minneapolis. Maybe you don't agree with my call to promote Latrice, but are you saying I can't do it?"

Tom sighed. "It's your decision. You know the way the corporation works—the guy in the field makes the call…and is held accountable."

"Okay, then, I say Latrice deserves this chance. I guarantee you this will be a home run." Mike was thankful to get off the phone.

The issue never came up again. Latrice accomplished every goal assigned to her, and over the next few years built a first-class operation with only two small layers of managers—a very flat organization.

In the early days at BLuR Financial, Mike and Latrice enjoyed trying unconventional methods to build and grow the organization. Neither had much formal management training, so they basically managed with as few rules as possible, and treated people the way they liked to be treated. Consequently, people embraced their jobs and accomplished things they didn't know they could do.

One of the things they experimented with was eliminating titles, or at least making them friendlier. Titles such as supervisor, manager, and VP were scrapped in favor of descriptions such as leader and coach. During the design meetings, one of the team leaders jokingly suggested that Latrice replace her old vice president title with "empress." They all laughed, but the title stuck and friends often called her "Empress Latrice" as a term of endearment.

Latrice led her staff with a unique style, rushing about with high energy and determination. She demanded honesty and directness and exercised both with disarming openness. "Wow! You look very handsome today, Lamar." "You did a great job closing that project last week, Gina! We're lucky to have someone like you on the team!" "You're late, Joey. I know you worked until seven o'clock last night, but it's important that leaders like you consistently set an example for others."

Back in January, when Latrice was in one of her more intense moods, she overheard Dwight tell Mike a joke that made fun of the King holiday. "What do the employees at Denny's call Martin Luther King Day?" Dwight paused. "Monday!"

Mike chuckled.

Waiting until she had him alone, Latrice confronted Mike. "I would like to know why you find it necessary to tolerate that kind of unprofessional behavior. That's the kind of insensitive, tasteless humor that causes bad feelings around here!" Latrice lectured.

Mike was flabbergasted. "Frankly, I didn't think it was such a big deal. I didn't even think it was funny."

"Well you are the top exec around here. You can't be part of crap like that."

"I agree that it was inappropriate, but don't you think you are overreacting here, Latrice? Dwight didn't mean anything hateful by what he said."

"That joke is ten years old. When are people like Dwight going to grow up?"

"Tell him yourself that you think what he said was inappropriate. But don't judge him. From my perspective, people like Dwight have come a long way from what they probably heard from people around them when they were kids."

"In other parts of the country, a remark like Dwight's would get him fired."

"That may be true, but other parts of the country don't have the same conditions as we have in Georgia. It's easy for Northeasterners to judge the South, but in many ways, areas like Macon, with half black and half white populations, have made more progress, especially when you consider the history of the past few generations." Mike continued, "Why don't you ask Paris for her perspective?"

"Paris may be black, but she comes from a different generation."

"There you go, judging again. I think Paris has the kind of wisdom that comes with experience."

"Dwight's comments were inappropriate."

"I agree, and I apologize for him. Okay?"

Latrice never said anything to Paris or Dwight.

+

Mike took great pride in his role as Latrice's mentor. He understood that she was quite young to be in such a position of responsibility and that with some fine-tuning, she might someday be his successor. To help her manage her temperament, Mike sat down with her every few weeks to review her performance and help smooth out the rough edges.

Over the years, Latrice had grown accustomed to having Mike's ear and found it a difficult adjustment when the growing organization required the expansion of the management team to include Jennifer as IT director and Dwight as division controller.

Latrice found the fast track exhilarating. Mike depended on her, and her daddy bragged on her. Her income rose to levels that she hadn't expected to make for several years, even if she had gotten her college degree.

The more Latrice's responsibility increased at work, the more isolated she felt about being a young, female, African-American executive. There were plenty of local women who were successful in medicine or education or who held high-level government positions, but few women in Macon had reached Latrice's level in private industry and few, if any, who were African American. Unlike Mike, who had a Rotary Club mostly full of white, male executives to relate to, there were few role models or mentors of a similar background with whom Latrice could confide.

One thought that made Latrice seethe was that less than open-minded whites and blacks who didn't know her personally might attribute her success to some unspoken affirmative action. She longed to discuss such unsettling issues with someone in a similar position.

As her awareness of others' perceptions of her heightened, so did her sensitivity to other subtle signs of prejudice. The more she noticed it, the more pressure she felt to take a stand. Soon she began to interpret a lot of the conflict and personality problems in the work teams as having an implied racial undertone.

Latrice's new racial consciousness at BLuR Financial created quite a stir. Issues that had not seemed important or relevant in the past were suddenly being openly and sometimes hostilely contested.

"I'm worried," said Mike, "that race issues are causing more and more disruption around here. The work is still getting done, but I can feel a certain edge around the lunchroom and after-work activities. The most innocent comments are interpreted as having racial overtones. Some people are tracking promotions or any other kind of employee recognition as competition between whites and blacks."

"I agree. I feel it, too," responded Latrice. "I don't like it, but I don't know what to do about it."

"Most of us, white and black, have learned to open our minds about race over the years. But there are blacks and whites who only learned to keep their mouths shut and their feeling to themselves, and these are the ones who seem to be embracing this new tension as a call to arms."

"Are you insinuating that I'm in that group?"

"I don't know how to describe you, Latrice, but you've changed. Just in the past few weeks you've made an issue of why there aren't more black males employed at BLuR and which departments have more black employees than others. Then there was the discussion about making Martin Luther King, Jr.'s birthday a paid holiday instead of having a floater day off. And you made an issue about banning the Confederate flag emblem on license plates of cars in the parking lot."

"Hey, Mike, those are important issues. I didn't create those situations, and I'm not going to ignore them. But I do sense that my relationship with a lot of white employees is deteriorating and I'm anxious to do something about that."

"It's just so damn ironic that our company is facing this. Our top leadership reflects the employee mix, we are more diverse than any other division in BLuR and probably more than any other major employer in Macon."

"What can we do, boss?"

"I'm not sure of what to do, but I know that you're a key player in this and we have to act quickly."

"Maybe we could pick a few representative people and have a couple brown bag lunch sessions to discuss this. We've got to get to higher ground, but we might have to break some china getting there."

"You know what's funny?" asked Mike. "We have spent so much time over the years brain storming about risks we face as a company. We have contingency plans around every conceivable disaster—fire, tornadoes, hurricanes, and winter weather. But you know the biggest disruption we've had so far?

"The flood of 1994?"

"That was a good one, but I was thinking of that time Vance, the third-shift computer operator, saw a snake slithering down the hallway late one night."

"Oh yeah! Mr. No-shoulders was in the house! And not much work got done until the cleaning lady killed it with the vacuum cleaner two days later."

"We had contingency plans for computer viruses, power outages, union organizations, fraud, sabotage, bomb scares, and biological attacks. But, out of the blue, a darn snake brought us to our knees."

"And now we face this 'race snake' issue," Latrice observed.

"And we're going to overcome this one too. Who do you suggest should come to these brown bag lunches? We'll get Paris to help put this together this week."

+

The Filipino government formally requested assistance from other nations after everything they tried failed to have any impact on slowing the spread of the disease. As Cory Sabugo was preparing to leave his home Monday evening to catch his flight to the US, scientists from the Centers for Disease Control in Atlanta were arriving in Manila wearing biohazard space suits and carrying strange looking laboratory equipment.

Cory gave his wife and kids an extra long hug and kiss goodbye. Despite his family's confidence about handling things at home, he couldn't shake the fear that taking this trip was a bad idea. No one in his family had the slightest flu symptoms, and they promised him they would stay locked up in the house until the health officials said it was safe to return to school and work. He promised he would call often.

The very first person that Cory came in contact with, a neighbor whom he asked to look after his family while he was out of town, gave him a big dose of influenza. Propelled by his sudden sneeze, the tiny droplets that carried the virus particles traveled more than forty miles an hour into the airspace shared by the men. Cory could have possibly fought off the relatively small amount of virus that he received from the neighbor, but the additional doses that he received from his taxi driver and fellow travelers at the airport allowed the virus to establish a strong foothold in the moist, warm fluid of his mouth, throat and lungs. Once this particular virus was entrenched, the odds were clearly on its side.

Particles too small to be considered a life form, the virus agents moved in unison with the precision and speed of an army attacking a defenseless village. Only the existence of counter agents within the bodies of certain humans allowed them to survive the invasion without getting seriously sick. The symptoms, as well as the progression of the virus, varied in every victim. Most people would get sick for a day or two and recover. Some would suffer no flu symptoms. And many would die.

Upon arriving at Manila's Ninoy Aquino International Airport, Cory checked his locker and suitcase. His PAL flight to Los Angeles was scheduled to depart on time. He called his wife from the concourse. Everyone was still fine. Nothing had developed in the hour since he had seen them.

Meanwhile the influenza viruses were having a field day as they attacked Cory's body. Millions of virus agents were penetrating the much larger, healthy cells and multiplying so fast that they forced the wall of each cell to explode, releasing new particles to invade more cells. The influenza particles attacked the tiny air sacs in Cory's lungs that normally took the air he breathed and mixed it with his blood. In a couple of hours Cory would probably feel cold symptoms, as the tiny sacs in his lungs would fill with fluid. Unless his body waged an immediate counter offensive, he could contract pneumonia before his plane landed in the United States.

Chapter 7

Tall Cotton

Sunday, September 13

The hymn echoed through the stark white sanctuary as the pipe organ strained to drown out a couple of off-key voices. A big, good-looking Dwight Williams focused his eyes firmly on the cross in front of him. He made his way down the center isle of the large Baptist church, which he had attended every Sunday for the past twenty-three years. His cadence kept perfect time with the other ushers, all middle aged males dressed in dark suits, as they delivered the heavy brass offering plates filled to the brim with loose bills and folded checks to the altar.

Dwight impressed his congregation with his willingness to serve as an usher every week, when in truth, it was the freedom to sit in the back where he could slip out for a quick smoke during the sermon that provided the real motivation.

Despite his devout attendance, Dwight was not particularly religious. Going to church every week had provided a rare calm in his otherwise stormy and turbulent childhood, and now, years later, he felt guilty if he missed a Sunday.

Getting his two boys there was another story. Ever since they had been given the choice, they seldom attended. His wife, Claire, followed suit.

Dwight slipped out before the benediction in order to beat the crowd. His religious Sunday ritual included a stop at the nearby Waffle House for some coffee, biscuits and gravy, and a little fellowship more in step with his own theology.

"Well hey, Dwight! Want the usual this morning?" The waitress behind the counter yelled as he entered the diner. Dwight nodded and she promptly turned to the chef to relay the order "One B 'n G with side grits."

The cook acknowledged Dwight without even turning away from the grill as he tossed an omelet over in the tiny frying pan. "How 'bout it, Dwight!"

"Hey there TwoBelly, you doin' okay?" Dwight responded.

"My doctor told me last week to cut back on cholesterol and salt, so I'm looking for a new doctor," TwoBelly joked. "Y'all know any docs that smoke and eat this kind of food? If so, send 'em my way."

Dwight took the only empty chair at the counter. A surprisingly diverse clientele packed the small diner to capacity. The church folks, older couples mostly, filled the smooth vinyl booths that featured a view of the parking lot. The squeaky swivel seats at the counter were generally reserved for single males and provided a grand view of the master chef at work.

Dwight greeted each of the employees and some of the customers by name as they scurried by him. The only patrons he didn't recognize would most likely be travelers on I-75 who were drawn to the familiar yellow block sign in front of the long narrow restaurant that resembled a single-wide house trailer. Even a mid-sized city like Macon had ten Waffle House locations, each with its own circle of regulars.

"What can I get you to drink, sweetie?" the waitress asked Dwight.

"I'll have the mother's milk of the South, Karen." Pinned to her ample bosom, the Waffle House name badge with "KAREN" engraved proudly reassured him that his memory served him correctly.

"You mean Coca Cola?"

"Nah, sweet tea." Dwight shifted his attention to the waitress. "Did y'all have a good weekend, Karen?"

"The Braves won four in a row. Life is good," she replied. She wiggled slightly as she smoothed the skirt of her chocolate-colored uniform over her full physique. The little brown handkerchief hat completed the ensemble.

"I know that's right!" said Dwight. "Hey Karen, why is it that Georgia Tech engineering school graduates can't break wind?" Dwight asked loud enough for everyone to hear.

"I don't know sweetie, why?"

"Because they can't keep their mouths shut long enough to build up enough pressure." Dwight laughed louder than anyone else.

"Hey Dwight!" Another regular jumped in to join the act. "What do you call a dead Tech graduate in the closet?"

"Don't know, Gene. What do you call him?"

"Last year's hide-and-go-seek winner!" The laughter moved through the diner in a wave.

The ruckus subsided momentarily as everyone returned to breakfast.

Conversations of the Waffle House regulars ranged from NASCAR results to presidential politics, high school football to medical breakthroughs, and could be heard by just about anyone in the diner who cared to listen.

The bill came to $3.80, and Dwight left a five-dollar bill. His chest swelled and he stood a little taller knowing he left such a generous tip—about thirty- percent, Dwight figured. Another sign that this local boy had made it big.

The hinge groaned as he opened the door of his twelve-year-old Cutlass. Dwight's real pride and joy was his old 1968 Chevy pickup truck that he only drove if getting somewhere on time, and staying clean, weren't essential.

It was such a nice day that he drove with his elbow out the window for the short distance from the Waffle House to a little convenience store that sold his favorite Sunday afternoon snack, boiled peanuts—raw nuts that had been cooked for hours in salt water. From there he drove home, taking his turns wide and slow, Southern-style, with nothing in particular on his mind. He smiled to himself as he turned into Country Club Estates and tooled up his driveway, humming along with a 1960s oldie on the local station.

Abruptly, Dwight's pleasant disposition disappeared as he slammed on the brakes to avoid running over the car wash paraphernalia left in the middle of the drive. Dwight struck the horn in the steering wheel with the palm of his hands, shattering the Sunday afternoon tranquility and disrupting the concentration of golfers on the course across the street from his house.

Seventeen-year-old John sauntered around the corner of the house only mildly concerned with all the racket. The rap music that poured from his earphones was audible from several feet away. His eyes met Dwight's with a blatant disdain. As Dwight glared at his son, he had an uneasy sense that he was looking into the face of his own father. The resemblance made him shudder.

+

Dwight's father, Roy Williams, had named his second son in honor of the thirty-fourth president of the United States, although he was only a famous general at the time Dwight was born. Roy served in Europe at the very end of WWII and frequently recounted the story of the time he shook hands with General Eisenhower in Germany.

Roy returned to Macon in 1947 and promptly started dating a neighborhood friend named Marianne whom he had known since childhood. The scarcity of good jobs right after the war provided Roy plenty of time for courting, and it wasn't long before Marianne became pregnant, and they got married. They named their first son Wayne, and eighteen months later Dwight arrived. Roy worked a series of factory jobs in downtown Macon. Though he made good wages, he often lost his entire paycheck playing poker on Friday nights and spent entirely too much time at the local taverns tossing back a few beers with his buddies after work.

It wasn't long before Roy transitioned from a clean-cut soldier into an all-American redneck. He wore his hair long and cut to one length, greased down, and combed straight back. His small, narrow eyes looked even meaner when they were blood-shot.

The Williams family lived in a small frame ranch house on the south side of town. The ever-changing inventory of a half dozen or so older model cars littered the grounds underneath the pecan and apple trees that graced the otherwise pathetic property. Neither the landlord nor Roy had much interest in keeping the place in good shape. The floors sagged and creaked with every step and the breezy crawl space ensured frozen pipes whenever the temperature fell below freezing for more than a few hours.

Wayne and Dwight learned a mean and narrow view of the world from their father. Roy believed that anyone who beat him at a game was a cheater, and any man who women found good-looking must be queer. He had little respect for women, or "split tails" as he called them: "Anything that bleeds for five days and lives must be evil."

Roy lost one good job after another and blamed it entirely on the "nigras" who were willing to work for less and the greedy, nigra-loving supervisors. He was an outspoken racist who became even more enraged by the civil rights movement in the late sixties and early seventies.

Dwight cut his teeth on the language of bigotry, knowing no better than what his father modeled. He secretly wondered if his father was involved with the KKK, but he never saw any tangible evidence of it. Dwight didn't dare mention that he had several black friends for fear it would provoke another round of Roy's late night drunken rages, when he beat his kids and wife.

+

John regarded his father mildly as he endured Dwight's tirade.

"If I've told you once I have told you a thousand times to put this crap away when you've finished with it."

"Yeah. Right. Well, Dad, I'm not finished yet. I still gotta buff out the wax. See how the paint looks real dull-like?" John said apathetically, his tone condescending.

"Don't you get smart with me," Dwight said, throwing John's floor mats into the grass. "Finished or not, get that stuff out of the way so I can put the car in the garage. And I mean now! Move, do you hear me?"

Aware that his response was out of proportion with the offense, Dwight's words were propelled by a rage that went far beyond the car wash stuff in the driveway. He watched John sneer as he tossed the bucket of dirty water across the lawn, drenching the family dog, a good-natured black Labrador retriever named Cleo.

+

One Saturday afternoon, when Dwight was twelve, a mutt named Casey, the family pet and his best friend in the world, gave birth to a litter of five healthy puppies.

"We can't afford any more mouths to feed around here," slurred Roy. "Kill 'em."

"I'll find them homes, Daddy."

"I said kill 'em, and I mean now!" Roy snapped. "Go get that bucket on the side of the house, fill it with water and drown 'em."

"I can't do that, Daddy." Dwight began to cry with the realization that his father was quite serious.

Brother Wayne sauntered over to join the raucous. His mother came outside from the house.

"I said now!" Roy hollered, nearly falling over as he tried to kick the boy with his boot. Dwight jumped up and did as he was told. The sight of the boy gagging from crying made Roy even madder.

"Give me the goddamn bucket," he screamed, grabbing the sloshing bucket and carrying it over to the box holding the puppies. "Get over here, boy!" he yelled as he picked up one of the pups by the back of the neck and submerged it in the bucket. "You ain't nothin' but a coward, you yellow-bellied, nigra-lovin' sissy boy!"

Wayne laughed, as he held Casey at bay. Marianne returned to the house.

"I can't do this, Daddy. Please, I'll find homes for the other puppies, I promise!"

Roy grabbed Dwight and forced his hands to drown each of the four other puppies.

Dwight would never forget the sickening feeling of the squirming puppies going limp in his hands, or the sad look of betrayal in the eyes of his best friend, Casey, as she witnessed the murder of her newborns.

+

Several years later, Dwight's mother died at the age of forty-eight, the same year his little sister graduated from high school. It came as a shock to the family and the doctors, though it shouldn't have after all the years of overeating and smoking. She failed to take her estrogen prescription following a hysterectomy, and typical for her passive nature, she ignored months of bleeding caused by colon cancer. Within a few weeks her heart failed, just before the cancer would have killed her. Dwight considered it a case of involuntary suicide and a reprieve from being married to Roy and the hell of her existence.

Perhaps now that she was gone, the mother he dreamed of who would cook tasty meals, help him with his homework and slay the dragons of childhood could become a reality, if only in his memories.

+

Dwight parked the car next to the pickup truck in the three-car garage. As he reached for the door to the house, it flew open with great force and his younger son, Charles, bounded out of the kitchen and down the steps to the garage, nearly knocking the cup of boiled peanuts out of his father's hand.

"Goin' to Jason's. Back by six." The words lingered, though Charles had already mounted his bike and wheeled halfway down the drive before Dwight could respond.

"Huh? Okay." Dwight didn't have the energy to argue after the exchange with John.

Charles applied the brakes and spun the bike around to face his Dad. "Oh, yeah, Dwight, Mom said to tell you that she had to go in to the office to do some paperwork, and that she would see you later tonight. Bye." He sped off without waiting for an acknowledgment.

The elation that Dwight had felt driving home had now been completely eliminated. He walked into the kitchen, tossed his keys on the kitchen table, and grabbed the Sunday paper from the counter. He opened the refrigerator for a beer on his way into the den and his favorite easy chair. The smorgasbord of take-out cartons and pizza boxes on the kitchen table served as an annoying reminder of Claire's absence and her growing obsession with work. Dwight grumbled under his breath. Finding the house far too quiet, he flicked the remote in the direction of the television to provide some background noise.

He removed the rubber band from the tightly rolled newspaper to reveal a front-page headline: DEATH TOLL RISES IN PHILIPPINES EPIDEMIC, CDC OFFICIALS WORKING TO IDENTIFY KILLER VIRUS.

"This has gotta somehow be the work of those yellowed-bellied terrorists," Dwight mumbled. Until recently, Dwight had never thought much about the influence of Islam in Asia, but the constant link of Muslim extremists in the Philippines brought home how effectively the religion had spread to every corner of the world. *Makes relations between blacks and whites in Georgia mild in comparison,* Dwight thought.

Before he could get to the stock quotes in the business section, a name in the state and local news made him do a double take. "Police arrested Wayne Williamson Saturday evening on charges of…."

Dwight double checked the name and breathed a sigh of relief. Williamson not Williams. He feared for a moment he had seen his brother's name and the circumstances certainly fit.

Dwight had not laid eyes on his older brother since Wayne was fifteen years old; he never returned home after serving time in jail for stealing. Dwight didn't miss his brother, he just wondered if he was still alive.

+

In an odd twist of rebellion, Dwight responded to a childhood of poverty and dysfunction by working hard in school and displaying a sense of responsibility uncharacteristic of his upbringing. When his mother died, he helped provide for his younger brother and sister. Thanks to a life insurance policy from his mother's employer of which he was sole beneficiary and of which his father was unaware, he managed to graduate from the University of Georgia with a degree in accounting. Later, he attended graduate courses at Mercer University and passed the CPA exam on his first try.

Though he never escaped the grip of his past, Dwight worked diligently to create a solid family life for his kids. But, over the years, Dwight's relationship with his two sons turned from total immersion to frustration. Their childhood admiration for the smartest, fastest, strongest man in the world, who coached them through soccer, Little League, Scouts, and the whole gamut of father-son activities, turned to disinterest. Now, Dwight was getting slower and his sons were getting more independent. Dwight viewed their typical teenage rebellion as an affront to everything he had tried to build. Seemingly overnight his two boys transformed into wise guys, more interested in playing video games and watching TV than spending time with Dad. With no personal experience to draw upon, Dwight responded in kind. *Let 'em go smoke dope or get tattoos or whatever the hell it is they want to do*, he thought.

Dwight's involvement in many of the outside activities that he had once loved dwindled to zero. He liked to play golf, but had never joined the first-class club in his own neighborhood, assuming that there was no way the board would accept a south Macon boy into their ranks. He liked to go hunting, but the season always seemed to end just as he got serious about getting out. He had a nice bass boat that they used a few times for water skiing, but that was hardly a solitary activity.

Dwight's marriage to Claire wasn't much to brag about either. After years of staying at home to raise two boys, Claire now enjoyed a challenging job as a buyer at a local department store. Dwight resented that her career was taking off just as his had reached a plateau. The only reason he tolerated the whole situation was the money she earned, which was more than enough to cover the tuition for the boys to go to private school.

+

Scanning the fine print of the stock market listings in the paper, Dwight grinned at what he saw—a few stocks down, but most up. He took a long swig of the cold Bud and refolded the paper.

`Looking up from the paper, Dwight spotted Claire's mother passing by the den window and waved. Helen lived behind them in a mother-in-law studio that was attached to the back of their house by a covered walkway. Dwight didn't mind having her live near them mainly because she was quite wealthy and would probably leave all her money to her daughter. Besides, she cooked some mean fried chicken and helped out a lot with the boys.

Not having much else to do, Dwight retrieved his briefcase and began looking over some reports from work. After his public accounting experience, joining BLuR had been a great career move for Dwight. He felt proud that he made a significant contribution, and was perpetually challenged by the growth and complexity of the business. He had a real knack for building the right relationships and playing the politics needed to get things done within the corporation.

Dwight enjoyed his relationships with the managers at BLuR. He looked forward to every minute he spent around Jennifer—watching the beautiful but lethal tigress stalk her prey. And Latrice was another kind of wildcat—fast, decisive, and always hungry. Paris was great, but she nagged him too much about always doing the proper thing. Screw it, he thought, all this touchy-feely, someone-moved-my-cheese crap was just a passing craze. Trying to become politically correct overwhelmed Dwight—quit smoking, no drinking, sexual harassment training—it was all getting to be too much. Plus, he secretly believed that women belonged home raising their kids. If only Claire was as concerned for her sons as she was about work, maybe his boys wouldn't be so distant and difficult.

Dwight was in decent shape for being fifty-one years old. His wardrobe included short-sleeve shirts that were a bit too tight and pants that were a little too short. The single most notable thing about Dwight was his full head of silver hair that encircled his dome like a helmet and gave him the appearance of a televangelist or a used car salesman.

Folks found Dwight charming and amusing most of the time. He always had a joke, although they were often inappropriate in mixed company. He was decidedly traditional and a bit conservative, as you would expect a financial executive to be. To the casual observer, he appeared to be on top of his game—nice family, beautiful home, lots of friends, and a great job—but these last few years were proving to be a very difficult period in Dwight's life. Despite the jokes, he felt lonely, isolated, and unfulfilled. He needed to feel needed, and in Dwight's mind, no one needed him much anymore. From his vantage point, the world had long since left him behind, and he was feeling discouraged.

Dwight knew all too well that there was a thin barrier between the nightmares of his childhood and the great success he had achieved as an adult. He wondered if his thieving brother Wayne was more content with his lot in life. He probably was happier, assuming he was still alive. Maybe crime did pay.

+

Cory Sabugo boarded his flight from Manila to Los Angeles at 8:30 P.M. on Monday, which was Monday 7:30 A.M. Eastern Standard Time. In addition to the security screening, the airline employee at the gate was asking people if they felt alright, explaining that they didn't want anyone who felt poorly to board the plane and get sick in route or possibly spread the virus.

Trying unsuccessfully to relax, Cory settled into his seat. The older gentleman beside him was reading a newspaper, and the headlines immediately drew Cory's attention. Shocking headlines and column after column of articles about the spread of the influenza from Manila to Taiwan, Hong Kong, and Tokyo covered the front page. Cory closed his eyes, unable to deny his growing anxiety about the welfare of his family.

Using the in-flight telephone, Cory called home while somewhere over the Pacific. As arranged, his wife Rosa answered immediately to avoid waking the kids with a call so late at night. She reported that their older daughter had the sniffles, but she was sleeping soundly as were the other three children. Cory had told himself that if anyone were sick when he called, he would return home from Los Angeles. The casual, nothing-out-of-the-ordinary tone of Rosa's voice helped convince him that he had made a good decision to leave home, but the reassurance faded soon after he hung up the phone.

Reclining the seat fully, Cory took off his shoes, slipped his feet into a pair of soft slippers, and unfolded the blanket provided by the smiling attendant.

Cory thought that he had boarded the airplane alone, but he was actually traveling with what had grown into billions of companions—the flu viruses. After a few hours of flying, his head became stuffy and his joints started to ache. He had a runny nose and began running a low-grade fever. Sleep eluded him. He prayed that it was just a cold and repeatedly denied the possibility that he was getting the deadly influenza.

Unknowingly, Cory infected every one of the 189 passengers and crew on the plane who was not already sick with influenza. The aircraft was too big for him to directly infect all the people on board, but the flight attendants travelling up and down the aisles and Cory's two trips to the lavatory helped. Those who didn't come into personal contact with Cory became exposed through the plane's ventilation system. Recirculating the cabin air was good for fuel economy, but it was even better news for the virus.

The death toll from the virus already qualified it as an epidemic, and now its rapid spread over a wide geographic region was quickly escalating it to the realm of pandemic. Mankind has been plagued by such events since the beginning of time—the bubonic plague, the death of American Indians in colonial times, the1918 influenza. But life moved faster now. In the age of international aviation and discount fares, scientists would need to come up with a new term that describes a pandemic that travels by jet.

Chapter 8

Not Really Stealing

Mid-June (three months earlier)

Dwight considered himself a pretty honest guy about most things. He tried to set a good example for his boys and managed to conceal most of his occasional moral lapses from them. They would never know that he exaggerated charitable deductions on his tax return, or that he had bought a "black box" to watch the premium channels on cable without paying. Then there were the occasional personal long distance calls at work and a few supplies taken home without reimbursing the company. He knew better, but rationalized all of this petty stuff under the "everybody does it" and "they'll never miss it" defenses.

Dwight's journey into the world of big-time crime began at a Monday morning executive staff meeting several months back. Mike announced a new corporate decision to change the method for allocating stock options.

"Who the hell at corporate came up with this Charlie Foxtrot?" fumed Dwight, unable to contain his frustration. Everyone knew that this was Dwight's way of swearing in mixed company— "Charlie Foxtrot" for "cluster fuck."

"Well, Dwight, as I explained, it was the consensus…"

"I don't give a flying flip what the consensus was! All I know is that I have been counting on these options to build my retirement and I just got screwed. It's a royal case of Egyptian football, moving the dadgum goal posts all over hell."

"Think about it, Dwight. I hardly think that an option for 600 shares constitutes getting screwed. You've already made more money than last year." Mike struggled to maintain his own composure in light of Dwight's surprisingly vehement reaction.

"That's 200 shares fewer than last year, Mike! Did your options get cut by twenty-five percent?" Dwight's anger stemmed partly from his suspicion that corporate fair-haired favorites like Mike were probably getting more shares than ever.

"I hardly think that this is an appropriate discussion for right now, Dwight, and you know it. I think you need to…"

Before Mike could finish, Dwight stormed out the door, leaving the rest of the team in an awkward silence, trying to figure out what just happened. Such outbursts were highly unusual in what was normally a very amiable working environment.

Dwight mentally kicked himself all the way back to his office. He now felt rather foolish over his childish display.

He realized that his bad mood stemmed largely from a weekend of boredom and self-pity. As had become the norm, his wife and boys were off doing their own thing, engaged in activities that didn't include him. He had celebrated his birthday on Saturday paying a mountain of bills. Even with Claire working, their debt load seemed to grow each year in direct proportion to the boys' growth spurts. Between insurance premiums, orthodontic bills and private school tuition, Dwight figured that the light at the end of the tunnel must be a freight train.

Later on Saturday he had zoned out in front of the television watching all 400 laps of a NASCAR race with a fifth of bourbon, a two-liter of Coke, and a pack of Marlboros to keep him company. His family had barely remembered to get him a card. He looked down at his calendar and grunted aloud at the notation of Father's Day for the following weekend. "I guess I'd better stop by the package store," he said to himself.

The female voice on the intercom jolted Dwight out of his deepening state of self-pity, as the switchboard paged "Debbie Patterson line 4, Debbie line 4." Knowing that she was not at her desk, Dwight picked up the phone and dialed the code for the parked call.

"This is Dwight Williams. Debbie must be down the hall. Can I help you?"

"Yes, this is Nancy Knox with U.S. Commerce Bank calling from Atlanta. I spoke with Debbie earlier regarding a loan transaction. I need a bank account number to deposit the proceeds of a new three-million-dollar loan."

"I'll give Debbie the message when I see her, and someone will call y'all back with that information in a few minutes."

"That's fine. I will need the account number before 2:00 P.M. if the transaction is to be processed today as planned."

"You'll have it. Let me get a number where we can call you back." Dwight reached for a pen.

Multi-million dollar loans were a frequent activity for the BLuR Financial Center in Macon. The $300 million portfolio of leases for laboratory animal cages made by BLuR in Richmond, Virginia, was funded by multimillion-dollar loans from several big international banks, including U.S. Commerce Bank. Debbie Patterson headed his team that tracked all the debt activities and attended to details such as disposition of the loan proceeds.

As Dwight hung up the phone, still fretting over the stock options, he had the fleeting thought that he should call her back with his own account number. The fantasy quickly became more serious as he began to brainstorm various possibilities for the loan proceeds. He settled on a surprisingly simple yet viable blueprint for instant wealth. Within just a few minutes he had gone from the depths of despair to climactic elation. The felonious flash that went off in his mind ignited a sense of adventure that had been lying dormant for many years.

He sat there for several minutes pondering the situation. This fatefully misdirected call could provide an unbelievable opportunity to temporarily redirect the $3 million for his personal use. The mere thought of misappropriating the money both excited and scared the hell out of him.

Should he just call the bank with the company account number or should he get creative? The cerebral debate raged. *It wouldn't be stealing unless I actually used the money, right? I could just invest it and use the earnings over a period of a few weeks to make up for money the company really owes me anyway. I could pay back the company at any time. Why should Mike and the corporate big shots get all the big bucks? It's managers like me who are the real workhorses of this organization. Hell, even if I got caught I probably wouldn't go to jail. Worst case, I'd repay whatever money they could find, serve a light sentence, and move to St. Simons Island to enjoy the good life.*

He decided to go for it.

"I'm going out. I'll be back inside of an hour," Dwight announced to whoever was within earshot.

Dwight drove downtown to the main post office where BLuR had its mail delivered. He opened a new post office box under the name BLuR Financial Center.

"Mr. Williams, do you want to come by later with a check for the fee?" asked a post office clerk who knew Dwight.

"No, I'll just give you cash and get reimbursed," Dwight replied.

After a post office box was secured, Dwight went to the downtown branch of the bank where BLuR kept its accounts, and where he had his own personal checking account. He opened a new bank account in the name of BLuR Financial Center with the new post office box number that he had just established.

The bank's assistant manager handed him the new account paperwork. "Mr. Williams, please bring these signature cards back and we'll give you a temporary checkbook."

Dwight carefully forged the two other corporate signatures, while he sipped a cup of coffee at the nearby Barnes and Noble. He strolled through the aisles looking for books on investments before returning the cards to the bank. He returned to the office shortly after noon and promptly called the bank in Atlanta to give them his new bank account number. As of 12:38 P.M. on June 15, the three million dollars was safely deposited in the account and available to Dwight. His heightened level of excitement made sitting still impossible, so he slipped out once more for a private celebration lunch at the Waffle House.

He returned from lunch refreshed and invigorated with a spring in his step, whistling as he crossed the parking lot. He smiled and spoke to everyone he encountered on the way back to his desk, then sat down to complete his work. He felt so good that he even went to Mike and apologized for his earlier outburst.

But he couldn't go on a shopping spree just yet; recording the entry on the books of the company would be a bit trickier. He had to figure out how to enter the loan on the ledger of BLuR so that they would pay the interest and pay off the loan slowly over three years. There was no easy way to do this without attracting the attention of others in the accounting department. To his credit, Dwight had established a thorough system of checks and balances.

Bringing someone like Debbie into the scheme as a partner would dramatically reduce his odds of getting caught, but he was pretty sure that she was too honest to go along. Besides, he didn't want to split the loot with anyone.

Dwight decided to wait a few days until the accounting team was swamped in their normal month-end activities so that he would have a little smokescreen to fix the books. June being the end of a quarter, they would be even busier.

In early July, on the eve of reporting deadlines, Dwight was in the office helping his staff close the books. "Dawn, would you please record this loan," he asked one of Debbie's assistants as he handed her the wire transfer.

"Sure, Dwight," replied Dawn. "To what do we owe the honor of you helping us tonight?"

"Claire's working this evening and the boys are at friends', so this is the happening place for me tonight. Besides, I took the call on this loan a few days ago and wanted to follow it up because the account on the deposit slip is wrong and needs to be corrected to show our regular account." Dwight pointed to some notes he had scribbled on the form. He hoped that he appeared calm, but his heart was racing.

Dawn reviewed Dwight's notes on the advice and did as instructed without hesitation. "Sure, I'll take care of it, Dwight." Recording bank deposits in the millions of dollars was routine, and there was no reason to question what Dwight had said.

Now the loan was recorded, but the cash had not been deposited, and a routine bank reconciliation would easily identify the irregularity. Dwight had to get creative to fix this last step.

As part of their normal monthly billing, customers who had not paid their previous month's rent were charged a late fee that was added to the billing. Since only a fraction of the late fees would be paid, BLuR followed the conservative accounting practice of taking late fees into income only after the customer paid them. This left a balance of several million dollars of "billed but not collected" late fees on the books.

The auditors had been hounding Dwight for some time to clean out these accounts. It was painstakingly difficult to track the detail because of the continuous high volume of small balances flowing between the billing and cash ledgers.

Dwight wrote one journal entry that both increased and decreased the cash account to record the bank's supposed error in depositing the loan. A second entry recorded what appeared to be a harmless write off of late charges due from customers against the offsetting deferred asset. In the crunch of closing a busy and successful month, no one questioned why four entries all for exactly three million dollars were written up as journals. And no one noticed that when Dwight entered the journals into the system, he scrambled the line items and only recorded a reduction in the cash balance and a write down of deferred late fees.

Now the cash account would reconcile with the bank statements. The three-million-dollar reduction in the late fee deferral account would not only go unnoticed, it was exactly the reduction that the auditors were recommending. *Brilliant*, Dwight thought to himself. *Just plain, friggin' brilliant.*

To invest the funds, Dwight would depend on his personal computer to provide the large volume of small transactions needed to avoid detection. Dwight's expertise with spreadsheets and ability to trade online would make managing his "borrowed funds" a breeze. His Dell laptop at home was powerful enough to share files with his PC at work to provide anytime, anywhere access.

One by one, Dwight carefully transferred funds out of his new, special bank account into a variety of investment accounts. He used several Web-based services to buy securities in various well-known corporations and mutual funds. With everything handled electronically, no broker or human agent ever laid eyes on Dwight's securities trading. The few statements that weren't paperless went to his special PO box.

For the next few months, Dwight's investment strategies yielded gains that would outpace the market averages. His plan to become wealthy without ever touching the original three million dollars was well on its way to reality. Meanwhile the loan accountants at BLuR would pay the quarterly interest on the three million dollar note right along with all the other bank borrowings as part of the normal routine.

Limiting his risks of being caught required some ingenuity. He kept each investment account small so that if someone found one of his accounts, it would be reasonable that someone in Dwight's position could have potentially saved that much money. Dwight lost some sleep in the first few weeks, but as more time passed, the trail got colder and it became unlikely that anyone could figure out what happened.

The success of the scam also acted as a potent aphrodisiac on Dwight, significantly raising his libido. He started to give serious consideration to having a little fling. It wouldn't be hard to keep Claire from becoming suspicious, as infrequently as they made love. There were several attractive and available women at work, but Dwight knew better than to "dip his pen in the company inkwell." He knew too many successful execs who lost everything because they couldn't "keep their pecker out of the payroll."

Going out to single bars was out of the question, and Dwight didn't know if prostitutes even existed in Macon. He even spent a good bit of time thinking up ways to get into position in case the attractive divorced woman who lived two doors down from his house needed a little companionship from time to time. Maybe he could hook up her computer or fix a broken appliance or help with her tax return.

Dwight was well on his way to reaping what he felt he deserved out of life.

Chapter 9

Motionless Stacks

Monday, September 14

By Monday, the media focus intensified to a near frenzy over the tens of thousands of influenza deaths in and around Manila. In an uncharacteristic openness to Western assistance, the panicked Filipino, Malaysian, and Chinese governments invited American medical officials and representatives from the Centers for Disease Control in Atlanta to cities like Beijing to assess the situation. With American experts now involved, alarm bells began to ring in the United States. Television and newspaper reporters traveling with the scientists covered the big airlift to various destinations in Asia. With the U.S. taking every precaution to prevent this plague from spreading across the Pacific, people came to the realization that indeed it could.

Typical of the modern day media propensity for the sensational, images of the dead bombarded the television screen in a gruesome minute by minute commentary on the latest accounts of the plague. Fear mounted worldwide as the virus escaped the boundaries of Southeast Asia and began to wreak havoc in distant places such as India and Pakistan. The cinematic images of middle-class men, women, and children stacked up dead along a curb like cord wood somehow proved of greater shock than those of malnourished natives from developing countries to which America had become so accustomed. Dressed for work or school in the latest fashions, the dead looked far too much like "one of us" for comfort.

Broadcasts took on a surreal quality with images from the Philippines. Commodity traders panicked as sellers far exceeded buyers. Empty store shelves resulted from the hysteria of buyers as well as the destruction of farm animals that supplied the meat. Corpses lay along the streets as the demand for coffins and body bags far outstripped supplies, and graves could not be dug fast enough to bury each victim.

The speed with which the flu claimed its Asian victims compounded the fear it evoked. In many cases, as few as twelve hours separated the difference between normalcy and death, providing little time to react. The dead and dying littered public bathrooms, restaurants, and office buildings. Hospitals and clinics, strained far beyond capacity, offered little hope as many of the medical personnel succumbed to the dread virus along with everyone else.

Americans had become used to the threat of diseases spread by insects or human contact. But death by inhalation brought back the worst fears of recent bio-terrorism warnings and images of medieval plagues. Even from half a world away, the desperation was palpable, and at home people began turning off their televisions out of an irrational, unspoken fear of exposure by viewing.

+

Alarmed by the growing coverage given to the virus, Mike Spiker took advantage of his contacts within the corporation by calling the executive in charge of the Atlanta BLuR operation, a research doctor by the name of Pete Farr, to get an expert's view of the pandemic situation.

"Pete, do you think this Philippines plague will spread to the US?" asked Mike.

"There's no way to stop it. The only thing we can hope for is that it changes into a harmless or less serious strain before it gets here."

"But they say it's just the flu! Why are people dying?"

"It does appear to be some type of influenza, and you're reaction is very common. People don't realize that influenza has been steadily killing people through the ages—sometimes millions of people annually. Often the worst toll is in third-world countries with unsanitary living conditions and terrible medical resources. But every few decades, new strains develop that are particularly virulent and attack in the U.S. and other developed countries."

"We hear about AIDS and mad cow and e-coli and West Nile, but it sounds like influenza can be a bigger threat," Mike injected.

"Well, technically it's not actually influenza that kills people, but the pneumonia or other complications that set in."

"So it really is transmitted through the air?" asked Mike.

"Yes, but you don't just walk outside and breathe in flu viruses. The viruses travel on tiny droplets of moisture in our breath. The cells and the viruses die within seconds if they don't land on something moist and warm where they can reproduce. But yeah, it really does travel by air, mostly between people within a few feet of each other."

"Unbelievable, doc. Is there any cure?"

"Sure, we have vaccines for all of the strains that we know about. You get your flu shot every year don't you? Unfortunately the virus mutates all the time, so we have to keep chasing new strains with new vaccines. And the big challenge in attacking any kind of virus is that they live and grow in healthy cells, just like cancer. We have a long way to go in understanding and treating viruses."

"Why do these epidemics always seem to start in Asia?"

"Because of dense populations and poor public health practices overseas. The USDA inspects our livestock all the time. American growers make sure their chickens and livestock are inoculated and they don't hesitate to destroy sick animals. We don't let cows near the chickens, or chickens near pigs. Many animals like dogs can carry forms of influenza all the time, but we can't catch it from them. We only get it from pigs, which is why they call it swine flu."

"If terrorists are behind this, don't you feel vulnerable living and working near the CDC in Atlanta?"

"I don't put much stock in conspiracy theories. Chances are this pandemic was started by natural causes. Every city has some potential terrorist target. You've got one of the biggest Air Force bases in the country in your back yard at Robins. And your Medical Center gets some complicated disease cases from all over the region."

"Good point." Mike paused. "Well, tell me one final thing. Are you scared? What are you doing to protect your family? Is it time to find an old bomb shelter and bunker down?"

"Remember Y2K? Same thing. Don't overreact. When it gets to the U.S. it will probably hit some distant city and we'll have time to react. Wouldn't hurt to buy some extra food that you can eat later, but if everyone does that we'll have a panic."

"I appreciate your time, Pete. Thanks for scaring the shit out of me," said Mike. "I hope the next time I see you is on a golf course like the one in Nevis last year!"

"Take care, Mike, and say hello to Courtney."

+

The strain of flu that developed on the Maylon farm in Batangas City had successfully accompanied Cory Sabugo and his fellow passengers on a Philippines Airlines jet across the Pacific to Los Angeles. The passengers deplaned at LAX along with an indeterminable number of virus particles. Longer customs lines due to tighter, post-9/11 clearance of foreigners entering the U.S. forced more people to spend more time in a limited space—another big advantage for the virus.

Some travelers stayed in Southern California, others caught connecting flights. Every passenger and crewmember on the plane had been exposed to the virus long enough to allow them to grow to communicable levels in the hours between Manila and LA.

Cory had endured a bad sinus headache on the descent into LAX, but once on the ground the pressure equalized and his pain went away. He deplaned for a few minutes to stretch his legs and buy some Sudafed. He called home to Manila where it was now morning. No one picked up before the answering machine came on. He tried again. And again. Still no one picked up. Now he was getting scared. Maybe they were still asleep. Maybe they were in a hospital. Maybe it was worse. From half a world away, he considered flying back to Manila. They announced final boarding for his flight. A decision would have to wait until he arrived in Cincinnati.

About 135 people boarded the plane for the flight to Cincinnati. Thanks to Cory, the cabin of the plane soon became so rich in airborne viruses that it took no time for everyone to become exposed. Cory felt achy and stuffy, but no worse than a few hours before. For inexplicable reasons Cory's body, like a select few, could ward off the ravages of the virus, at least in its current form.

The flight arrived in Cincinnati four hours later. The decongestant pills had prevented another sinus headache and even cleared up some of Cory's flu symptoms. Upon deplaning in Cincinnati, Cory looked for a men's room to relieve himself and wash up. Streams of passengers from other flights entered the river of people walking through the concourse. Cory spotted a bank of pay phones where he could call his family as soon as he finished in the bathroom. If they still didn't answer he would call his sister or perhaps alert the authorities. If he couldn't make contact pretty quickly, he would turn around and fly back home. Something, he sensed, wasn't right.

Chapter 10

The Lovely and Talented

Saturday, September 12

"Hey Eddie, what does someone from the University of Georgia call a graduate from Georgia Tech?" Jennifer's deceptively sweet voice dripped with Southern drawl, transforming her references to Georgia into "jaw-ja".

"I don't know. What?" Eddie knew what was coming, but, unable to resist her charms, he played along.

"Boss," replied Jennifer. Her husband, R.T. and their friends, Eddie and Cam, all laughed.

The two couples lounged on a blanket on the grass lawn of the Alumni House on the campus of Georgia Tech in Atlanta. In a couple of hours, the Georgia Tech Yellow Jackets would play the University of North Carolina Tarheels.

"Does all this take you back a few years?" R.T. directed the question to his friend Eddie who had graduated from Emory University, a large school with no football program.

"Oh yeah. I used to love coming to Tech games," said Eddie. "How's that go? *I'm a Ramblin' Wreck from Georgia Tech and a helluva engineer! A helluva, helluva, helluva, helluva, hell of an Engineer!*" he sang out the fight song with help from Jennifer and R.T.

"Y'all sound like a bunch of wrecks," said Cam, who attended Agnes Scott, a women's college near Emory.

"You're right, Cam," said Jennifer, "but it's half drunk, middle-aged, fat cats like these two that make this village come alive on fall Saturdays, you know?"

R.T. breathed in deeply, sensing a hint of autumn crispness in the still warm September air. "Y'all, this is why we work our butts off all year and invest in these expensive tickets—an exciting game, great friends, and I'm with the most lovely and talented Yellow Jacket in the history of the school."

Eddie and Cam exchanged glances, grimacing at R.T.'s overt adoration of his wife. If Jennifer heard the remark, she didn't react. She was too busy checking out the local talent.

In their familiar fall ritual, the couples had arrived on campus early to eat lunch near Bobby Dodd Stadium. The party-hardy foursome drank beer and feasted on fried chicken and pimento cheese sandwiches. While thousands tailgated on campus, the festivities spilled out into the city as other hungry fans made their home game pilgrimage to the Atlanta Mecca known as the Varsity, casting caloric caution to the wind as they consumed greasy fries, overcooked hamburgers, and Cokes served over chipped ice. An hour before the game was to begin, the four friends broke camp and put the now much lighter cooler and picnic basket back into the Suburban. They strolled leisurely to the gates of the stadium past the surprisingly polite scalpers hawking tickets at ridiculous prices for the sellout game. Thousands of fans funneled through the narrow entrances as watchful guards barked instructions to pour out open containers and prepare for an inspection of all bags. Since 9/11, searches for weapons made smuggling liquor bottles into the stadium much more challenging.

Once they settled in their seats, Jennifer made small talk with two guys seated to her left. "If Mettler's shoulder is one hundred percent, we ought to mop them up with our rushing game. Of course, UNC's defense will key off Goodman. And if Henley has a good day at safety..."

Jennifer surveyed the scene before her. Only a small patch of blue and white in the visitors' section interrupted the endless sea of yellow and black. Stands full of white faces cheered on the predominately black players as they warmed up on the field. The faithful masses formed a colorful mosaic in motion. Wind-swept white clouds painted the perfect blue sky. The performance of the Star Spangled Banner sung by an unseen soprano with a booming voice silenced the sellout stadium if only momentarily. The inspirational moment of patriotism gave way to a collective battle cry that shook the arena as the fans yelled and stomped like Romans awaiting gladiators.

In the interest of viewing this brute spectacle, 48,000 fans relinquished their normal demands for personal space, each body occupying a mere two-foot-by-two-foot plot of hard metal and concrete. A near-perfect scenario for the rapid and epidemic spread of a virus was at hand. Indeed, billions of little germs traveled from person to person on the tiny droplets expelled with each yell of the throngs. Today, fortunately, most of the germs were harmless, or at least easily defeated.

Tech beat North Carolina by two touchdowns. Heavy traffic delayed the drive home to Macon, but Jennifer kept the group entertained with her play-by-play highlights of the game.

"Dadgum Jenn! You know more about the game than the announcers! The coaches ought to give you a headset and ask you to join them on the sidelines!" declared Eddie.

"I've been attending my brothers' football games with my Daddy since I was four years old," she replied nonchalantly. "The Tarheels could've made it more interesting if they had established their running game earlier."

Jennifer looked out the window at the non-stop wall of pine trees along the highway—quite a contrast to the parched fields surrounding her childhood home outside San Antonio.

+

Jennifer would always regret that she never had a chance to tell her mother goodbye. Her family functioned in perfect denial up until the time that her mother, age thirty-six, slipped suddenly into a coma from which she would never return. Though not appreciated at the time, it was actually a compassionate end to a two-year battle with cancer. Jennifer was ten at the time, and she still carried the image of her seventy-pound mother in her mind as clearly as the pictures of her children in her billfold. Every vein and tendon in her mother's bony, frail hand remained visible in her mind's eye. Left unattended, the wounds of the experience left a deep emotional scar that Jennifer did not understand or even recognize. Unconsciously, she associated love with loss and pain. Distance and control over all future relationships would assure her that she would never again endure that kind of anguish.

After her mama died, Jennifer's father took advantage of an offer from his company to transfer from Texas to a new plant in Warner Robins, Georgia, near Robins Air Force Base. He elected to live in nearby Macon so Jennifer and her four brothers could attend the local Catholic high school. Despite the fact that they were raised Baptist, he figured the nuns could bring some much-needed discipline into their motherless lives.

A classically tall, handsome Texan, Jennifer's father cast a big shadow. While memories of her mother were painfully visual, it was her father's voice that she would recall—loud and rowdy, always living life a little too large. He loved his daughter as deeply as he knew how, but had no idea how to raise a young lady. He simply treated her like another son, and as a result she grew up talking about sports, cars, and politics. They taught her to ride horses and four wheelers at an early age. He taught her his trade skills as an electrician, and she became comfortable with wiring and electronics, working first with appliances, which led to her interest in computers.

In many ways, she was the spitting image of her father—thoroughly entertaining, but possessing little emotional maturity. Football and politics weren't the only male attitudes Jennifer would be exposed to growing up. In a household inhabited by five men and unrestrained by a mother's boundaries, conversations frequently turned raunchy. Her insight into the male mentality took a decidedly naughty twist as she adopted their view of sex as more act than intimacy, more conquest than commitment. In the process she discovered the irresistible power and means of control for which she longed—sex. She listened and learned, silently, secretly taking in lessons from her brothers that would later be used like lethal weapons against their own kind.

With her sharp mind and highly competitive spirit, Jennifer got straight A's in school with little effort. After graduating from Georgia Tech with a degree in computer science, she took a job with a Fortune 50 firm in Atlanta. After four years of marital bliss, her first husband became a raving lunatic when Jennifer quit her job, divorced him and took their three-year-old daughter to Macon.

"I just don't love you anymore, Chuck," Jennifer reported coldly. "I'm going back to Macon to be closer to my family. You can see Molly any time you want to drive down to see her. It's been great, but it's over!"

Jennifer aced out the competition and landed the position as IT director at BLuR Financial Center in Macon within days of her return.

She met her second husband in Macon, had a son named Matthew, and divorced number two, all within three years. Fortunately, her father and his new wife were happy to help her raise the children while she took care of business.

Before long she met and married R.T. Sanders, her third husband. Together they had a son Cliff, which brought the total to three children for Jennifer, all with different fathers. The kids got along famously, even though they each had different last names.

Every other Friday night, husbands one and two met in the driveway, sometimes with husband three, to coordinate weekend custody of their kids. Potentially explosive exchanges always ended without a fight. Her two ex's had not completely gotten over Jennifer and, in her presence, they melted faster than an ice cube in August. They sure didn't want to upset her, knowing full well that the only thing that exceeded her beauty was her temper.

+

R.T.'s family was "old Macon" with roots that reached back generations. His grandfather had started Sanders Funeral Home in a premium downtown location on Cherry Street. For three generations, the Sander's men, in their black suits and starched white shirts, had provided the best mortuary services in town—"dignity and quality at a fair price" as R.T. always said. Of course the funerals were far more dignified than many of the folks they buried, but R.T. loved his work and dreamed of someday teaching his son the tricks of the trade and passing the business on to him.

According to R.T., being a mortician was one part chemistry, one part ministry, and two parts politics. Proving the point, he remained active in the community. As a past president of the Rotary Club, he was assured lifetime stature in the Macon good ol' boy network.

A long-standing agreement with the county and city police ensured that R.T. got at least his fair share of calls. In the absence of a special request from the family, calls to pick up bodies were simply rotated between the local funeral homes—by color, of course. Segregation remained alive and well when it came to mortuaries, based on nothing more than the desires of both races.

Never really comfortable with the funeral business, Jennifer could not bear all the death and suffering, and she wondered how R.T. could make it his life's work. She avoided the Sander's facility because she feared stumbling into that room where they put all the body parts that don't go in the ground, or open a door and see her frail mama lying in a casket.

R.T. and Jennifer lived in one of the majestic antebellum mansions in the city. In typical urban style, you were as likely to see the well-to-do out walking the dog as the homeless making their way to the local soup kitchen. The grandiose brick home loomed only feet from the street. Like the bodies he embalmed, R.T. had gutted and restored the entire structure with new plumbing, electricity, and central air conditioning. The porch wrapped around three sides of the house shielding a dozen rockers from the ravages of the Middle Georgia elements.

While R.T. and Jennifer were professionally prominent and socially popular, both individually and as a couple, those who knew Jennifer and R.T. were amazed that their marriage endured. Jennifer's friends didn't understand what she saw in R.T. He was a nice guy and a gentleman, just not in her league. Mr. Mortician meets Miss Cosmopolitan. Affections were decidedly lopsided, but then perhaps it was not as strange as it might appear—as a mortician, he was accustomed to corpse-like coldness.

+

"I'm really pleased with your performance as IT director. You're doing a great job, Jennifer!" Mike told her during one of their recent performance reviews at BLuR. Her responsibilities over the information technology department included oversight of all of the computer equipment, networks, and applications for the operations in Macon. Her team of forty highly skilled technicians managed the data center twenty-four hours, seven days without a break, while a second team developed software applications. Her experience at the Fortune 50 facility in Atlanta had exposed her to the latest and best technology systems. In just three years under her direction, BLuR had grown from a primitive computer shop to a world class technology center.

"You seem to have an excellent rapport with your workers. I have never seen a leader quite as skilled at motivating technical people as you seem to be. You're very impressive, Mrs. Sanders."

She flashed Mike a smile as if to encourage him to keep talking.

Mike remained formal to keep some distance, but after the words left his lips, he regretted that they probably came across as forward. He often felt awkward around beautiful women because anything he said usually sounded like a come-on.

"I am particularly pleased with the improvement in the up-time stats. The system hasn't been down since you arrived on the scene."

"Well, I have an excellent team." Jennifer feigned modesty. "Have you had an opportunity to review the training schedule I left for you? I know it is ambitious, but I believe it is essential for us to maintain our level of service."

"It's already been approved and is in route back to you." The room filled with silence as Mike made a few notes and signed her review form. "I hope you're happy working here, Jennifer." Mike watched for her reaction and saw no indication otherwise. "Let me know if you get that IT itch to move on. By the way, how is R.T. doing? I haven't seen him in a few weeks." Mike always inquired about R.T. Knowing Jennifer's track record with ex's, R.T. offered the best hope for keeping Jennifer in Macon, even though she could be making a much higher salary in Atlanta or New York.

"R.T. is great," reported Jennifer. "I know that we IT-types enjoy a reputation as Gypsies, but I really like it here, Mike. It's a world-class operation in a town that's easy to live in. Don't worry about me getting any urges." The innocent phrase couldn't help but rouse a man into thinking about what kind of urges she could be referring to, even a cautious guy like Mike.

One of her employees had commented recently, "Everyone loves her, but she's unlike anyone I've ever met. I've never seen her raise her voice or get frustrated, maybe because I've never seen her not get her way. All the guys have a school-boy crush on her."

Mike knew exactly what he meant. He too found himself somewhat enamoured by her charm and quick, sassy wit, but he made a conscious effort to keep things on a strictly professional level.

Chapter 11

Tires, Brakes, Cocaine?

Monday, September 14

A beautiful day greeted the new workweek for team BLuR.

Dwight left his house for work at 6:45 A.M., allowing plenty of time to stop by the Waffle House for a cup of coffee and to catch up on the latest news. He walked through the door of the suburban BLuR office complex at 7:30 A.M. on the dot. By eight he had already checked and responded to several email messages and attended to the obligatory Monday morning chitchat with co-workers. He held three quick meetings before nine, reviewed some financial reports that he would present at the executive meeting, and answered some questions from his staff as he visited them at their workstations.

By 7:00 A.M. Latrice was methodically making her rounds to be sure that the computer systems were all up and running, the reports run over the weekend had been distributed, and that the early shift was busy at work.

Latrice's morning had not begun so smoothly as yet another shooting had occurred overnight in Unionville. Police discovered a black male shot seven times in a yard less than a mile from her house. By the time she drove by on her way to work, plainclothes investigators mingled with the uniformed cops in an area cordoned off with bright yellow crime scene tape. In the safety of the office, such a scene seemed like nothing more than a bad dream, except for the fact that her daughter had to walk past the carnage to get to her bus stop. The first thing Latrice did when she arrived at work was to phone her parents and ask them to drive Regina to school using a different route.

Mike's morning routine defied a predictable pattern. If he woke up before dawn, as he often did, he might arrive at work by 6:30 A.M. If he slept in until 5:45 or so, like this morning, he would take the opportunity to spend as much time with the kids as he could. Today, he pulled in at 7:50, and immediately began thinking about the agenda for the weekly executive meeting that morning.

Halfway to his office, Mike was interrupted by a silky "Good morning" behind him. He turned to see Jennifer.

She smiled warmly as her blond hair hung jauntily to one side. "Have a good weekend, Mike?"

"Fine, Jennifer. I guess you and R.T went to Atlanta Saturday."

"Oh yeah, it was a great game. You ought to join us sometime." She smiled again.

The fifth member of the executive team walked up. "Good morning, y'all!" sung Paris, jovial as always and perpetually running late. She often arrived at work tardy, which was not exactly acceptable behavior for the human resources director who was responsible for setting the example of proper employee conduct.

Paris had the furthest to travel from her home in rural Jones County where she was the unofficial matriarch of the Hawkins family compound—more than a hundred relatives living on one hundred acres that had been passed down through the generations. A controversy with her cousin Jimmy Mack over ownership of the property was consuming a lot of Paris's time and energy recently.

Paris was probably late because she stopped at McDonald's on the way to work. With only her aging father to care for, Paris spent little time in the kitchen. Her dedication to her BLuR family came first.

"See you in a little while," Paris said in passing as Mike and Jennifer went their respective ways.

Jennifer arrived for the executive meeting just before nine, followed closely by Dwight.

"Hey, Jenn! How 'bout dem Dawgs! Whooped the Tide big time!" Dwight let out a few patented UGA Bulldog 'woofs'. "I see the Jackets did great against North Carolina, too." Dwight had to be careful not to encourage his Tech rivals too much because the big Georgia-Georgia Tech game was only a few weeks away.

Mike entered the conference room, but not the conversation. His alma mater, the University of Maryland, was having another lousy football season, and Dwight and Jennifer made fun of Maryland's mascot, the terrapin.

"How'd the mighty turtles do, Mike? I didn't see the score." The subject provided a legitimate means for Dwight to torment his boss and he delighted in it.

"They lost to Virginia. They have a lousy team again this year. But, hey, way to go Dawgs!" Mike didn't feel like defending his alma mater's mascot, even if they were one of the most ferocious animals in nature. Since moving to Georgia, he simply adopted UGA as his new home team, but he lacked the true fighting passion of diehard Bulldog alums such as Dwight.

Paris and Latrice entered the room engrossed in their own conversation about whether they had probable cause to drug test an under-performing employee.

"Hey, did y'all see where O. J. Simpson visited his alma mater's football practice?" said Dwight, continuing the football banter as the five leaders settled in around the conference table. "Why doesn't that creep just go away?"

"Now, what do you mean by that, Dwight?" Latrice responded, stopping her own conversation. "Hasn't the man paid his dues? Can't he visit his school's scrimmage without making the headlines? I'll bet most of the players were glad to see him."

"He's a murderer, for God's sake!"

"That's your opinion, Dwight," responded Latrice, thrusting her face his way.

"Let's move on," Mike broke in.

"No, Mike, let's talk about this. Picking on O.J. when the man was found not guilty of a crime is just another example of racism," Latrice said curtly.

"Me, a racist?" countered Dwight. "I'm just relaying a story I saw in the news yesterday. O.J.'s the one who played the race card! Hell, he pulled out the whole deck!"

"Guilty or not, the evidence was corrupted. The jury couldn't overlook that a racist cop planted evidence—"

"What a load of crap, O.J. was—"

"Latrice! Dwight! This all happened many years ago. Let's stop this arguing and start the meeting," Mike demanded.

"You're the one making this a race issue, Latrice," Dwight jumped right back at Latrice, ignoring Mike's plea for a truce. "Black or white, it was O.J.'s celebrity status and money that got him off. He slaughtered those two people, then signed up the best defense team money could buy!"

"Maybe it was just a little justice after 300 years of oppression. Was it money that got off the white cops that beat up Rodney King? How about the white guy who murdered Medgar Evers? And what about—"

"Okay, that's enough!" Mike raised his voice. "This is going nowhere. Let's stick to business."

Paris sat with her mouth open, anxious for the pain to end.

Jennifer stared at her notes, hoping the rest of the meeting would go a lot more smoothly.

"Dwight," Mike began the meeting, "why don't you start us off with a look at the August financials."

Dwight reviewed the results for the previous month. Latrice interrupted him three times to ask about details for her department: "Have all the extra overtime hours from that last weekend in August been accrued or not?"

Dwight didn't like her tone, and didn't know the answer off the top of his head, so he shrugged her off. Latrice was in no mood to be shrugged off.

"How can I find out, Dwight? It's important," responded Latrice.

"Do you want me to go right now and find out or can I get back to you later this morning?" Dwight replied sharply.

"That's enough," Mike said sternly. "You two better knock it off. I have enough children at home." Mike couldn't remember a time when Dwight and Latrice got along so poorly. The usually jovial mood of the group had gotten off to a bad start—and fallen off from there.

"Hey, y'all," Dwight said with a smile. "How can you tell when you've met an extroverted accountant?" Dwight paused. "While he's talking to you, he's looking at your shoes instead of his own."

Everyone chuckled, including Latrice. Paris breathed a sigh of relief that Dwight's joke only insulted accountants, and not an entire protected class.

+

Back in August, Latrice and Dwight both attended a national operations meeting at BLuR Headquarters in Wilmington, Delaware.

"Hey Empress, what do you say we hire a limo and drive to Atlantic City tonight?" Dwight asked Latrice as the first day of a two-day meeting was wrapping up.

"You mean bag the recognition dinner tonight? What if one of us gets Employee of the Year? How will it look if we're not there to accept the award?"

"Yeah, right. I'll call the limo service."

Once in the casino, Latrice and Dwight played craps, blackjack, and talked over cocktails until midnight. They returned to the limousine for the trip back to the hotel.

"Well, we certainly left an impression on our New Jersey American friends, didn't we, Empress!" Dwight turned to the window. "Youse guys love Georgia accents up here, don't youse?" he said, pretending to yell out the window.

"They do like to hear us talk, don't they?" Latrice asked of her fellow Macon native. "Do you figure they think you and I are a couple, because we were together and both talk funny?"

"Yeah, they're fascinated by us. You're a recently released slave girl and I'm a cruel, narrow-minded cotton plantation owner," Dwight said laughing.

"They were probably going crazy wondering if our kids have straight redneck hair like you or a beautiful, kinky black 'fro like me," Latrice said, cupping her hair.

"Yeah, I'm sure we were great entertainment. They think we're perfectly charming—sluggish and dumb as a post, but real nice."

"That was until you told that dealer that he was "slower than a crippled turtle." They laughed.

"One thing that had to impress them was how you were throwing all that money around tonight," Latrice said. "You were so nonchalant about losing quite a bundle in there."

"You win some and lose some, I guess." Dwight said, immediately regretting his words. "I hit the jackpot playing craps up here a few months ago," Dwight explained quickly. "I figured I'd better let 'em win a little back."

Dwight stared out the window as if the darkness demanded his attention, and Latrice was left to silently wonder what had caused his dramatic mood swing. Like a couple of Cinderella's after midnight, the spell was over and they were once again just a pair of tired executives trying to get back to Wilmington for their meetings in the morning.

Within ten minutes Dwight's head was extended back on the seat, his mouth wide open and eyes closed. A long snore escaped from time to time. Latrice took the half-full drink out of his hand and placed it in the cup holder. She looked over at Dwight with fond amusement, then curled up on her side of the seat and dozed off.

+

The Monday morning meeting resumed as Latrice highlighted several operational process changes. She was several minutes into her talk when Jennifer found herself in the middle of a decadently inappropriate fantasy involving Mike.

"Well, Jennifer…can you do this by December or not?" Latrice's voice broke in.

"That shouldn't be a problem. Why don't we discuss the details after this meeting." As the meeting continued, Jennifer wondered exactly to what it was that she had just committed.

+

At Jack's Auto Repair on Gray Highway on the east side of town, another Monday morning meeting was underway. Wayne Williams, Dwight's long lost older brother, forked over a pile of twenty-dollar bills to one of his suppliers. The sackful of tiny bags of crack cocaine were already safely in Wayne's pocket.

Unbeknownst to Jack Walker, the shop's owner, his most regular customers came in for new tires, new brakes—or a bag of crack, not necessarily in that order. The auto repair store provided a great base of operations because both suppliers and customers could find Wayne at regular times at a convenient location.

Every penny Wayne earned at the shop or from selling drugs went to support his lifestyle. He drove a new Jeep during the week and a Harley on the weekends. If he wasn't at work, he could usually be found on his way to the nearest NASCAR event with a gang of friends.

Jay, one of his buddies, reminded Wayne of a South Georgia gnat. No matter how many times he swatted at him, he never went away. The two were virtually inseparable. They had met several years earlier when Wayne was dating Jay's kid sister. While the relationship with the sister fizzled quickly, Jay and Wayne struck up an immediate kinship based on all the vices they had in common.

Jay's vast knowledge and experience with firearms, especially automatic rifles and exotic weapons such as machine pistols and grenade launchers, captivated Wayne's interest. They often hunted birds and squirrels with Uzis and high-powered rifles. Recently they began experimenting with homemade bombs.

In recent months a third member had joined their band, Jimmy Mack Hawkins. He came into Jack's one day shopping for tires, and walked right into one of Wayne's crack transactions. Wayne and his client panicked until they realized the large black man in uniform was a Georgia National Guardsman, not a cop coming to bust them. Jimmy Mack waited until the drug buyer left before he approached Wayne and extorted half off the price of a new set of tires in return for keeping his mouth shut. When Jimmy Mack stood up to Wayne's threats to kill his black ass, Wayne recognized some real potential and came to appreciate Jimmy Mack's initiative.

With Jimmy Mack's Guard unit's periodic drug tests, he had to stay clear of the drugs personally, but he had no problem selling the stuff.

"Today I was taking this banker dude back to his house while we put tires on his shiny new Lexus," Wayne told Jimmy Mack and Jay over beers one night. "The whole time he's in the car, he's talking to his wife on this cell phone about going to Jekyll Island for the weekend. Y'all should've seen this house! It was friggin' huge! And get this, no dog and no alarm. And it was like way out in the middle of nowhere! Y'all game for a little visit to Mr. Banker Man's big house this weekend?"

"Crap Wayne, don't you have enough going on without breaking and entering?" Jimmy Mack jested.

"If you think it's a good deal, Wayne, I'm in," Jay answered mindlessly.

Wayne proceeded to describe all the electronic gear and loot he managed to spot in the house after he asked the guy to use the can. Jimmy Mack's greed kicked into overdrive as he listened.

"What do you say, Jimmy Mack? You in?"

Jimmy Mack nodded.

That Saturday, the trio ransacked the house, mainly stealing stuff they could use or sell to friends. The loot was great, but it was the thrill of a successful mission that gave them a real buzz.

+

Cory Sabugo was fortunate to only suffer mild cold symptoms after being exposed to the influenza virus in Manila. Agents in his body were able to keep the virus from attacking his lungs and causing any significant infection or damage. But unfortunately for those around him, that didn't make him any less contagious.

A middle-aged airport worker in a blue uniform removed the little yellow barricade from the entrance to the Cincinnati airport men's room just as Cory and two other travelers entered. A faux pine scent still hung in the air and the chrome fixtures glistened. The freshly cleaned facility provided travelers with a false sense of security as the virus traveled through the seemingly disinfected air. Cory exhaled a long weary breath of jet lag and exhaustion that contained sufficient virus particles to infect both of the innocent bystanders that had accompanied him into the room.

Outside the bathrooms, Cory found a pay phone to call home. It was now evening in Manila. The phone at the Sabugo residence rang six times before the answering machine came on. Cory left another message, wondering if his wife would check the messages before the machine reached capacity.

Nobody could answer the phone because no one left in Cory's house was conscious. His little boy was in his bed thrashing about, moaning from the high fever and spitting up blood. The two older girls had run from the house in their night clothes and bare feet, and out onto the street. They were terrified to have found their mother lying still in her bed, her eyes wide open. They couldn't wake her up and she wasn't breathing. They needed to get some help. None of the neighbors on their street answered their doors, so they fled to their grandmother's house two kilometers away.

Chapter 12

McDirty

Tuesday, September 15

As Cory Sabugo was deplaning in Cincinnati, Harry Miller was three gates away, anxiously awaiting the arrival of his son. While people greeting arriving passengers were relegated to the street side of the security checkpoints since 9/11, Harry had obtained a special pass from the Delta ticket counter to meet Austin because he was only five years old. Harry stood on his tiptoes and stared intently down the jetway. It had been two months since he had seen his little boy, and Harry couldn't wait to begin their planned trip to Disney World.

In an instant, Harry's face transformed from weary worrier to grinning father when he spotted Austin walking down the ramp holding the hand of a flight attendant. Harry dropped to one knee to greet his son as he came running.

Austin gave his dad a big hug, then looked up at the Delta agent. "This is Angie. Can she come to Disney World with us?"

Harry laughed. "Well, Angie is more than welcome, but I'm sure she has other commitments."

She smiled and nodded her head.

"Thanks for taking care of him, Angie."

"You're quite welcome. He's a good little flyer, sir." She patted Austin on the head and disappeared back into the jetway.

"How was your flight, Austin?" Harry asked as he noticed the Delta wings displayed proudly on his shirt.

"It was great, Dad. We flew over the Grand Canyon and Angie showed it to me out the window. Can we go there on our next trip? Can we Dad?"

"Maybe. We'll talk about it on our way to Florida. Do you have to go to the bathroom? It's a long drive." They headed toward the men's restroom.

"Nah-uh. I went on the plane. It was a really cool bathroom and I couldn't find the thing to flush the toilet, so the flight lady showed me." Austin followed his dad inside the restroom.

Harry entered the restroom without touching a door or any other any surfaces. The urinal flushed itself when he turned away. The sink sensed the presence of his hands and turned on the water. The paper towels pulled down from their dispenser. Gravity was all that was required to dispose of the towel in the waste can. Fresh air circulated continuously, with the slight hint of pine scent. The facility had been flawlessly designed to minimize the spread of germs.

But in a most unfortunate turn of fate, Harry happened to stand at a urinal next to a Filipino fellow who had what appeared to be a bad cold. Harry innocently breathed in the toxic air that surrounded a highly contagious Cory Sabugo. Although Harry was perfectly healthy, the invaders got past all his defenses and were now ready to incubate themselves in his body. Soon, they would reproduce and send their offspring on to Austin, who was dutifully waiting behind his dad.

+

Two hours into the fifteen-hour journey to Orlando, the father and son stopped for gas outside of Lexington, Kentucky. Harry infected several people with whom he came in contact.

Influenza had also invaded Austin's body. Had his great, great grandfather been with them, he would have used the occasion to teach Austin an old ditty:

I once had a bird, its name was Enza
I opened the window and influenza.

But Grandpa had died of influenza in 1918 at the age of twenty-eight.

They stopped at a restaurant in Knoxville, Tennessee, for dinner and infected several members of the staff and many of the patrons. The cashier received a big dose when she touched the twenty-dollar bill Harry gave her. She also received a large airborne dosage by standing only a few feet away from Harry when he sneezed suddenly and sprayed down an area six feet wide and fourteen feet long. The tiny droplets of saliva and phlegm suspended in the air were swimming with viruses.

While the virus spread easily, it was not particularly vigorous. After a few moments in the open air, it died. A few single microbes might not infect a person in reasonable condition, but once a big dose got into the mouth, eyes or nasal passages, the warm, moist environment encouraged rapid growth.

Harry and Austin began to feel the symptoms of the flu as they drove through Atlanta and headed south on I-75 toward Macon. As scheduled, they pulled off at the Arkwright Road exit, just north of Macon, and checked into the Hampton Inn a block off the highway. They infected several more unfortunate souls in the lobby when they registered.

Normally Harry and Austin would have a big time together at the hotel swimming pool or going out to eat at one of Austin's favorite establishments like Chuck E. Cheese, but tonight, weary and achy, they both fell asleep by 9:00 P.M.

+

Mike turned from his PC to find Jennifer standing at his desk. The pleasing scent of her perfume and brightness of her smile failed to conceal that something troubling and urgent was on her mind. "Hey, Mike, can we talk in private?"

"Sure. That conference room over there looks open." As Mike followed her down the hall, he couldn't help noticing how the tear-shaped muscles in Jennifer's calves stiffened, then relaxed with each stride. Mike took a seat across the table from where Jennifer stood, but she came around and sat next to him. Each pushed their chair away from the table to face one another, their knees almost touched.

"Latrice just told me that she thinks I made a bad choice in who I hired for the open help desk position this morning." Jennifer leaned forward until Mike could almost feel her breath. "Mike, I made a good decision, a great decision. I followed the book in finding the person. But because I didn't hire one of the black candidates that Latrice was pushing, she's insinuating that I made the call based on race."

Mike leaned back in the chair, put his hands behind his neck and looked at the ceiling. "Latrice has not been herself over the past several days, I think we both know that. But now we have no choice except to review this case."

"Just ask Paris about the process we followed—posting the position, letting the team interview the applicants, finding external candidates as well as internal applicants. It took five weeks to make the final offer, then Latrice sticks her nose in it."

"Well, the person is hired, right? Move forward and let me deal with Latrice. Bear with me here, Jennifer."

Mike couldn't help noticing how tan and smooth Jennifer's legs looked as she rose from her chair. "Thanks, Mike." Jennifer extended her hand. "I make an effort to hire African Americans every chance I get. But I'd be letting my IT team down if I followed some quota instead of offering the position to the most qualified person."

"I hear you, Jennifer. This is a thorny issue that we must resolve carefully. I'll get back to you on this soon." Jennifer brushed by Mike as he opened the conference room door for her.

"See you later," Jennifer said with a smile.

As Mike walked over to talk to Paris about the help desk hire, he was thinking about what a huge maintenance issue Latrice and her race sensitivity had become all of a sudden.

+

Wednesday, September 16

Harry and Austin rose early the next morning despite feeling terrible. Harry dismissed the body aches as the price of driving all those hours from Cincinnati to Macon. He worked hard to will away the nausea and other symptoms.

"How ya doin', buddy?" Harry asked his son.

"Not good, Daddy. I feel sick," Austin barely had the energy to respond.

"You can sleep while I drive, okay? We don't want to miss Disney World, right? What do you say we go to McDonald's?"

Accepting the bribe, Austin allowed himself to be showered and dressed. They drove down the street to the golden arches for some breakfast. Harry was sitting at a table in the restaurant, drinking his coffee when a sharp pain cut through his bowels, and the urge to vomit suddenly hit him hard.

Harry tried to act normally as he hobbled into the men's room, trying hard not to lose control where people were eating. He fumbled frantically with the doorknob, and, for a moment, he panicked at the thought that it was locked. Once inside, the virus proceeded to exit his digestive system through both ends. He hugged the toilet as his body convulsed. There were hints of blood in his vomit. Then he sat on the toilet and experienced a violent bout of diarrhea.

Once the wave had passed, he struggled to stand on wobbly legs and walked slowly back to Austin. He felt dizzy and close to passing out.

Such a stench radiated from the restroom when Harry left that a couple of the customers complained and one of the employees took a mop and pail into the bathroom to wash down the floor. Unfortunately, the virus ravaging Harry's body was at such a heightened volume that it saturated the air and covered everything that Harry touched. The design of the men's room created a veritable viral haven with doorknobs, fixtures, and toilets that all required the human touch.

After finishing his task, the teenage worker returned to the kitchen and casually rinsed his hands at the sink with cold water for a few seconds. Without soap and several minutes of hot water, the rinsing was totally worthless in removing any virus. He then wiped his hands on a towel that he threw back on the food prep counter. The influenza agents that he picked up in the restroom remained all over his hands, arms, and face. It wasn't long before another employee picked up the infected towel, and a third employee touched the counter and the contaminated faucets.

The employee went back to taking orders at the counter. "Here's your order, Miss Paris!"

"Thanks, Derek. Say, is that man over there going to be alright?" she asked, indicating the ill-looking man at the other end of the counter.

"I think so, ma'am. Looks like he's gonna need some help, but we'll handle it. I think he was asking for directions to the doctor or somewhere."

Paris had stopped at McDonald's for some breakfast, but what she got was a big dose of the virus by touching and later eating the food served by the kid who had cleaned the restroom after Harry.

In the few minutes that it took for Paris to get her coffee and sandwich and drive to work at BLuR, the flu agents had already begun to multiply by the millions. In less than four hours, Paris would be highly contagious.

Realizing that he needed medical attention, Harry asked the employee at the counter for directions to the nearest hospital, which turned out to be a MedCenter clinic just a few blocks away. Harry considered asking them to call an ambulance, but decided to tough it out. He didn't want to frighten Austin.

Chapter 13

Day One

Wednesday, September 16

It took Paris five minutes to drive from McDonald's to work at BLuR Financial, and thirty minutes to make her way from the front door to her desk.

"Paris, Rhonda's husband came to the lobby here yesterday and said he was gonna kick somebody's ass if he didn't see his wife, and she slipped out the back door…"

"Paris, Shawna was selling Avon products around here. She's been told about it before, but she must think she's above the rules just because she works the late shift…"

"Paris, the girls in the front of Building A won't use the ladies room because Melinda goes in there. They think that just because she's a transsexual that she's going to give 'em all AIDS or something…"

"Paris, this is the third day Daryl has been absent without so much as a call…"

And so it went. From the time she left her car until she sat down at her desk, she had already held a half dozen hallway meetings, as she like to call them. But company communications had now taken on a new communicable twist.

Paris ate her half-cold breakfast in the break room, then stopped in the "smoke shed" for a cigarette on the way to her desk, speaking to several more coworkers who were catching one last smoke before the workday began.

Finally in her own cubicle area, Paris deposited her pocketbook in a drawer and was checking her calendar when another employee appeared at her desk. It was times like this that she missed having an office where she could close the door, but the environment that Paris helped design had as few walls as possible. Everyone had a cubicle, even Mike, and groups of cubes were arranged in team pods. While the purpose of this openness was to encourage interaction and teamwork, the unintended result currently was to help the flu virus circulate with greater speed and intensity.

The schedule for Paris's day would be full—an exit interview, a training session, a new employee lunch, and a meeting with Mike. That didn't even count all the unexpected crises that popped up in a typical day with a family of several hundred.

+

While it had been many years since Mike had endured big city traffic jams, he was forever grateful for his leisurely seven-minute commute to work. Before getting down to business, he stopped in the cafeteria to visit with the employees and get some juice or an apple.

He spotted Paris sitting at one of the tables eating out of a paper McDonald's sack. "Have you had a chance to look into Jennifer's help desk hire?"

"Yes. I've talked to the white man she hired and to the two black men that Latrice encouraged. I compared their resumes to the position requirements. No doubt about it, Jennifer made a great hire. The qualifications of the two other guys weren't even close."

"Thanks, Paris. Good work," Mike smiled as he looked at the ham and egg biscuit Latrice was eating. "And you're in charge of our wellness program, lady? Can I get you one of those bananas or apples?"

The mouthful of McDonald's breakfast biscuit prevented Paris from her usual come back about her eating habits being none of his business. She could only manage a wide, sarcastic grin.

Mike smiled and left to join Jennifer on a conference call with corporate to seek approval for a capital request to expand the computer network. Mike watched as Jennifer convinced the corporate officers—including Tom Mumford—on the other end of the speakerphone that the benefits were several times the cost. She gracefully cleared every hurdle they presented. Mike was convinced the entirely male corporate hierarchy would have caved even faster had Jennifer been in their presence.

Toward the end of the discussion, Tom Mumford realized that Mike was on the line with Jennifer and his attitude immediately changed from agreeable to argumentative. "Mike, you of all people should know the pressures we're under. I just had that conversation with you last week. Surely your memory isn't that short, is it? If we waited twelve months to spend this money, what harm would it do?" Tom's tone was decidedly condescending.

"The benefits both to customers and to productivity would be delayed. Why would we wait? Do you want us to arrange some financing to help get us through the next twelve months?" replied Mike firmly. "BLuR Financial borrows more than a $100 million per year, another $1.2 million for this project is not a big deal."

"Mike, I don't think you understand..." Even over the phone Mike and Jennifer could both see Tom bowing up.

Jennifer interrupted him. "Fellows! Y'all, lets get back to the request. I can work out the financing with Treasury later. Do we have approval for the project?" Jennifer's assertiveness amazed Mike.

"Yes, Jennifer," said Gordon McLain, a senior vice-president and point man for these decisions. "We'll send you the approved request. You and I can work out the details over the next few days."

"Thank you very much gentlemen," Jennifer purred as a chorus of congenial good-byes concluded the call.

"What the hell is with Mumford?" Mike asked throwing his hands in the air at the instant the phone call ended. "That son of a bitch launched at me! And it had absolutely nothing to do with this project. What is his problem?"

Jennifer glanced uneasily at Mike. "Don't worry about him, Mike. We got our request. Let's just move on." Jennifer gripped Mike's forearm as she spoke.

Realizing that they had indeed gotten what they wanted, Mike blew off his boss's silly antics. "You were amazing, Jennifer. They never had a chance." As Mike shook her hand he unconsciously cupped his other hand over hers. He couldn't help but notice the firm but delicate texture of her skin and the warmth of her touch.

By 10:00 A.M. the virus population within Paris reached critical mass and became infectious. She spread a few particles of influenza to each of the seventeen people in her training class. A few would fend off the influenza, but most would get sick. The virus was demonstrating a condition the experts call "extreme amplification," multiplying at an extraordinary rate. In a few hours the virus count in each individual would total in the hundreds of billions.

Oblivious to the potential time bomb ticking within them, the employees of BLuR worked diligently on the execution of their duties, as the viruses worked just as hard to execute their host. For some, the early onset of pneumonia—difficulty breathing, fever, and coughing—would escalate to total failure of the lungs, in just a few hours. As the viruses grew silently, it never occurred to any of the employees that in the next few days, many would literally drown in their own body fluids.

For numerous reason, the influenza had begun in this results-oriented corporate environment to meet its own clear objectives: invade a human host, take over, and spread to the next victim. Repeat.

+

At 11:00 A.M., Mike met with Dwight to go over the August financial results in more detail. Dwight had purposely pushed the meeting right up to the final deadline for sending the statements to corporate. Expenses came in below plan, and everything else appeared in order. Looking at the company's performance figures was as familiar to Mike as shaving in the morning.

"Why are interest costs rising faster than finance revenues?" Mike asked Dwight.

Dwight avoided Mike's eyes. "I believe that the, uh, the spread we are paying has more load for, uh, the fees they charge us to match funds…"

"Come on, Dwight. What does that mean?" Mike said sternly.

"Well, uh, I'll have to get back to you on this," Dwight stammered, his mouth now as dry as a bone. He could feel the blood rising to his head. Beads of perspiration formed on his forehead.

"Is something bothering you, Dwight?" Mike probed, concerned.

"Nah, I just wish I could give you a good answer. I'll have to check the details and get back to you."

Mike furrowed his brow and considered Dwight silently. The interest expense was only off by two tenths of a percent, but it was worth understanding why.

"Anything else? I have to go to a meeting with the auditors," Dwight asked, still out of sorts.

Mike shook his head and watched Dwight retreat. He made a note on his calendar to follow up with Dwight.

+

At noon, the members of the executive team had lunch with the company's new hires for that month.

"Paris, please hand me one of those chocolate eclairs, would you?" Dwight requested.

"A man after my own heart!" Paris replied as she attempted to reach the large tray of sweets at the end of the table with her short arms.

"Shoot, darlin', don't bother with that big 'ol tray. Just hand me that big one on the end."

Paris picked it up and passed it on down to Dwight who was licking his chops.

The virus particles hitched a ride on both the éclair and the napkin, which were promptly transferred to Dwight and the new employee next to him. Smooth hard surfaces like door handles or toilet seats significantly reduced the shelf life of the viruses. A soft, moist, sugary substance like a pastry was an ideal place to thrive and reproduce rapidly.

Mere contact did not allow the virus to infect a human body because it could not penetrate the skin, but their human hosts usually always cooperated by touching their eyes, nose or mouth with their hands, providing the virus with the warm moist environment it needed to grow.

+

Mike excused himself early from the lunch to pick up Courtney and attend the funeral of a close friend from the club. The sight of Emmitt's wife and young kids sitting there without their dad brought tears to Mike's eyes. He turned his thoughts to happy times with his own kids to keep from losing control of his emotions.

The procession of hundreds of cars driving through red lights with their police escort between the church and cemetery was a public tribute to a great man. Mike loved the way Southerners showed respect for the dead by pulling off the sides of the road until the procession passed. The burial at Rose Hill Cemetery put Emmitt in company with nineteenth-century statesmen and well-to-do citizens, overlooking a field of hundreds of Civil War casualties marked by rows of small simple stones.

Mike attributed his own sniffles and aches to the heavy heartedness he felt at the funeral. But the dozens of hands he shook and necks he hugged each received a good dose of type-A influenza virus that he received from Paris, that she received from Harry, that he received from Cory from the other side of the world.

+

When Mike returned to work around three to meet with Latrice, it was a toss up as to which one of them had the most bloodshot eyes or droopy expression.

"You look like I feel," Latrice kidded.

"Gosh, you feel bad too, huh?" Mike tried to return the banter, but he didn't have the energy. "We have something important to talk about, then I'm ready for this day to be over."

"You must feel bad, mister. I can't get enough of this place."

Mike just grunted. "Jennifer said that you told her that she made a mistake hiring the help desk woman instead of one of the two African-American men you recommended."

"Yes, I thought she should have made a greater effort to hire someone from within the company instead of an outside person."

"Paris checked into the credentials of all of the applicants and spoke with the top three applicants. She says that Jennifer made the right call, that we hired a great employee, and that the two men really weren't qualified."

"Okay, well the decision is made and the IT department still has the fewest blacks of any team in the division."

"No, it's not okay, Latrice. First you got mad about Martin Luther King Day. Then the O.J. issue. Now the help desk hire. Why does everything have to be a race issue with you?"

"You're generalizing, Mike. Let's look at each of those situations."

"No, I need to generalize. You have got to look at the forest instead of the trees! Maybe each episode was a difficult judgement call, but you are tearing this place apart with your over-sensitivity to race. We can't even have a meeting without it erupting into a shouting match."

Latrice sat silently for a moment. "You're right. There is too much tension around here. But are we going to put equity on hold in favor of productivity?"

"We have equity around here for the most part. We can't solve centuries of race problems in a matter of months. I want us to be colorblind, not use color in making decisions. Yes, we will overcompensate where we can to try to reverse the injustices of the past, but if we dilute the efficiency of this company too much, everyone loses.

"You know I think the world of you, Latrice," Mike continued. "I hope you run this place some day. But you have got to stop letting your hypersensitivity to race drive a wedge into the heart and spirit of this operation. Being patient and cutting your coworkers a little slack will get a lot farther than beating them over the head with principles."

Despite the logic in what Mike said, Latrice's pride would not let her back down.

As the two of them talked, it was evident that something serious had physically gripped them both, something more than a cold. Mike's eyes were dark and red. His body ached.

"I'm going to think about what you've said," replied Latrice reflectively. "You and I may not agree on how to deal with these issues, but we both want this place to flourish. These haven't been good days for me recently either."

Paris walked into the room carrying a small pack of tissues in her hand, dabbing her runny nose. "Can I join you?"

"Sure," Mike said to Paris, then turned to Latrice. "One more thing: I hope you know that I've said all these things with you in mind. The company will survive. I want *you* to grow from these experiences. Choose your battles wisely, Empress."

"I appreciate that, Mike."

"What's with everyone feeling bad, Paris?" Mike tried not to sound alarmed. "Aren't you in charge of health around here?"

"I don't know," Paris tried to be positive, "but we've got whole teams dropping like flies out there. A lot of people are going home." Visions of the morning news flashed through her mind. "I hope this has nothing to do with the news in Asia."

Mike kept his Chicken Little thoughts to himself. "Macon is not exactly the first stop out of the Philippines."

"I'm sorry, y'all, but I am fading fast," said Latrice. "Let's get back together on this tomorrow. I need to get home."

"I'm right behind you," Mike quipped. "Paris, why don't you encourage people to go home if they don't feel well. We're probably making things worse by sticking around."

Mike, Dwight, Paris, and dozens of other employees went home early. Jennifer on the other hand, wondered what was going on with everyone. She worked until six, then joined some supplier executives for drinks and dinner downtown.

Chapter 14

Manila Flu

Wednesday, September 16

Austin would never get to see Disney World with his dad. In fact, Harry and his son never resumed their journey to Florida. Within minutes of arriving at the medical clinic, Harry lay in the back of an ambulance on its way to the Medical Center hospital downtown. As soon as the doctors realized Harry was coughing up blood, they knew he would have to be admitted. Harry's condition deteriorated dramatically as the ER personnel attempted to identify the source of his condition. They drew blood for testing, gave him an IV for fluids, and called in the infectious disease specialist.

Before he could even be transferred to a room, Harry vomited blood all over one of the nurses who was huddled near him studying the blackish blue tint of his skin. Moments later, he slipped out of consciousness from the high fever. Consumed by his own misery, Harry had no way of knowing that Austin had also succumbed to the ravages of the virus.

The boy's temperature topped 105 degrees, while Harry's fever skyrocketed to a blistering 107. Even in the hospital, an atmosphere accustomed to disease, this particular pestilence prompted an unspoken uneasiness. The symptoms indicated influenza compounded by pneumonia, but the abrupt onset and rapid deterioration added a frightening dimension. None of the hospital personnel could recall ever seeing anyone get so sick so quickly. After repeated attempts to clear Harry's lungs with suction, doctors resorted to a tracheotomy to eliminate the chance of blockage in his throat. The infectious disease doctor ordered some antibiotics, but none of the customary procedures had any impact.

The doctors pronounced Harry dead at 5:30 P.M. on Wednesday, September 16. Thirty hours after Harry had picked up his son in Cincinnati, he suffocated from the inability of his lungs to deliver oxygenated blood to his vital organs.

“Ever seen anything like this before?” asked one doctor to another, yet oblivious to the fact that people had already begun to die the same way in Cincinnati.

“Looks like a bad case of pneumonia to me. He’s got respiratory failure and his lymphocyte count is very high. He’s in such good shape otherwise; I wonder why he didn’t put up a better fight. And his son, too.”

“We took a lot of risks treating him so openly. We should have had him in a positive pressure room where we can isolate any contagion.”

“The blood tests were all negative. This is some kind of super infection. I’m getting real uneasy about this, too, but let’s not cause a panic.” He turned to the nurse nearest him. “Have this body isolated in the morgue. And get a team of orderlies in here. I want this entire area thoroughly disinfected.”

“Right away.” The nurse looked into the doctor’s eyes for reassurance, but found none.

As they discussed containment measures, virtually everyone in the ER managed to inhale some of the virus particles left in the air from Harry’s fit of coughing and projectile vomiting. The biohazard suits remained untouched in a special closet down the hall and the new decontamination facility built after the anthrax scares in 2001 sat vacant. Within hours, nearly everyone in the hospital had come in contact with the virus.

Earlier, the doctors had called the Centers for Disease Control and Prevention in Atlanta. Normally doctors didn’t contact the CDC in cases of influenza, but conditions in Asia changed that. Having been alerted to similar outbreaks in California and Ohio, the CDC sent two disease detectives and an FBI agent to Macon. The federal entourage arrived inside of three hours and searched Harry’s car and belongings. An airline ticket in Austin’s luggage led them to San Diego and Austin’s mother. Panicked by the phone call, she caught the next flight to Atlanta and rented a car. She arrived in Macon only a few hours after Harry died.

“Excuse me, ma’am, but you can’t go in there.” The nurse placed a hand gently on the women’s shoulder as she started through the door to the isolation unit.

"You don't understand. That's my son in there." Her panic was apparent.

"Yes, ma'am, I do understand, but you still can't go in. Your son is in quarantine. Why don't you come with me to the nurse's station and let—"

"Damn it, let go of my arm! You can't keep me away from my child," the mother cried.

By the time they made it down the hall the two women were in a full-fledged wrestling match. Realizing she was outnumbered, Austin's mother collapsed onto the cold tile floor, put her head in her hands, and wept.

"Damn you to hell, Harry Miller. This is all your fault!"

+

Record numbers of Americans flocked to their televisions Wednesday evening hoping that their city was somehow not in the path of the killer plague that was sweeping across the globe.

At 6:37 P.M., the country froze in fear.

"We interrupt our local broadcasts for this urgent news bulletin. Doctors in Cincinnati, Ohio, report that several people have died from a condition that appears similar to the flu that has killed millions of people in Asia. As yet there is no clinical confirmation that it is the same virus; however, similarities in the symptoms seem to indicate a connection. At this hour, six deaths have been confirmed. Area hospitals have reported the death of two middle-aged men, one older woman and three children. Officials from the Federal Emergency Management Agency in Washington and the CDC are currently in route to Cincinnati."

The media immediately tagged the virus the "Manila Flu" and the phrase quickly became as terrifying as terms such as AIDS, West Nile, or Ebola.

After Federal authorities agreed that air travel probably brought the Manila strain to the US, the president held a special urgent meeting of top health officials in Washington. Several leaders argued that the spread of the virus was inevitable and that it was cruel to keep families from traveling to reunite. They lost to the scientists who felt strongly that the only way to protect the majority of citizens was to quickly close all borders. In an unprecedented action, the U.S. government immediately terminated all flights to or from anywhere outside the U.S. and asked that other countries do the same.

The huge volume of products that flowed continuously from Asia to all points within the U.S. ceased immediately. All boats and trains were quarantined, and car and truck traffic to Canada and Mexico was stopped as soon as the existence of Manila flu in the U.S. was confirmed.

Goods perished in trucks abandoned at U.S. border crossings and in container ships off the east and west coasts. Restaurants, malls, and other public places began to close as customers and employees alike hastened home.

The police in Manila received a phone call from a man who identified himself as Khaddafy Janjalani, one of the leaders of Abu Sayyaf, the Muslim militant group linked to al-Qaida, claiming credit for spreading the virus in the Philippines.

+

Wayne threw a dart that ricocheted off the dartboard, hit Jimmy Mack's beer bottle and sent it crashing to the floor. After five rounds, the three stooges laughed like children, then ordered another round from the Whiskey Creek bartender.

Wayne punched Jay on the arm and nodded toward the television behind the bar. "Shut up and watch the TV, you moron."

Most of the people in the bar went home immediately after the announcement about the Manila Flu, but the three pals stayed. Doing his best thinking after a few beers, Wayne announced, "Hey fellas, this could be our big break!" He turned to face the other two. "If everybody gets sick, that means fewer cops, right? This flu just might be our opportunity to make a fortune."

"What makes you immune from this shit?" Jay cocked his head.

"Meanness, my friend, pure unadulterated meanness." Wayne smirked.

+

Cory Sabugo recovered from the flu in Cincinnati without ever going to the doctor or hospital. He watched the news bulletin on the TV in his hotel room with the same shock and horror as everyone else in North America. He still had no clue that he might have been the first point of entry in America for the virus, so it never occurred to him to talk with the officials. It wasn't like he had boarded an airplane with a box cutter or sneaker laden with explosives, he just had cold symptoms. The government never traced the trail to him—he was just one more name on a passenger list.

He had been able to meet with his American customers, but because of the quarantine, there was no way for Cory to get back to his homeland and no way to ship his products. The trip had been a living nightmare. Now he was helpless, lonely, scared, and several thousand miles from home. Cory wished that he had never left his family.

No one answered as Cory continued to call his home in Manila. The answering machine was full. He ached more from guilt and homesickness than from the remnants of the virus. He missed his family and prayed that they were being spared from the plague.

Alone in a motel room with thousands of questions, answers were thousands of miles away. He watched the TV images of the mounting Asian casualties and wondered if his family was under one of those tarps. Every time he blew his nose, he tried to convince himself he just had a bad cold. Suddenly the entire world posed a threat and there was no place to flee.

Chapter 15

Special Bulletin

Wednesday, September 16

The drive home took Dwight about ten minutes. Traffic seemed unusually heavy as he waited to turn left into his north-end subdivision. Rambling old ranch-style homes inhabited predominately by doctors, lawyers, and bank executives lined the streets. In real estate vernacular it would be considered an established, exclusive neighborhood. Roughly translated that meant that the air virtually reeked of old money Macon.

Dwight drove past the meticulously groomed Idle Hour golf course and pulled into his driveway. He moved a bicycle from his path before parking. As he entered his house, he sarcastically yelled, "Honey, I'm home" in his best Ricky Ricardo voice. He yearned for the days in the not too distant past when his wife and sons would greet him enthusiastically, as if his arrival home provided a highlight of their day.

The note on the counter said John went to his friend Danny's house. "Punks," Dwight muttered as he wadded up the note and tossed it into the trash.

Claire had told him that morning that she was going to be working late and the sounds of electronic automatic weapons coming from upstairs meant that Charles was bunkered in his bedroom playing his video games.

Dwight leaned down to pet Cleo the family mutt, and when he stood up he nearly stumbled from dizziness. He sat down in an easy chair in the den to get his bearings. After a few minutes, the dizziness subsided and he stood up slowly and walked over to the foot of the stairs.

"Charles!" Dwight yelled up the stairs. No answer.

"Charles!" he yelled louder. After a long moment, Charles appeared at the top of the steps.

"Yeah."

"Has your Mom called?"

"Nope."

"Do you want me to order a pizza for dinner?"

"Sure."

Dwight regarded his son's lethargic one-syllable replies for a moment and turned to call for delivery. An hour later, Dwight and Charles were eating pizza when the news from Cincinnati interrupted the show they were watching. Dwight called Claire at work.

"You heard about the flu in Cincinnati?

"Someone just came back from dinner talking about it. Sounds awful. You don't think we have to worry about it here, do you?" And then out of the blue Claire asked, "Have you checked on mother?"

Dwight rolled his eyes. "Uh, I was just headed back there to check on her, but I wanted to check on you first." *Good save*, he thought to himself.

"Never mind, Dwight, I'll call her myself. I'll be home a little after nine." She hung up without allowing a response, her irritation zipping through the phone line like an electrical charge.

Dwight called Danny's house, but no one had seen John or his friend.

By 8:00 P.M., nine hours after the virus entered his body, Dwight felt terrible. His head ached, he was nauseated, and chills wracked his body. John came home around 8:30. Dwight tried to talk with him, but he just mumbled something under his breath, took the stairs two at the time, and slammed the door to his upstairs bedroom.

A few minutes before nine, after watching some of the flu reports on TV, Dwight went upstairs to bed. He stuck his head into Charles's room to say goodnight, but got no response. John's door was locked and Dwight was too tired to make a scene. Before climbing into bed, he placed the bathroom trashcan near his side of the bed in case he got sick. He was sound asleep when the local stations announced that a man had died in Macon from influenza-related complications.

Claire came home around ten. When she checked on Dwight, he moaned as he tossed fitfully under sheets that had been pulled loose from the foot of the bed. She reached down to feel his forehead, but stopped short when she could feel the heat radiating from his skin.

"You need an aspirin or something?" Claire shook his shoulder as she asked, but Dwight did not respond.

Dutifully, Claire replaced the trashcan liner in which he had vomited and carried it outside. The quantity of virus Claire received from Dwight would cut by hours the time it would take for her to feel the effects.

+

"Daddy's home! Daddy's home!" yelled Mike's kids in unison as he walked through the door. He gave Courtney a peck on the cheek, and blew kisses in the direction of his four children.

"Have you had a good day?" Courtney asked.

"Oh, I quit today. Too much stress for too little pay," he quipped.

"I'll tell you what. You stay home with the kids tomorrow and I'll take your place."

"I wish I could," Mike said chuckling. "I don't feel too good. I'm coming down with something and I think it's gonna be a doozie. Hey, anything new on the flu outbreak in Asia?"

"Cindy next door said that she was at the hospital today when a guy was admitted in bad condition with the same kind of symptoms. She said that when her shift ended at three o'clock, the man and his son were in pretty bad shape," Courtney reported.

"Scary stuff," Mike said as he went into the great room to play with the kids until dinner was ready.

Within a matter of minutes, his fever spiked and abdominal cramps gave way to a violent bout of diarrhea. He took two Tylenol and spent a few minutes in the bathroom splashing cold water on his face and focusing on deep breaths to ward off the nausea.

"You okay in there?" asked Courtney, through the bathroom door. "Dinner's ready."

"Go ahead and eat without me. I don't feel too good."

He stayed in the bathroom while the rest of the family ate supper. He resurfaced after dinner just as the big headlines about the outbreak in Cincinnati came across the local news. He and Courtney silently watched the story unfolding, sitting on the sofa with their arms around each other. Mike kept his distance from the kids for fear of giving them whatever he was catching.

"What if I'm getting the Manila flu?" Mike said, finally expressing his fear. "I don't feel good at all."

"Did you jog to Ohio and back today, Running Man? Besides, you're in too good of shape to get sick," said Courtney.

"Well I sure hope that means something to those germs. I think I'm going to go lie down."

For the first time in memory, the kids stayed up later than their Dad. Five-year-old Amy came into the bedroom to check on her Daddy just before she went to bed. She sang him a quick round of her own version of "You Are My Sunshine" which he had told her always cheered him up. But Mike was already fast asleep, not knowing that there was a possibility that something might take little Amy's sunshine away.

Before Courtney went to bed, she tucked in Mark, Amy, and Emily and gave them each a tender kiss as she whispered "I love you." She put the baby in a portable crib in the first floor master bedroom. As she lay down in bed next to Mike, she tried to dismiss her own sudden aches as the result of another long day. Despite her exhaustion, she lay awake worrying for what seemed like an eternity.

+

Paris left work at 4:45 P.M. and drove twenty-five minutes to her home on the Hawkins family property. This was the night when the entire clan would meet to discuss how to subdivide the land to protect the rights of each family. If something wasn't done, the oldest son of the oldest uncle would inherit the entire 100 acres, and no one trusted that Jimmy Mack had anything but his own interests at heart. Paris struggled to combat the biological war waging within her, but she had spent weeks preparing for this meeting, and she wasn't going to miss it.

"I just need a little something to get me through this meeting," Paris said to the cat as she made her way to the bathroom to check out the medicine cabinet.

Later that evening, the entire Hawkins clan was invited to the family meeting in the big picnic pavilion on the property. Patriarchs Horace and Otis Hawkins had chosen Paris as the leader because she held the respect of all and understood the legal details.

By 7:00 P.M., most people had finished eating. Paris stood up to speak, climbing atop a picnic table at one end of the pavilion. A feeling of light-headedness swept over her, then passed. The festive chatter gave way to an anxious hush as everyone waited to hear what Paris was going to propose.

"If I could have your attention… please go ahead and keep eating while I talk." Paris felt a sudden wave of nausea that soon passed with a few deep breaths. "Thank y'all for coming to this important meeting. Let me start with a few comments, then we'll open it up for questions." Her bowels suddenly boiled up, as if being flushed out under pressure. No one noticed the little grimace in Paris's expression. Surely she could make it a few more minutes.

"Our great-great-great grandfather, Quincy Hawkins, is up there in heaven right now smiling down on us all tonight. I know he would be pleased to see how his family has grown and that each of y'all has chosen to live here on what was his property. I know too that he would approve of what Uncle Horace is fixin' to do."

Everyone was getting excited and started to chatter among themselves. As Paris waited for the crowd to quiet down, she looked out, relieved to find cousin Jimmy Mack not present. "Uncle Horace has agreed to legally record two-acre plots for each of the families living here today. Soon you will all own a piece of…"

Paris stopped speaking in mid-sentence and doubled over in pain. Her legs buckled and she collapsed onto the picnic table. Her father and uncle, who had been standing up front with her, rushed over and helped her stretch out on the table. Everyone ran to the front of the pavilion and huddled around her. They quickly cleared away when she began to vomit.

"Let's carry her into my house" said Albert, a cousin who lived closest to the pavilion, about 100 yards away.

Within a few hours, cousin Albert's house, a house trailer, was transformed into a makeshift infirmary for family members. Instead of everyone returning to their own homes with their family, the pavilion and houses around it became makeshift sick bays to treat the stricken.

+

When Jennifer arrived home at 9:00 P.M. from her dinner meeting, her kids were in bed. R.T. waved to her as he talked on the phone. She could only hear his side of the conversation, but what she heard sent chills down her spine.

"...I understand. We'll do the best that we can if the need arises, but we can only process so many bodies at a time. You should line up an overflow facility just in case."

R.T. looked as pale as the corpses with which he spent his days.

"That was the hospital. Actually it was a CDC official at the hospital. They are developing a contingency plan in case this flu thing escalates the way it did in Asia." R.T. stopped to blow his nose.

"Yeah, I heard about it at the restaurant, which was just about empty with everybody headed home. Are the kids okay?"

"They're fine for now. How are you?"

"I'm fine."

"I am too. I'll bet you and I have been exposed to this virus. Either the bug hasn't had a chance to make us sick yet, or our systems are somehow able to fight it off."

"Well don't be a hero-turned-martyr tomorrow. There's no need to take unnecessary risks. And don't bring any germs back from the hospital." Jennifer gave R.T. a peck good night as she went upstairs to bed.

+

Latrice left work feeling poorly from flu symptoms like most of her coworkers. She stopped by her parents' house around 6:00 P.M. to pick up Regina.

When she got home, Latrice drew a steaming hot bath and climbed in to soak her aching joints. A ringing phone interrupted her retreat.

"Baby, it's Poppa. Let me talk to yo Momma, please."

Regina handed her mama the phone.

"Treesy, you watchin' the news?"

"No, Daddy, I'm in the tub."

"Git out an turn on the news, girl. That flu mess they been talkin' about over in the Philippines, well it done come here to Macon!"

"What are you talking about? You mean the thing in Cincinnati?"

"Jest go turn on the news. People's gettin' sick right here in Macon."

"Okay, Daddy, okay. Let me call you back. I'm turning it on now." Latrice had already gotten out of the tub and thrown on a robe. She checked out CNN for a moment, then switched to a local station.

The earlier announcement from Cincinnati had been shocking. This was horrifying. "We interrupt coverage of the influenza outbreak to give you this very important bulletin. Officials have confirmed that a man died earlier this evening at the Medical Center of Central Georgia of flu symptoms identical to those being reported in Cincinnati. The Manila Flu, as it is being called, is suspected to be the same strain that has swept across the Philippines and much of Asia. The man, identified as Harry Miller from Cincinnati, had driven to Macon on his way to Florida yesterday. His young son is still in critical condition at the Medical Center.

"Hospital officials now report that more than a hundred people have come to the emergency room this evening with severe flu symptoms which include pneumonia, vomiting and high fever. They say that the signs of pneumonia include severe congestion, a slightly blue skin coloring, and signs of bleeding in the lungs, intestines, and around the mouth and nose.

"Please stay tuned for more details. Please do not attempt to call the station or the hospital. Telephone lines are jammed. Please stay tuned to this station as we continue to pass on news and advice as soon as it is available from the authorities."

+

Courtney lay down to sleep after tucking in the children. Her body was beginning to ache with flu. Once she settled her nerves, all she could hear was Mike breathing next to her—a raspy exhale followed by a wheezing inhale.

She rolled out of bed, got a cold capsule from bathroom, popped it in her mouth, and downed it with a cup of cold water.

She laid back down and got comfortable, determined to not move until she fell asleep. She thought of pleasant things—how well the kids were doing in school, that the kids were healthy, the hope of cooler weather that usually accompanies the upcoming state fair.... But each train of thought returned to a prayer that everything she cared about would still be okay in the morning. Surely this was not a dangerous plague, but another nuisance of a bug that soon would pass.

Chapter 16

Oh My God

Thursday morning, September 17

"What is that noise?" Claire Williams struggled to open her eyes and focus on the room. Normally a morning person, she felt confused and disoriented. She struggled to roll over and turn off the alarm that now echoed in her head like a giant bell. She reached down to pull the covers around her shivering body, only to realize they were already twisted around her. Each move produced a barking cough as every joint in her body ached at its core. She moaned involuntarily as she rolled to one side to shut off the alarm.

"Dwight, honey, are you awake?"

No answer.

"Dwight! Dwight!" she strained to yell.

She pulled the chain to turn on the lamp on the nightstand, and let out a gasp. Lying on his back, Dwight's arms rested in an unnaturally stiff position along his body. At first she feared he was dead, but his loud breathing quickly dispelled that thought. The air rattled noisily through his throat and lungs. Sweat poured from his pores as the fever consumed him. He had vomited without making any effort to get out of the way. She could not wake him.

"Oh, my God!" Claire cried.

She picked up the phone on the nightstand and dialed 911. It took twenty rings for anyone to answer.

"Please hold." The 911 operator immediately put Claire on hold without waiting for a response.

As the minutes passed, Claire tried to calm herself with slow deep breaths. The calming effect wore off as soon as she looked over at Dwight's expressionless face. For the first time in years she actually felt sorry for him as he lay suffering from something he hadn't brought on himself.

"Poor thing." Claire started to cry. The panic set in the moment she thought about the boys down the hall.

"John! Charles!" The severe congestion in her throat and lungs muffled her yell.

No answer.

"John! Charles!" she called feebly.

Silence.

She resisted the urge to run down the hall to the boys' room. *Get help first*, she thought.

An eternity later the operator came back on the phone. "911 Emergency. Can I help you?"

"Yes, my husband is very sick. He has a high fever and he's not breathing right. He won't wake up."

"Ma'am, you are one of hundreds of people calling in this morning with the same situation. All of our ambulances are out. The emergency rooms are packed. I will take your name and address, and someone will be out to see you as soon as possible. But, it could take several hours."

Claire couldn't believe her ears. The nightmare just got worse and worse.

"Then could you please tell me what the hell I am supposed to do for my husband and kids until someone gets here!" she screamed into the phone.

"There is nothing I can tell you, ma'am. I have your address here from the system and we'll send someone as soon as anyone is available. We're telling people to take aspirin and any cold medicine you have on hand and stay tuned to the radio. I am sorry, but I have to take another call." The line went dead.

Claire just sat there, stupefied and scared, listening to the dial tone.

Soon, Claire stirred herself, hung up the phone and hobbled down the hall to Charles's room, stopping at the doorway to catch her breath. Her son's resemblance to Dwight took on frightening dimensions as Claire entered and found her son lying unnaturally still. She stood a moment and watched him breathe. She couldn't wake him.

Desperate for one of her boys to come to her aid, she made her way down the hall to John's room hoping he could help her with Dwight and Charles. Her hopes dissolved as she surveyed the scene that surrounded her older son. Dark phlegm and bright spots of blood were fresh and thick in the vomit that covered his neck and chest. Delirious with fever, he tossed and turned fitfully. Each breath was tortuous and his skin looked blue. Not even Claire's frantic pleas could rouse him.

Claire clutched her son and began to cry. The blood frightened her and she quickly wiped it away with the sheet to make it go away. Helplessness swept over her like a wave. As the strength slipped from her, she fell to the floor beside John's bed and lost consciousness.

A few hours later, unmercifully, Claire woke feeling a little better. She found John's condition had deteriorated and he now lay still as death. In a brief moment of lucidity, she remembered her mother. She managed to sit up and lean against the side of John's bed but could make it no further. She tugged on the phone cord until the phone crashed down beside her.

"Mama, it's Claire."

"Oh thank God, Claire, are y'all okay? I've been trying to reach you for hours. When no one answered the phone, I came over, but the deadbolt was locked. I pounded on the door, but I guess you couldn't hear me. I've been worried sick."

"I don't know what it is, but it's bad, Mama. Dwight and the boys are so sick. They are burning up with fever and won't wake up."

"Oh honey, you sound real bad yourself." Her mother tried to conceal the depth of her concern. "Claire, have you seen TV or listened to the radio yet this morning?"

"No, Mama."

"Some sort of horrible flu epidemic has hit Macon. Things are desperate and getting worse. No point calling the hospital—lots of folks are dying and they're turning people away."

"I know. I called 911, and no one can come for hours. Oh God, Mama! I don't know what to do." Claire suddenly sounded like her mother's little girl.

"Do you have any antibiotics? Take any penicillin or any medicine you have. Give them to Dwight and the boys too. I'll be right there. Can you make it downstairs to unlock the door?"

"No! Mama, don't come over here. I don't want you to—"

The phone went dead.

Claire crawled down the hall to the master bedroom where all the medicines were stored in the bathroom cabinets. Dwight looked no worse than a few hours earlier. She took three aspirins and filled a cup with water to take to John. With great effort, Claire willed her way back down the hall into John's room.

Claire stood frozen in the doorway, the water and pills spilling to the floor. Afraid to enter, her eyes fixed on John's contorted face that appeared as if he had died mid scream. A combination of dried sweat and vomit clung to his bedclothes. He had lost control of his bladder and bowels and a stench filled the air. Claire clutched the doorjamb for support, unable to bear the sight.

Claire moved to his bedside and called the name of her son softly, as if she were waking him for Christmas morning. "John? John, wake up sweetie."

Claire reached down and brushed his hair from his face. She closed her eyes as she forced her son's lifeless lids over his glassy eyes. Not knowing what else to do, she pulled the sheets around him as if she were tucking him into bed. The muffled sounds of her mother pounding on the back door went unheard as Claire collapsed on the floor and slipped once again into unconsciousness.

+

Claire's mother pounded and screamed at the door for about five minutes before resorting to more desperate measures. She took a nearby piece of firewood and broke one of the glass panes in the kitchen door. Just as she threw the log down, a van pulled into the driveway. An EMT wearing a biohazard suit stepped from the van. Nearly six hours had passed since Claire had called 911.

"I'm the mother of the woman whose family owns this house. Thank God you're here!" Claire's mother would have hugged the young man, but his biohazard suit sent a very clear message.

"I'm with the Bibb County Fire Department. Please stand clear, ma'am. Don't go into the house. How many are in there?" Claire's mother didn't recognize the body bag he held under his arm.

"Four—my daughter, her husband, and their two teenaged boys. Oh Lord, please look after them. My daughter called and said John was so sick."

He didn't have the heart to tell her that his job was simply to bag and remove the dead to help contain the plague. He reached through the jagged hole in the glass and unlocked the door, careful not to tear the suit.

"Ma'am, I need for you to stay out here while I check out the house. You don't need to get exposed to this flu. In fact, you need to stand a few feet away from me since this suit has been exposed. I'll be back in a few minutes with a report for you." The tech went inside and Helen went back toward her apartment.

The medical technician located all four persons before tending to John. He dragged Claire out of the boy's room and put her on the bed in the guestroom, tossing a clean towel from the closet over her. He grunted as he struggled against John's dead weight to place him in the large plastic bag along with the soiled linens. He threw the body over his shoulder and carried him fireman style out to the van.

Helen reappeared just as he slammed the van door. She wore a hardware-store variety gauze mask that she kept on hand for working in her garden during the spring pollen season.

"Where are Claire and Dwight? Where are the boys? Is everybody okay?"

"The dark headed boy is dead. Do you know his name?" the EMT asked.

"Oh God, John? Oh dear God, no! He can't be dead already. Claire just called."

"Ma'am, I'm sorry for your loss, but I have to go to the next call. I have your grandson in the van, but I need his name so you or his parents can find where he is buried later."

"John Paul Williams," she said between sobs. "Where are the others?"

"They're all upstairs. Pretty sick, but hopefully they'll all pull through. I suggest that you don't go in there though."

The EMT slowly and clumsily took out a pen and pad to write the information.

"Is there anything you can do for the others? Can we take them to the hospital?" Helen kept talking while he wrote.

"There's nothing anyone can do. There's no medicine and there's no room at the hospital. Just pray they come through. Not everyone dies, but there have been a lot of fatalities today already.

"And by the way," added the EMT, "you might as well not wear that mask. It's like trying to keep out mosquitoes with chicken wire.

We're dealing with a virus here." He got in his van and drove to his next call down the street.

Helen ignored the advice of the EMT and went directly into the house. She combed through the medicine cabinet, then managed to wake up Dwight, Claire, and Charles to give them each an antibiotic cocktail spiked with a mega-dose of acetaminophen. After sponge-bathing each of them as they slept, she sprayed the bedroom areas down with a heavy mist of disinfectant, if only to make herself feel better. When she had done everything she could think to do, she sat down in the middle of the hall and cried and prayed.

It took about three hours for Helen to begin feeling the effects of the virus. Her general health was good, but her age worked against her. She collapsed on the floor near Charles's bed between her frequent rounds to check on her loved ones.

+

Early that evening, Dwight woke up feeling as though he had been on a long drinking binge. Driven by an overwhelming thirst, he fought the lightheadedness and managed to make it to the bathroom for some water. The spinning gradually slowed and settled into a dull ache behind his eyes. Totally disoriented, the 7:16 on the digital clock registered in his mind as A.M. instead of P.M.

The eerie silence sent chills through him. Daylight peaked around the edge of the window shades. Except for a strong sour scent that lingered in the air, everything seemed normal. Unable to focus fully, he closed his eyes and listened to a dog barking in the distance and the drone of the air conditioner as it circulated cool air through the house. But something wasn't right. He listened harder. It wasn't what he heard, but what he didn't hear. No traffic or lawnmowers. No children yelling or golf carts humming. No TVs or stereos or voices. Instead of tranquility, the stillness screamed doom.

Dwight looked around the room for signs of Claire. *Maybe she never came home last night. She and the boys must have gone to Helen's to avoid catching what I had.* Dwight shuffled back into the bathroom and splashed some cold water on his face. He relieved himself and cringed at the sight and smell of his own urine in the toilet, the water turning a dark brownish amber. *Not a good sign*, he thought. He walked down the hall and discovered Claire lying on the bed in the guestroom. *She must have slept here to get away from me when I was sick.*

Claire stirred as he entered the room. Dwight helped her sit up.

"Oh, Dwight!" Claire fell into his arms with an abandon he had not seen since their early years of marriage. "I thought you were going to die. I've never seen you so sick. Charles had it bad, too. John—" Panicked that the nightmarish image of John that came to her mind might be true, Claire headed for his room without a word.

"Claire?" Dwight followed behind her. "Claire, what's wrong? What about John?"

She froze in the doorway to John's room. There was no sign of their son. The bed had been stripped, but as Claire stared at the bare mattress the image of her dead son's face flooded into her memory. She gasped audibly and fell to her knees.

"Claire! What the hell is going on? Talk to me!" Dwight's tone became angry.

"Oh, God, Dwight. John is dead! I remember now. Dwight, he's dead! I tried to help him, but nothing worked. Oh, God. Oh, God." Claire collapsed further to the floor, shaking her head. There were long gasps between sobs.

This was more than Dwight could deal with. Was John really dead or had Claire lost her mind? Where was his body? Dwight helped Claire up as she held on to him tightly. They walked slowly down the hall to check on their other son. Charles sat on the floor next to his bed holding his grandmother in his arms. Helen barely clung to life. The bluish tint to her skin already gave her the appearance of death, and her skin was cold to the touch. Her eyes stared expressionlessly at the ceiling. Rather than fueling life, every breath drained the strength out of her body. Charles looked toward his parents pleadingly.

"She's been taking care of all of us. Now she's got this crud," said Charles.

"Let's get her into your bed." Helen didn't weigh much more than a hundred pounds, but it took all three of the Williamses to hoist her tiny frail body into her grandson's bed. They straightened the blankets and covered her, then sat on the side of the bed.

"Mama, Gram said John died."

"Yes, baby, John…," Claire began.

"She said a fireman came all dressed in a space suit and took his body away. He said people are dying all over town. What's going on? What is this, Mama?"

Claire looked at Dwight.

"You just rest, son. You've been sick, but you're going to be just fine in a little while. We can figure all this out later. Do you feel like eating something?"

"God, no." Charles placed his hand over his mouth. "I just need something to drink."

"Do you think you can make it downstairs? Let's go get something to drink and see if we can find out anything on the news. Your mom will take care of Gram."

Charles and Dwight helped one another down the stairs and into the kitchen. As soon as Dwight opened the refrigerator, he wished he had stopped by the store the day before. The cupboard was pretty bare. He managed to find a half-full bottle of Sprite behind an expired carton of milk.

For the first time in years, father and son sat down at the kitchen table together. Dwight reached for the remote and flipped through the channels on the television in the adjoining den. Static sounded from many of the regular channels and all the rest were broadcasting the same telecast. Bedraggled reporters standing in front of hospital emergency rooms gave minute by minute accounts of the latest devastation from the Manila flu.

After a few minutes, Dwight told Charles to stay downstairs while he went up to check on Claire and Helen. He stopped before he got to the bedroom door. He could hear Claire whispering an old children's story to her mother. "*I'll love you forever, I'll like you for always, as long as I'm living, my Mommy you'll be,*" a story that her mother undoubtedly had shared with Claire as she held her daughter in her arms many years earlier.

Claire came over and held Dwight when she noticed him in the doorway.

"We're losing her, Dwight." Claire spoke quietly, careful to not let her mother hear her. "She's getting worse and worse. She may not make it."

They continued to care for Helen as best as they could, but her condition deteriorated quickly. Her every breath became more difficult. Her lungs filled with fluid and her heart pumped faster and faster. The fever spiked to over 106 degrees. Within a couple of hours, her struggle ended. Her death was a grotesque end to a long, gentle life.

Charles came into the room to join his mother and father shortly after his grandmother took her last breath. He had no previous experience with death of any kind. Awkwardness punctuated his fear. He was reluctant to touch his grandmother and when he did, he pulled back at the cold, clammy lifelessness of her skin. He stuttered and stammered as he tried to express his feelings, then fell silent and wrapped his arms around his mother, averting his gaze from Helen's stony expression.

Dwight disappeared into the bathroom under the guise of fetching Claire some water. He splashed cold water on his face and stared at the stranger in the mirror. He found his own face virtually unrecognizable. He considered for a moment the possibility that he too had died and that these circumstances were punishment for the many sins of his life. Surely Hell could be no worse than this.

Chapter 17

No Baby's Breath

Thursday morning, September 17

Mike woke up at 5:00 A.M. feeling as sick as he could ever remember feeling. His flu-fraught mind reran a recent show he had watched about patients who regained consciousness during surgery because the anesthesia had worn off. They reported that they could feel every move of the surgeon, but their limbs and vocal cords were too numbed by the anesthesia to let anyone know.

His teeth chattered as chills wracked his body, now exhausted from the act of shivering. He opened his eyes wide trying to adjust the focus. The slightest movement magnified his lightheadedness and disorientation. His stomach gurgled. Courtney lay asleep next to him and he could feel the heat from her body from across the bed.

Mike managed to sit up. His head spun and he placed his hands at his sides on the mattress in an attempt to stop the spinning. He looked around for the source of a strange gargling sound.

He got out of bed slowly and peered into Beth's crib at the foot of the bed. It hurt to listen to her breath. He laid the baby on her back. Her breathing got worse. He laid her on her belly. She threw up, bright red blood streaking her vomit.

"Oh, shit! Oh, my God!" he cried.

Now oblivious to his own pain, he bolted to the phone on the nightstand and dialed 911 before he even had the receiver to his ear. Thirty rings into eternity, he slammed the phone back in its cradle. He frantically looked to Courtney for help. His gentle nudge turned into a forceful shake when she failed to respond.

"Courtney, wake up! Please, honey! Wake up!" he yelled.

Her words sounded like lumpy oatmeal, sticky and mushy. Mike couldn't make out what she said. His knees buckled, and he collapsed on the floor beside the bed.

"Flu…fucking flu. Please, God," he moaned, "don't take my family! Please don't let them die. Please, please," he wept the words, "don't let any of us die."

Mike escaped into unconsciousness.

After three hours he woke up. Rising, he glanced down at the baby in her crib. Her condition was no better. After his earlier experience, he was afraid to even touch her. He hobbled up the stairs to check on the other children. He wanted to carry them down to the car and drive them all to the hospital, but he knew he didn't have the strength.

The three older kids were nestled in their beds. Mark and Emily were feverish and wheezing with fluid-like rattles, but Amy was sleeping in relative peace.

"Daddy, is it time to get up?" Amy asked with one eye closed.

"Baby, you have to stay in bed a little longer. Everybody's sick except you and me, and I don't feel too good. Hear Emily breathing funny? I think you should—"

A scream came from downstairs.

"Amy, baby, stay in your bed. I'll come back up and check on you in a few minutes. Now you stay there!" Mike said sternly, pointing to Amy in her bed on his way out the door. Amy just looked at him, no longer the least bit sleepy.

Mike staggered down the stairs to the master bedroom. Courtney was kneeling on the floor, leaning against the crib as she gazed with glassy eyes at baby Beth.

"Mike, do something, please. I think she's dying," Courtney pleaded.

"Mark and Emily are sick, too." Mike regretted his unnerving tone as soon as the words left his lips. "But they're okay," he said. "Amy seems to be perfectly fine."

"Oh, God, no!" Courtney cried. "Please, not the children."

Mike knelt next to Courtney, and held her tightly. Her body was hot, but not the kind of warmth that attracted him. This heat was ugly, radiating sickness.

"I already tried to call 911, sweetheart. No one answered. We're going to beat this thing, Courtney. I swear to you, we're going to beat this."

Before she could speak, Courtney's body went limp in his arms. Mike laid her gently on the floor, covered her with a sheet, and placed a pillow under her head.

He turned on the radio on the nightstand. The FM station he normally listened to was broadcasting simultaneously with another station in accordance with the Emergency Broadcast System procedures. The EBS's shrill signal filled the room. Mike knew something big was going on. The Spikers were not alone in this.

A moment later a recording declared, "This is the Emergency Broadcasting System. Macon and the seven-county metropolitan area have been declared a medical disaster area. A large segment of the population in this area has been affected by an influenza outbreak now referred to as the Manila flu. Hundreds of people are known dead. The death toll is expected to rise dramatically. A strict, total curfew is in effect. Federal officials are well aware of the situation and expect to ship vaccines to the area within a few days. Until further instruction, you must stay home. Do not leave your house. The city of Macon and surrounding areas are under strict quarantine. Law enforcement officials will take extreme measures to maintain control. Do not go to the hospital. Do not call 911 for at least the next twenty-four hours. Do not visit friends or family. Do not use the phone unless it is absolutely necessary. The governor has put all military personnel and the National Guard on high alert. All police, fire, and other officials should remain close to a phone or radio to await further instructions. Once the situation is better understood, emergency teams will mobilize to provide necessary assistance."

In a moment, the announcement began again. Mike turned off the radio and stared at the ceiling in dazed disbelief, then drifted off once again.

+

Mike woke up abruptly a few hours later, feeling a little better. He moved his head to one side to block the intense rays of sun that penetrated the shutters on the far end of the room. Despite the bright sunshine outside, a cold, dark eeriness painted the room and dripped from the high vaulted ceiling. Mike shuddered.

Courtney was still lying on the floor between the bed and the crib. Her breathing was pained, but she was no longer sweating from a high fever and she appeared to be stable. He stepped over her to reach the crib.

He held his breath and peered down at the tiny child. He found no comfort in the absence of her labored breath. His baby girl lay perfectly still. Her flawless, rose-colored skin now had a bluish-black hue. An expressionless mask covered her face. Her skin, no longer soft and supple, chilled the touch. After several long moments of waiting for her to breathe, Mike gasped. He picked up her still body and held it close to his chest. She seemed suddenly much heavier than usual.

Holding the poor baby at arm's length, Mike stared into her face, holding her head up. Her eyes stared back blankly and her limbs dangled like a rag dolls.

Tears washed down his face onto Beth's matted wisps of curls as he clutched her tiny body again to his chest.

His grief gave way to rage as he laid her body on the bed. "Damn! Damn! Damn!"

As Mike went to the closet for a clean blanket, he thought about how dangerous it was for him to leave Beth unattended on the bed. Courtney would yell at him if she were awake. But the baby did not move, even to breathe.

Stooping over the toilet, Mike vomited. When it appeared clear that his body would not spare him by losing consciousness again, he returned to the bedroom.

Mike wrapped Beth in the blanket, then closed the shutters to darken the room. It seemed somehow an appropriate reflection of the light that had been extinguished within him. He walked past Courtney, asleep on the floor, in search of fresh air. The urge to run overwhelmed him.

Mike walked out onto the deck and plopped wearily into the wrought iron chair. Tears streamed down his cheeks.

"This is insane." His thoughts escaped verbally.

He glanced at his watch and longed to turn back time a few short hours. How much things had changed in just twenty-four hours. And yet, the sky remained blue, the trees tall, and the grass green. Everything outdoors looked normal and healthy. He glanced at the security alarm stickers affixed to the windows, and laughed cynically at the irony of it all. Something had violated his family's space all right, but he couldn't even see it.

He watched the neighboring yards for signs of life. A sudden terror washed over Mike. Would anyone survive this plague? Where would they get food? Would things ever return to normal? He rushed into the kitchen and tried to call his mother. The phone lines were busy. In a moment of rational thought he ran some water and flipped the light switch on and off. He turned the burner knob and the gas flames ignited. All the utilities were working fine. He found some comfort that there was at least some semblance of normalcy.

He walked back out onto the deck, then over to the property line. "Kathryn! Julius! Are you okay over there?" he shouted toward his neighbor's house.

No answer.

He would have walked over and knocked on their door, or even broken into their house. But what if they were dead? What if they needed help? What if they hadn't been exposed? He had more pressing problems in his own house, and went back inside.

The aches and dizziness persisted, but Mike improved by the hour. *How could an older man like him survive and not poor Beth?* he wondered. He kept a regular vigil tending to Courtney and the older children.

On one of Mike's many trips up to check on the three older kids, Amy was nursing her little sister by wiping her face with a cool washcloth, while big brother Mark finally stirred.

"Daddy, where's Mommy?" asked Mark.

"She's downstairs. How're you feeling, sport?"

"I want Mommy. I feel real bad."

"I know, son. Your mom's sleeping. Is there something I can do for you?"

"I'm hot. Can you turn up the air conditioning?"

"You have a fever, son, but I'll see what I can do. Go on back to sleep. Amy is up here if you need anything. Send her for me if you need to. I'm going back down to see how your mom is feeling. Amy, take care of Mark, okay? I'll come back up to check on y'all in a few minutes."

Mike went downstairs to check in on Courtney. She hadn't moved from beside the crib. He realized he had to do something with Beth's body that still lay on the bed. He went to the garage and got a plastic leaf bag. The news reports had stressed the importance of containing the spread of the disease and mandatory procedures for disposing of bodies. He came back into the bedroom, and lifted the baby in her blanket onto the black plastic. He tried not to think about what he was doing, but he still couldn't bring himself to cover the baby's face. Such precautions might be necessary, but he couldn't help feeling like he was treating his precious child like some kind of rubbish.

How in the world was he going to tell Courtney? There was no sense delaying it. The sooner, the better in helping her deal with the horrific sequence of events. He tried again to wake her.

"Courtney? Wake up, Courtney."

Nothing.

"Courtney, can you hear me?" He shook her by the shoulders.

Courtney stirred but didn't answer. Mike held his wife closely, closed his eyes and cried. He considered ways to soften the message that her baby was dead, but came up empty. He avoided the possibility that he might lose her, too.

A few moments later, Courtney awoke to Mike's sobbing.

"Mike? What's the matter? Why are you crying? What's going on?" Her eyes were only half open and her pupils were rolling up into her head.

"Courtney! Thank God you're okay. You've been asleep for a long time."

"What time is it? Are the kids okay?" She slurred her words. "What am I doing on the floor?"

"There's some sort of crazy flu epidemic. It's not just us. The whole damn city is sick. There have been a lot of deaths." Mike tried to ease into the inevitable.

"How are the kids?"

"Amy is fine. Mark and Emily are still pretty sick, but they are getting better."

"Where's Beth? She's not in her crib." Courtney propped herself up on her elbows and glanced into the crib to double check. "Oh, no! Mike? Where is Beth?"

"Beth is gone. She died a little while ago in her sleep." Mike wept as he told her.

"Oh, God, no!" gasped Courtney. She attempted to jump to her feet but her legs would not support her. She started screaming: "Why didn't you wake me? Why didn't you do something? Did you call the doctor? Where is she?"

Mike tried to hold his wife closely, but she struck at him with her fists.

"She's gone, Courtney, there was nothing I could do. There was nothing anyone could do. Her body is on the bed."

"No!" Courtney shrieked, her face contorting in pain.

Courtney lunged at the bed, nearly losing her balance. The small bundle lay motionless beneath a blanket and the plastic sack in the middle of the bed. Courtney froze momentarily, staring at her daughter for a long time. She slowly reached out to touch her, but snapped back angrily just as the tips of her fingers touched the baby's cold cheek. She turned to Mike with rage in her eyes.

"How dare you put my baby in a plastic bag!" she snarled.

"Daddy?" Mike whipped around to find Amy standing at the door.

"Mommy, what's going on? Why are you crying?" Tears streamed down her face.

"Oh God, Amy! You have to get out of here!" Mike blurted out, moving toward her. "You have to go back upstairs! Everything will be okay, but you have to go back upstairs and take care of Emily and Mark."

"Get upstairs, Amy! Now!" Courtney yelled.

Amy turned and ran.

Mike closed the bedroom door and moved closer to Courtney.

"I didn't know what to do about Beth." Mike was sobbing and working hard to find the right words. "We can't just leave her lying here and they say we can't leave the house. You have to say your good-byes now. What else can we do? She's gone, Courtney, and it wasn't my fault or yours."

Courtney held the lifeless baby close to her chest. She wept uncontrollably and moaned like a wounded animal.

After a few moments she looked up at Mike with red, swollen eyes. Her face was wet and flushed from crying. The dark circles under her eyes and smudged make-up exaggerated her look of despair. Her lips quivered and her body trembled.

"Why didn't you do something, Mike?" Courtney asked woefully. "How could you let me sleep while our baby died?"

"I'm sorry, Courtney, I'm sorry," Mike said, shaking his head helplessly. He looked at her for a moment and then turned and left the room.

Mike went upstairs to check on the kids. Mark and Emily showed steady improvement. He thought about waking Emily when he heard a whimper coming from the other side of the girls' room. In the very narrow space between her bed and the wall, Amy was sitting on the floor, crying. Her face was red and she could not talk for sobbing. Mike lay across her bed, his face inches from Amy's.

"Hey, baby, come on up here and lay next to me. I'm so sorry you went downstairs. You're going to have to stay up here until I tell you it's all right to come down, okay? Please don't be so upset," Mike said. *How is a five-year-old supposed to deal with seeing her parents break down?*

"Why is Mommy crying? Why was Mommy yelling at you, Daddy? Is Beth okay?" Amy struggled to speak between sobs.

Mike took a deep breath. "Mommy is upset because Beth has been so sick. Mommy was sick herself and when she got better, Beth was feeling real bad, and that made Mommy feel really bad. You see, baby, all of us except you have been very sick. For some reason you didn't get sick. You must be a really special kid to fight off those bad germs!" Mike reached over to hold Amy.

"I'm scared, Daddy. I'm hungry. And there's nobody to play with. Can I go to school, now?"

"Tell you what, you are going to have to take care of Mark and Emily. You need to wipe their heads with the washcloth and try to wake them up to see if they're hungry. Before we do all that, why don't you and me go down to the kitchen and get something to eat? But please promise me that you won't go into Mommy's room. Mommy needs some peace and quiet so she can get better. Okay?"

+

After he got Amy situated with her snack, he went into the family room and turned on CNN. The reporter on the scene looked as if he had dressed for a space mission. He stood in a gymnasium. Bodies on army cots lined the walls, and row after row covered every inch of floor. Mountains of blankets towered behind him. The place buzzed with activity as people tended to the sick, carried bodies on gurneys, and visitors checked on their loved ones. The caption at the bottom of the screen said "Live from Lexington, Kentucky."

"...is a long line of people waiting to get inside the gym, but unfortunately there is nothing for them once they arrive here. Local officials tell us there is no medicine available to treat the Manila flu. And unfortunately, latest estimates indicate that there is about an eighty- percent chance of contracting the airborne virus if you are exposed. People continue to be urged to stay at home and avoid contact with those infected if at all possible."

Mike flipped to another station. Even the Weather Channel had gone on flu alert. They plotted the spread of the disease using their existing library of maps. The weatherman explained how the pandemic spread in all directions from Cincinnati and Los Angeles by travelers who unknowingly carried the disease. On another channel, the newscaster made frightening comparisons to the 1918 flu.

"The tremendous growth in population density and widespread use of high-speed travel allowed this flu to spread much faster to more people."

The next report came from Cincinnati where the plague was in its most deadly stages. Out of 900,000 people in the Cincinnati area, about 600,000 had gotten the flu. Of those, nearly 26,000 people had died so far. In Lexington, Kentucky, several thousand had died. Reports from Knoxville and Chattanooga were still preliminary as emergency crews were just beginning to enter those areas. Reports from Atlanta and Macon were unreliable as the plague was in its early, ravaging state. Orlando, Tampa, and Jacksonville were just entering the initial stages.

From the attic Mike retrieved a beautiful antique cedar chest that Courtney used to store mementos from the kids—artwork from school and church, photographs, and news clippings. The sum accumulations from Beth's life were the newspaper from the day she was born and her baptism certificate from the church. Mike choked back tears thinking that Beth would never have a refrigerator art showing like her brother's and sister's or even see her first birthday.

He emptied the contents of the chest neatly on the floor and carried the elegant little wooden box down to the master bedroom. Courtney was lying on the bed staring at the baby beside her.

"It's time to say goodbye, Courtney. You have three more kids who need you. We all need you."

"Why Beth, Mike? Why our baby? Look how innocent and helpless she is."

Mike was not particularly religious but he thought he might try appealing to Courtney's more fundamental Baptist upbringing.

"Jesus will take care of her Courtney. You have to trust God."

Courtney stared at the box that Mike held in his arms. "What are you doing with that chest?"

"We have to get the baby out of the house. You don't want the kids to have to face this. They're way too young."

She said nothing, but clenched her teeth and walked out of the room leaving Mike to take care of Beth alone. Courtney had unwrapped the body and changed Beth's clothes.

Mike rewrapped the infant in her favorite blanket, then wrapped her securely in the plastic bag, and laid her in the chest. He tucked another blanket around the little body to hold it in place. He closed the chest and carried it through the house toward the garage.

He opened the rear hatch of the Expedition, and delicately placed the chest in the cargo space. He returned to the kitchen and called 911. It was busy. He kept trying until he got through.

"911 Emergency. Can I help you?"

"My child died a few hours ago in our house. Can someone come get her or should I take her somewhere?"

"If you've been listening to the radio you know that the death toll has been very high and the city is locked down. The government has set up an emergency morgue at the Macon City Coliseum. If it weren't for the curfew in effect right now, you could take your child there. I will put your name on a list and someone will be out to your home to pick up the body. But it will be several hours, probably even tomorrow, before they arrive."

"My other children are still sick. What can I do?"

"There's no medicine available yet. Just keep the news on; they're airing medical updates every fifteen minutes. Sorry, I've got to take another call."

Mike threw the cordless phone onto the counter toward the base unit. It bounced off the counter and struck a big bright fruit bowl, sending shattered pieces of pottery and pieces of fruit rolling all over the kitchen floor.

It would be dark outside before long and Mike became consumed by the need to do something, anything, to protect Courtney and the three older kids. He needed to leave soon in order to get to the Coliseum and back before dark.

He walked up the steps to find Courtney sitting on Amy's bed. The little girl was lying still, her mother gently scratching her back.

"I'm taking Beth down to the Coliseum. They have set up a citywide…" His voice trailed off, unable to utter the word "morgue" in the same breath as his child's name. "I'll be back in an hour or so if I don't run into any problems."

Courtney just closed her eyes and didn't speak. He stood there for a moment, then turned and left in silence.

He had plenty of fuel in his car, but it dawned on him that he better use what he had judiciously. All the gas stations were closed, along with everything else. He drove slowly out of reverence for the precious cargo in the back of his vehicle.

The vacant streets had the look and feel of a B-rated science fiction movie. No cars. No people. Just an occasional stray dog running across a yard. The traffic lights worked, but there was no one around to pay any attention to them. Mike crossed over Pio Nono Avenue on his way south when a police car squealed out onto the road behind him. The policeman caught up to him quickly and his mechanical voice blared, "Stop your car! Pull over now!"

Mike pulled over.

The officer jumped out of his car and drew his revolver.

"Get out of the car slowly and put your hands behind your head."

Mike did exactly as he was told.

"I have a dead child in the car and I am taking her to the coliseum. I called 911, and they told me about the morgue. I'm going home as soon as I leave there."

Seeing the sorrow in Mike's eyes, the officer softened his approach. "We are under a very strict curfew. We cannot let anyone drive around. Get back in your car and drive quickly to the coliseum. I will lead you. If you go anywhere else, I have strict orders to use whatever force is necessary to enforce the curfew."

"Thanks officer. I'll follow you."

The policeman nodded his agreement, put his pistol back in its holster and got back in his squad car.

Following directly behind the officer, Mike drove to the coliseum on city streets to avoid the military roadblocks that had set up along the major highways. As he turned into the parking lot of the huge public arena, armed military guards promptly approached the car and ordered him to stop at the entrance. They inquired about the absence of a permit on his windshield, but after he explained his purpose, they let him through.

Proceeding to the opening on the north end of the mammoth structure, Mike headed for the big overhead doors that were used to load equipment onto the main floor of the arena. Mike felt as if he had stepped into a sci-fi movie set, and gasped in disbelief. People with biohazard suits scurried about in golf carts, forklifts and other small vehicles or pushed gurneys loaded with bodies. Mechanical sounds mixed with muffled voices reverberated off the walls of the make shift morgue. Mike involuntarily covered his mouth and nose with his hand to filter out the stench of exhaust and death.

Emergency technicians with clipboards busily took notes and placed large tags on the corpses that were encased in coffins or wrapped in waterproof fabric. Other bodies sheathed only in sheets were being rewrapped in body bags. Hundreds of bodies laid neatly in rows on the arena floor behind the overhead doors. All sizes, all shapes, all ages, all colors…all dead.

The men in the bio suits unloaded the small wooden chest from Mike's SUV and carried it to the first staging area. They recorded all the personal data Mike gave them on the forms, and put a label on the chest that stated "B003537C." Bibb County, victim number 3,537 processed at the coliseum.

A steady stream of vehicles continued to pull into the loading area. Most were vans and cube trucks that were out picking up bodies in neighborhoods and from hospitals and school infirmaries. Pairs of military recruits manned most of the vehicles that displayed permits in their windows allowing them to be out on the streets during the quarantine. A few civilians like Mike were bringing bodies of family members, despite repeated warnings of the curfew.

Mike tried to talk to the emergency technicians to get some details about the burial. They just looked at him with blank stares, exhausted and numb from their duty. Having made no previous plans for a cemetery plot, Mike wanted to secure several adjacent plots so that he and Courtney could eventually lay next to Beth, plus any of the kids or grandparents who later chose to join them. The EMTs simply shrugged and shook their heads apologetically when Mike asked what would happen to the bodies. Mike was given a receipt with the reference number for follow up in a few days and he walked off.

Mike wandered about, staggered by the sheer numbers of dead. A team of men busily made ice on a section of the floor that would have soon been the rink for the Macon hockey team. As morbid as it seemed, it provided an effective method for keeping the bodies from decaying until they could be buried.

A military policeman wearing a gas mask approached Mike. "Hey you! What are you doing here? This building is off limits to civilians."

"I've brought my daughter's body and I am trying to find out what will happen to her," Mike explained.

"Well there's nothing back here to help you. You'll have to leave. Follow me please." The officer took Mike's arm and turned him around. As they walked toward the shipping area the officer continued. "These bodies will all be taken to a new mass cemetery in Jones County."

Mike looked for names he recognized as he walked down the aisles of dead bodies. Lorra Harris, Mary Jo Morrow, and Trent Harper—all names of BLuR employees.

"Can I arrange for her to be buried in another cemetery or…"

"Mister, I don't know anything about those kind of details. We've got our hands full here. I have to ask you to leave now or we'll have to take you into custody."

Mike exited the building and stopped to get his bearings. The loading bay looked familiar, but could he have come out a different door? He looked around frantically for the small chest that held his infant daughter. It was gone.

Chapter 18

Pleas for Mercy

Thursday morning, September 17

The ends of the well-worn blanket flapped behind her as Latrice ran down the deserted street to her parent's house. The weight of her young daughter in her arms barely slowed her pace. She had been afraid to leave Regina at home sick, but Latrice became alarmed when her parents didn't answer the phone.

The rocker on the front porch moaned in harmony with Regina's pained breathing as Latrice eased her into the cushioned seat. She quickly unlocked the front door and scooped Regina back into her arms. They entered the house to find her parents sick and sleeping fitfully in their bed.

After checking her parents' pulse, she carried Regina into her old bedroom. As she pulled the soft covers around the young girl's flushed face, Latrice smiled hopefully at the thought that this was the same bed in which her Mama had nursed her back to health from virtually every known childhood sickness—measles, mumps, chicken pox.

She checked in again on Muh-Dea and Poppa. Now stirring from her sleep, her mother was ailing and groggy, but conscious. Her father was another story. Deep furrows appeared in Latrice's brow at the sight of a half-empty pack of cigarettes sitting on the nightstand next to her father. The pack disappeared into the pile of tissues in the wastebasket as Latrice reached for the phone.

"No sense in tryin' to call nobody, baby. I already tried," reported Latrice's mother.

"We've got to get Poppa some help."

"I know, Baby. I called the doctor and the hospital several times. Ain't nothin' they can do, is what they told me."

Latrice looked helplessly from her mother to father and back. "Well, we'll just see about that!"

Latrice struck the 911 keys hard as though it would help. She got no response. She tried several doctors' offices and even called their residences. Each call brought a system busy signal.

After an hour of watching her father's condition worsen, Latrice made an executive decision. "That does it. I'm taking Poppa to the Medical Center."

"I'm not so sure that's a good idea, Latrice. You heard what they was sayin' on the radio."

"It's not more than five miles away, Momma. We'll be fine. We can't afford to wait any longer. Poppa's getting worse by the minute. We need to go, especially now that you're up, and Regina is feeling a little better. Can I take your car? I don't want to have to go all the way home. Besides, I'm almost out of gas, and everything's probably closed up."

"Keys are by the back door. You call me once you get there."

"Yes, ma'am. Just keep a close eye on Regina, and call me on my cell phone if she doesn't keep improving." Latrice gave her mama a peck on the cheek and jotted down her phone number.

+

Latrice drove around the block at the hospital twice before she realized that the long line of cars double-parked on Pine Street was the line to get into the emergency room. She maneuvered between two parked cars, jumped a curb, and shimmied into a parking space. "I'll be right back, Poppa." She expected no response and received none as she exited the car and walked down the sidewalk dodging parked cars in her path. She saw a friendly face in the line.

"Are you waiting to get to the—," she began to ask.

Startled, the person quickly rolled up his window. Not expecting such a response, Latrice backed up a few steps. The guy rolled down the window halfway after she had backed off.

"Yeah, this is the line for the emergency room. We've been sitting here for three hours. I'd leave if I had any idea where else to go to take my wife." He reached over and dabbed the sweat from his wife's forehead.

Latrice went back to her car, cracked the windows and locked the doors. She hated to leave her dad alone, but lugging him from place to place would be even worse. She jogged the few hundred feet to the ER entrance.

The entry area of the hospital resembled a scene from *Gone with the Wind.* Battle-weary nurses tended patiently to the hopeless masses. Like wounded Confederate soldiers, the victims littered the entire area outside the hospital and spilled out onto the sidewalks. But unlike war times, many of the victims were women and children crying out pitiful pleas for mercy.

In contrast to the compassionate nurses and technicians, Air Force MPs in biohazard space suits guarded the doors with automatic weapons. No one appeared to be going into the hospital, except the few medical personnel with their hospital IDs clearly displayed.

After a few minutes, a hospital worker came out of the ER entrance to indicate to a coworker that another sick person could enter.

Latrice intercepted her. "Could you give me an idea how long it will take to get through these lines?"

"I'm sorry, ma'am. I really can't give you any idea. I'm not even sure where the line ends. At this point the only time we can let someone in is when someone dies inside. No one from inside has been discharged."

"Is there any way someone can take a look at my father? He is in really bad shape."

"Sorry, ma'am. Seems everybody is in bad shape. We're taking children first. A lot of people have died here already today." Her voice faltered slightly.

"Is there anything you can suggest? I've got to get some help for him."

"Several folks headed over to the gym at Central High School. They said it had been set up as an infirmary. And someone else told us that the city is turning the Auditorium into a makeshift hospital to handle the overflow." The worker headed back inside.

The Macon City Auditorium sat a mere five blocks from the Medical Center. Latrice went back to her car. Her dad's condition continued to worsen. She started the car and headed for the massive copper dome of the City Auditorium.

The scene didn't look promising, judging from the absence of noticeable activity around the front entrance on First Street. She backed up a few hundred feet to the alley and looked down the lane to the loading dock area. She spotted several men milling around and decided to investigate. Latrice parked the car and walked over to the overhead doors.

The hospital worker had gotten the information wrong. The City Auditorium was not an infirmary, it was being set up as a logistics center. Military officers and professional types stood conversing in the middle of the huge empty hall.

Soon, Latrice spotted a member of her church, Dr. Thomas Bagwell, a leading surgeon and one of a growing number of African-American doctors in town.

"Latrice, what brings you here?" Dr. Bagwell asked, walking toward her.

"They told me at the hospital that the City Auditorium was being converted into an infirmary. I have my daddy out in the car; his condition is getting worse." Latrice choked back tears.

"No, I'm sorry, this is not an infirmary. We're setting up a crisis center here. But, you know we are desperately looking for help, so if you're available, please join us. Assuming that you've been exposed, you look like one of the fortunate few to have escaped the plague." The doctor felt her forehead. "Are you feeling okay?"

"I'm fine, and I'm almost positive I have been exposed. I had a mild headache and stuffy head, but that's even passing. My daughter is at my Momma's house. They're both sick, but nothing like my father."

"I'll tell you what. If you agree to help us, I can help your father. Call your momma and see how they are doing."

Latrice smiled, then excused herself as she moved aside and pulled her cellular phone out of her purse. She braced for endless system busy messages, but her call went through on the second try. She breathed a sign of relief. To her surprise, her daughter answered.

"Hello."

"Regina! It's Momma. How are you feeling?"

"I'm okay Momma. I threw up a little while ago, but I feel much better. My head still hurts though."

"How's Muh-Dea doing?"

"She's in bed, but I took her something to drink. She says she's feeling better, too. Just tired."

"Well you take care of yourself and Muh-Dea. I'm going to be here at the hospital taking care of Poppa. It's going to take a long time. Be sure to tell Muh-Dea that I called. I'll call y'all later. I love you." Latrice hung up the phone and returned to the doctor.

"Dr. Bagwell, I would like to help you here. My mother and baby are okay at home. So where can I get help for my Daddy?"

"As a precautionary measure, they are setting up an infirmary just for volunteers downstairs. Take your dad down there and I'll come down in a few minutes."

"Oh, thank you, Dr. Bagwell," Latrice threw her arms around the doctor's neck and kissed his cheek before turning and running to her car. She wouldn't have hugged him if she had realized that she and her father were among the doctor's first exposures to the virus.

She recruited assistance from the emergency medical technicians near the loading dock. The National Guardsmen had received a crash course in emergency procedures, first aid, and crowd control. Soon they had wheeled her dad down to the infirmary on the lower level of the Auditorium. Restricted access to the infirmary provided for a much different scene than Latrice had encountered at the ER. Calm and clean, the area was for the exclusive benefit of the people working in the crisis center and their direct families. There were only a handful of patients at present, but many more were expected.

Dr. Bagwell came down a few minutes later. Having checked out Latrice's father, he reached into his medical bag and removed a syringe and a small vial of medicine.

"This is penicillin. It isn't effective against this virus, but it helps fight the pneumonia," he explained as he administered the shot. "It should help slow down the build up of fluids in his lungs and give his body a chance to fight the flu itself. I think he will be okay in a day or so.

"We can't tell anyone about this medicine," the doctor continued. "We have a very limited supply to treat workers in the crisis center. If word gets out that we have medicine…well, I hate to think about it."

"Thank You, God!" Latrice said half as a prayer and half to her new found guardian angel. "God bless you, Dr. Bagwell!"

"He's not out of danger yet, but he should be stable soon. Okay, let's put you to work," he said, and led her upstairs to her station in the new crisis center.

+

"She's gonna die! Sweet Jesus, she's gonna die!"

"Shut up, Ruby!" Albert Hawkins yelled to another of Paris's cousins. "Stop acting crazy! You're scaring the children."

But the reality was that things were pretty much out of control. Nearly everyone who witnessed Paris collapse at the big family meeting was showing the symptoms of influenza just a few hours later. Fatigue gave way to numbness as the Hawkins clan shared in a nightmare from which some would not awake.

Paris took her last pained breath shortly after 1:00 A.M. It had been obvious for hours that something had attacked Paris that was stronger than she was.

Paris's father Otis put his head in his hands and sobbed. "I prayed harder than I ever prayed to you before, Lord. Why have you ignored my pleas? I begged you to take me and spare my baby girl."

+

Young Austin Miller's fever broke early Thursday morning as he lay beneath the sweat-soaked sheets of his hospital bed in the Medical Center. His mother, who had flown in from San Diego, could hold him now.

"But, Mom, Dad promised we would go on to Disney World when he got better."

"I'll explain later, but you and I are going back home to California right now. This is one promise your Dad can't keep."

"But I want to see my Daddy," cried Austin as his mom swept him up into her arms and rushed down the hall.

Ignoring the advice of the doctors, they drove back to the Atlanta airport, minutes ahead of the police and military who began erecting roadblocks behind them.

By the time they ditched their rental car at the deserted airport return area and reached the gate, all the flights had been grounded. Baggage handlers, airport workers, and airline personnel exited en mass, fleeing to their families, despite the pleas from officials trying to maintain a skeleton crew.

Pandemonium quickly followed. Thousands of stranded passengers wandered the airport corridors in hopes of finding one final flight to anywhere closer to home. As time passed, and the panic escalated, normally restricted areas of the airport were breached. Angry hoards in search of their luggage broke down the doors leading to the servicing level below the terminal. Some pillaged the bags of other passengers in search of food and supplies. They took over vehicles and airplanes in an attempt to secure some defendable territory. Groups rearranged the furniture at the gates, and broke into restaurants, shops, and vending machines. Alarms screamed frantically, but no one responded. Frontier justice reigned, and the scent of death hovered in the air.

Austin and his mother camped out in Terminal B. His mother huddled in a shivering ball on the airport floor, moaning in pain as the sickness wracked her body. With the innocence of a five-year-old, Austin simply couldn't grasp the horrors that surrounded him. His stomach let out a loud, empty growl. He hadn't eaten in two days. He put his thumb in his mouth and curled up behind his mother's legs, trying to stay clear of the coughing and vomiting.

Chapter 19

Center Command

Thursday, September 17

Communication now flowed through the floor of the Macon City Auditorium as officials waged war against the plague that decimated the city. The air hummed with activity as media representatives tracked television and radio broadcasts, engineers coordinated telecommunications, and doctors shared strategies and treatments with medical specialists around the country. Clergy from various faiths and denominations gathered to support the efforts in prayer. All this activity revolved around the executive center in the middle of the hall, which was wallpapered with maps and equipped wall to wall with phones. The military occupied an area adjacent to the executive center. On the opposite end, a press area had been constructed for announcements and conferences.

Officially, the mayor commanded the center, seeking expert advice from the fire and police departments and the coroner's office. But none of the top local government officials were present at the crisis center because they were either home sick, tending to family members, or unwilling to take a chance at being exposed to the plague. Zeke Jarrell, the local director of FEMA, took charge.

Dr. Bagwell introduced Latrice to Zeke and to Beverly Stewart. Like the doctor, Beverly recognized Latrice from Mt. Olive Church and greeted her enthusiastically. As the chief administrator to the mayor, Beverly headed up the administrative area at the crisis center. Latrice was immediately given a badge and put to work. When Beverly later became ill with the flu, Latrice assumed responsibility for the area.

Periodically, Latrice checked on her father in the infirmary. The once empty beds were now full. Gurneys crammed the space, extra cots had been brought in, and the more recent additions had been relegated to blankets on the floor. Service at the crisis center proved no defense against the rampant virus, although the rate of infection did seem lower here than in the general population.

The employees at BLuR had indeed been part of the first wave of exposure in the area. Now the general population of Macon was becoming ill. On one of her frequent trips to the infirmary, Latrice cringed to see Dr. Bagwell lying sick on a blanket not far from her father. She moved to comfort the good doctor, but found him unconscious and burning up with fever. Another doctor administered penicillin and antibiotics. They could ill afford to lose any doctors now. He would be given the best possible care.

In between answering the endless calls in the executive command station in the main auditorium, Latrice also called frequently to check on her mom and daughter. "How are you doing, baby?"

"We're okay, Momma," replied Regina. Muh-Dea is still in bed mostly, but she gets up sometimes to fix us something to eat. I saw you on the news, Momma. That's really cool. You were talking on the phone or something, and they were showing the crisis center thing."

"You think that's cool, honey? I'm glad. Can you get your grandmother on the phone? There's a phone in her bedroom."

"Okay, just a minute."

"Latrice, you okay, baby?"

"Hey, Momma, Regina says you're doing better. I just wanted to let you know that Poppa's doing okay, too. Coming here and running into Dr. Bagwell probably saved his life."

"Bless you, baby. It's good to hear that you and your daddy are all right."

"Now we need to pray for Dr. Bagwell. I'll call you later, Momma." Latrice added a heartfelt, "Momma, I love you."

She hung up as Zeke Jarrell approached. "I have an important job for you."

"Sure, Zeke. How can I help?"

"We need to track the death rates in Middle Georgia. It's a morbid task, but I need you to call the hospitals, schools, and other temporary care sites and acquire accurate death counts from them. Also, check with the temporary morgue they have set up at the coliseum. I'm afraid this epidemic hasn't peaked yet, and your findings will help us know when we have turned the corner."

"Okay, Zeke. I'm happy to help in any way I can."

"I may not be here much longer. My wife just called. The kids have taken a turn for the worse. Just do what you can if I'm not here."

Calling all the places receiving the sick was painstaking and mostly futile with the phones so busy. Even though the locations reported hundreds of deaths, Latrice quickly realized the limitations of her efforts. She remembered the lines outside the Medical Center emergency room. "The hospitals aren't where the deaths are occurring," she said to no one in particular. "People aren't leaving their homes." She called the 911 center.

"Lady, we're getting so many calls that our computers can't handle it. To top it off, most of our 911 operators never reported in to work today. Our reports show that most of the calls are hanging up. Can't say I blame them."

As staggering as the death rates were, she was only scratching the surface. Latrice felt like the captain of the Titanic realizing that it wasn't just a stray piece of surface ice that had struck the ship.

Latrice started checking around with the acting chief of police, the phone company, the National Guard and other experts at the center. She put together a plan to temporarily relocate the 911 operation to the crisis center. They would staff it with Guardsmen until enough 911 operators were available. The technical experts agreed it was a plausible plan. She called Zeke Jarrell at home and he gave his blessing for the strategy.

Within four hours all 911 calls had been redirected to a call center at the Auditorium. Thirty Guardsmen received a cram course in crisis response and were encouraged to give aid and comfort to those who called. Workers cheered as the first calls came in and the area took on the appearance of a telethon, though one with grave implications. Soon few calls went unanswered.

Hours later, Latrice called Zeke Jarrell at home to give him an update on the activities at the crisis center. "It looks like about two-thirds of the population around Macon has been exposed to the influenza virus. About eight out of ten infected people become seriously ill, one out of ten suffer only mild symptoms, and one in ten shows no sign of illness. Based on the preliminary data, one out of twenty will die."

"A staggering finding," Zeke said slowly. "Make sure you share those stats with the press and get some communication going with the FEMA office in DC as well."

"Will do. How's your family, Zeke?"

"They're sick, but stable. It looks like we are all in that lucky percent that pulls through. Call again when you get a chance, Latrice. I'm telling my people that as far as I'm concerned, you are now the official unofficial leader in charge of the center. Just until I get back, you understand." Zeke chuckled.

+

Next Latrice tackled the telephone traffic logjam. "The central office reports serious voice traffic overload situations," reported the ranking BellSouth official on site at the crisis center.

"Can we restrict outbound or inbound?" asked Latrice. "Can we block one or the other?"

"Sure. But that's not how we normally do it."

"Well I don't think anything is normal right now. Try letting people call out, but restrict inbound calls. People will contact their family outside the area. The load is probably coming from all the people trying to check on family and friends in Macon."

"I think that will work. I'll get my supervisor to approve it."

Latrice put a hand on the BellSouth official's shoulder. "This isn't any ol' day at the office. Times like this require focus and the guts to make decisions fast. I suggest that you forget checking with your supervisor. Just check it out and make the decision yourself. I have all the confidence in the world that you'll make the right call."

The official returned, his entire demeanor changed. He reported that he had decided to severely limit inbound long distance and to play a special message to the callers. Within an hour the logjam was largely relieved. Soon, they would be able to open and close circuits giving priority to lines necessary for police and medical activities.

"We're keeping a close eye on the activities of the medical experts," Latrice reported to Zeke Jarrell in her next update call to his house. "Everyone is holding their breath for news about a vaccine or some other treatment alternative. Our medical guys here are in constant communication with the relevant agencies about vaccines."

"What else are the doctors working on?" Latrice could hear one of Zeke's children crying in the background over the phone.

"They are working on a campaign to warn people against some of the crazy home remedies that keep popping up. You wouldn't believe some of the stuff they've been telling me, like wearing a scarf soaked in turpentine helps prevent infection. Or bathing the flu victim in ice water. Oh, yeah, one lady called and told them she made her child drink massive doses of vinegar to 'get the bugs out of her system.' The doctors are worried that in the panic, the desperate measures will only get worse.

"Another point of interest," Latrice continued, "is ministers from various churches have been coming by regularly. We've been putting them on our TV broadcasts. We get more favorable feedback on the preachers than on the medical experts."

"You're making great progress, Latrice! What would we have done if you didn't happen to come around?"

"Thanks, Zeke. One of the preachers told me yesterday that God answers prayers when we allow ourselves to become his answer."

"Well, Latrice you have become His answer many times over for hundreds of folks. You're an angel!"

Chapter 20

Parasites

Thursday morning, September 17

With the absence of law enforcement, Wayne went about making plans to profit from the influenza, his entrepreneurial spirit immediately grasping the huge opportunity at hand.

He called Jimmy Mack only to discover that he had been called in for duty. He left his number on Jimmy Mack's pager and headed for Jay's apartment.

He climbed the stairs littered with trash bags and cigarette butts and pounded angrily on the flimsy door t until he could hear Jay cursing in the background. Jay opened the door a crack.

"I don't feel good. I feel like crap, man. Leave me alone," Jay whined.

Wayne pushed his way past Jay.

"Oh, poor baby. Little Jayzie doesn't feel very good." Wayne laughed as he pinched Jay's cheek and twisted.

"Shit, Wayne, that hurts! Knock it off."

"You pussy! You've been watching too much TV. Get your bony ass moving and get dressed." Wayne grabbed a crumpled shirt from the back of a chair and tossed it in Jay's face. "We got things to do, man."

"Not today." In an uncharacteristic display of defiance, Jay threw the shirt back at Wayne. "I'm going back to bed. Call me tomorrow."

Wayne shrugged and headed out the door. "Your loss, man."

A few minutes later, he parked his Jeep out of sight in the back of Jack's shop and retrieved the keys for the unmarked white shop van. An old license plate that he had taken off a wreck months before would serve to throw off any ID checks. Wayne unlocked the pumps and gassed up before going home to finish equipping the van.

Once home, he pulled out a couple of handguns, his hunting rifle, and a box of shells. He packed several blankets, rope, duct tape, some food, and a cooler full of beer into the back of the van.

Jimmy Mack called Wayne around noon on Thursday. He had been assigned to daily ten-hour Guard shifts until further notice. The Guard infirmary had pumped the troops full of penicillin and other antibiotics in hopes of keeping them healthy.

"Hey Jimmy Mack," Wayne said. "Can you talk?" Wayne had to assume that he was within earshot of the entire U.S. military establishment.

"Yeah, I'm clear for a few minutes, what's up?"

"Here's the plan. You got to find us a way we can break curfew and cruise the streets in this van I got from work. Can you get us a military or EMT decal?"

"Could be. I'll check into it."

"And you have to find out where the police and MPs are and where they ain't. You know, what streets are they patrolling?"

"I can probably do that."

"I've got the shop van ready for the loot. It'll be like taking candy from a baby. Everybody's sick, including the cops. When this thing breaks, we'll be set for life, man!"

"When and where do you want to meet?"

"As soon as you're off."

"Six o'clock. I'll meet you at your apartment."

"See you then. Probably be just the two of us," reported Wayne. "Jay's pretty sick. I was over there earlier and he looked like crap."

"See you at six," Jimmy Mack said.

"I'll be armed and dangerous, mister military man," Wayne said with a laugh.

Wayne checked out a few self-storage places, but it occurred to him that the attic at Jack's would be ideal. It could only be accessed by backing a pickup truck onto the lift, raising the lift and climbing through the trap door from the bed of the pickup.

On his way home Wayne went over to check on Jay. He was still sick, but improved. If things went as well as expected, he'd use him tomorrow to unload all the loot. Jay came in real handy for grunt work.

Back home, Jimmy Mack turned on the television to check out the news. He got a map of Macon and identified several neighborhoods throughout the area. The police and MPs on patrol were concentrating on keeping traffic from entering and leaving Macon's major highways. He and Wayne would move around using the secondary roads and avoid the authorities. Jimmy Mack pulled out the permit he had lifted from the armory. Under the guise of picking up dead flu victims, they could go anywhere, anytime.

+

Mike returned home from taking Beth's body to the coliseum to find Courtney in the fetal position in their bed, whimpering like a little girl. The smell of sweat and vomit still hung heavy in the air and seeing Courtney brought back the despair of the situation.

"Honey, honey…" Mike gently nudged her.

"Stay away from me. I can't believe you could let Beth die. What kind of father are you?"

Any hopes that Mike held that Courtney would soon come around were shattered. Mike leaned against the bedpost.

"C'mon, Courtney, you must know how bad I feel about what happened. I was unconscious just like you when Beth died. I've already lost a beautiful little baby girl, but now I'm scared I'm losing you, too."

"You should have woken me up. What good are you if you can't protect your own baby?"

"I tried to wake you!" Mike went over and rubbed her shoulder. Her skin was cool and clammy.

"Don't touch me you fucking asshole!" Courtney shuddered at his touch and pulled away. "Don't you ever touch me again!"

Mike stood, thought for a moment, and then left the room.

He went upstairs to check on the kids. He changed their beds, gave them each a bath, and brushed their teeth.

Mark and Emily didn't resist returning to bed right away. Amy was in no mood to stay in bed any longer, so Mike lay next to her.

"I'm really proud of you for being such a good girl during all this fuss. It's no fun being around people who are sick, and you're really lucky that you never felt bad."

"I'm bored, there's no one to play with, and no TV. Can you read to me?

"Sure. When this is all over, we're going to write a book, just you and me, okay? We'll make up the story together, but you have to draw all the pictures."

Mike lay there tickling her face until Amy faded off to sleep. He went downstairs to check on Courtney. She was sleeping soundly in the master bedroom. He returned to the girls' bedroom with a sleeping bag and slept at the foot of the girls' twin beds.

+

That same Thursday evening, the first night of the epidemic in Macon, Wayne and Jimmy Mack methodically cruised the streets of Shirley Hills, an affluent, old Macon neighborhood. They encountered only one roadblock, but were immediately waived on due to the red emergency permit affixed to their windshield. They looked like any number of teams out picking up bodies.

The sun was just beginning to set and bright orange rays back-lit their first target house as they made their way to the front door. Selected largely at random, it had the added appeal of no signs of a dog or alarm system.

An elderly woman answered the door. Wayne immediately shoved the old woman inside the house and pushed his pistol against her neck, while Jimmy Mack put a nylon stocking over his head. As soon as he finished, Wayne followed suit while Jimmy Mack pressed his pistol hard against the woman's pale cheek.

"Who else is here and where are they?"

"My husband is in bed upstairs. There's no one else here. Please, don't hurt us."

"Let's go find hubby, shall we?" Wayne said, pushing her toward the stairs.

They followed her up the steps.

The old man proved to be no threat.

"Watch him and make sure he doesn't budge," Wayne barked at Jimmy Mack, then turned to the wife. "Where's your jewelry?"

"In that jewelry box on my bureau." She pointed to the other side of the room.

"How about cash?" Jimmy Mack added.

"I have forty dollars or so in that top drawer over there," she said pointing to her bureau again.

"Got any guns?"

"Heavens no, we don't have any guns."

"Now listen carefully," Wayne said, putting his face near hers. "I'm gonna ask you some questions. You help us, you won't get hurt. But we'll tear this place apart if you make us. And, if you lie to us, it ain't gonna be pretty, you hear?"

"Okay." Her voice trembled as she looked helplessly over at her husband.

"You expectin' anyone to come here to this house for the next hour or so?"

She shook her head.

"You got anything real valuable hidden around here?"

She hesitated.

"I'm warning you, lady!" He raised his hand as though to strike her.

"Alright. My husband has a stamp collection in a safe downstairs."

"Shit!" Jimmy Mack shook his head. "We don't want no stamps!"

"Is that everything? You sure?" Wayne pressed the gun harder into her cheek.

"Yes, yes, I swear."

"Where are your car keys?"

"They're on the kitchen table downstairs."

"Now, get over there in that chair."

Using duct tape they bound the old lady to a chair in the corner of the bedroom. She watched as they sat her husband up in the bed and bound his wrists above his head to each of the headboard posts. They crammed socks into their mouths and taped their eyes closed.

Jimmy Mack grabbed the car keys off of the kitchen counter, and went to the garage to pull the couple's Toyota out onto the street. There was no traffic of any kind. He backed the van into the garage and closed the overhead door. Meanwhile, Wayne tossed the jewelry box and cash into a pillowcase and scanned the bedroom for other valuables. He snatched the old man's Rolex from the bedside table and pried the wedding rings off the old couple.

Methodically, they proceeded to ransack every room in the house. They took a couple of televisions and a camera, but they didn't even recognize a large collection of Steuben crystal pieces—the most valuable possessions in the house.

They considered taking the car but decided against it because it would be too easy to trace. Satisfied with the booty of their first heist, they finished loading the van. "Must be three or four thousand dollars worth of stuff here!" Wayne exclaimed.

Almost as an afterthought, they took all the packaged foods and canned drinks they could carry from the kitchen.

"Hey, this flu thing lasts long enough, this food and drink may be the most valuable stuff we got," quipped Wayne as he went back upstairs to check on the couple.

He thought about unbinding the old man since he had never gained consciousness during their visit. Wayne cut the tape away from the headboard and the old man slumped back onto the bed. Hearing Jimmy Mack crank up the van, Wayne headed downstairs.

Wayne and Jimmy Mack moved quickly to hit another home a couple streets away. This time no one answered the front door, so they went around to the back and broke in. Inside they found a woman semiconscious in her bed, with two sick teenage sons down the hall. The presence of the boys startled the thieves, but they quickly realized everybody was too sick to resist. The thieves didn't even bother with masks.

One of the boys looked up at Jimmy Mack. Jimmy Mack announced in a very official military tone, "We're emergency medical technicians checking with folks to see that they're okay, son. Hope you feel better soon. Sorry to disturb you."

Taking no chances, Wayne and Jimmy Mack bound the mother to the bed and covered her mouth with duct tape, then headed downstairs and went to work. They grabbed a few big-ticket items and were out of there within minutes.

The pair of thieves ended up robbing three homes that night. Their pockets were crammed with cash and the back of the van was filled with electronics, jewelry, silver, guns, and food.

At their last stop the scene looked much the same, an entire family incapacitated by the virus. This time they bound mom and dad and the two kids by wrapping tape around their wrists.

On the way home, the thieves reveled in their loot.

"You see the look on that ol' lady's face when I put this baby in her scrawny little cheek?" Wayne waved his pistol.

Jimmy Mack laughed. "Where to tomorrow night?"

"Hummm," Wayne contemplated. "I like these ritzy neighborhoods. More bang for the buck. How 'bout we join the Country Club tomorrow?"

"You think they'll let a darkie in?" Jimmy Mack punctuated his question by picking up Wayne's pistol and aiming it at an imaginary target in front of the van.

Wayne reached across and backhanded Jimmy Mack in the chest with his forearm as they both laughed uproariously. "Affirmative action, bro, affirmative action!"

Chapter 21

Black Friday

Friday, September 18

Jennifer, R.T., and their three children escaped the onslaught of the virus. R.T. and the kids had bad colds, but the scope of what was happening across the city had miraculously spared them.

R.T. walked to Sanders Funeral Home and called each of his twelve employees at their homes. Two of his employees thought they might be able to return to work within the next few days. Several didn't answer their phones. One employee asked R.T. to pick up his wife who had died Thursday. The wife of another employee was crying so hard that she could barely explain that her husband had died. Two had lost children. R.T. spoke to each and promised to be out to see them as soon as he could.

After finishing the calls, R.T. noticed police activity around the City Auditorium a block away. He walked over to investigate.

Being on a first-name basis with the policemen at the front door gained him prompt admittance, and he was quite surprised when he asked for the person in charge and was introduced to Latrice.

"R.T.! What are you doing here?" Latrice said, looking up from her paperwork.

"I guess I could ask you the same thing," he replied.

"How are Jennifer and the kids?"

"Amazingly, everybody at my house is fine. We've been watching the news, but I didn't realize just how bad things really were until I got out of the house."

"Believe me R.T., I know."

"I could really help out here if I could get some helpers and the proper permits."

"Hmmm." Latrice stood and motioned for R.T. to follow. "Let's see what we can do.

"We're able to keep the larger TV and radio stations in Macon on the air by asking employees from smaller stations to fill in. Local coverage has been limited, with the majority of news coming from network broadcasts. Meanwhile, the Macon Telegraph provides an Internet site with a link to officials in Washington."

R.T. and Latrice paused in the media area to listen to the president who had just gone on the air.

"So far it is clear that the epidemic began in Ohio and California, and is spreading along major Interstates." The screen dissolved from the president to a map of the U.S. with red shading along I-75 and a large red splotch in the middle of Georgia.

One of the workers in the area commented about how pale the president looked, just about the time the commander in chief turned from the microphone to cough. In closing, the president touted optimism about the prospects of eventually beating the flu.

R.T. and Latrice walked toward the military affairs area. "Just between you and me," she whispered, "disaster recovery operations are still civilian controlled. But if we screw up, the military is ready to start running the show. You'll see what I mean here."

They entered the military operations post staffed with several high-ranking officers from a nearby Air Force base and local Army National Guard unit. Captain Martin currently had charge of the area.

"Hey, Miss Rutherford," he said with little enthusiasm. He looked back down at his report as if he were too busy to deal with a civilian. "And what is it that I can do for you?"

The captain heard and declined R.T.'s request for a military helper, citing the need for every available soldier at the coliseum. But he did accept the mortician's offer to help in the crisis, and as a military "need to know" individual, proceeded to update him on the situation from the military perspective.

"Within hours of the arrival of Harry Miller and his son in the Macon area, more than 4,000 people at the hotel, restaurant, and hospital came in contact with the virus. By Wednesday, those people had infected about 30,000 people and, by the end of Thursday, more than 200,000 of the 350,000 people living in the greater Macon area had been exposed.

"Lots of folks were caught in the wrong place when the panic hit. That's been one of our biggest logistical challenges. Business people traveling, kids off at college, people vacationing…while we're trying to contain this blasted thing, we're running headlong into mamas and daddies trying to get home to junior.

"The military is in charge of burial of the dead and that's where we can use your help as an undertaker."

"What can you tell me about terrorist involvement in this epidemic, captain?" asked R.T.

"The Abu Sayyaf terrorists in the Philippines claimed credit early; they're the same group that killed an American hostage a few years ago. They're a pretty primitive band of thugs, not well funded like the Arabs inside al-Qaida. They have no labs to create viruses and they aren't bright enough to pull off something this sophisticated. This is still classified military information, but our troops invaded their camps in the last few days and found hundreds of terrorists dead from the flu. The few survivors of the battle are squealing like pigs, saying that their leaders had nothing to do with this pandemic."

R.T. received his permit to drive during curfew and was provided vouchers for forty gallons of fuel. Latrice thanked the captain, and they made their way back to her desk where Latrice had a call from FEMA Director Zeke Jarrell.

"I just checked with the CDC in Atlanta and the National Institute of Health in Bethesda about their progress on a vaccine. They're not finished yet, but they are making steady progress and expect to make an announcement any day. Apparently, all the preparations for a possible anthrax or other biological attack on America a couple years ago are really paying off now. Hang in there, Latrice. I'm at home if you need me."

Armed with a mission from Latrice to coordinate efforts with the new makeshift morgue across town, R.T. drove over to the coliseum. All of his years as a mortician couldn't prepare him for the ghastly scene. Corpses arrived in a steady stream. The highest number of dead in a single day was expected to be about 1,500, a number incomprehensible for a city that buries 80 people in the average week. There was no time for embalming the bodies or for services for family and friends. Every effort would be made to maintain records for all the bodies so that loved ones could arrange for permanent individual grave markers and services at a later date.

The workers, mostly military enlistees from all over the US, were glad to meet a trained undertaker. They bombarded him with a variety of questions.

"This wasn't in the Air Force recruitment video," said one young soldier.

"We have to handle dead bodies like sacks of grain," said another. "They gave us these space suits, but they're so hot and confining that most of us came out of them."

"I feel like a garbage collector," reported another soldier. "Unbelievable how many young children have died. Makes your soul harden up real fast."

Suddenly feeling very fortunate that his family had survived all the death, R.T. stopped to call Jennifer and check on his family.

"R.T., I'm glad you called," said Jennifer. "Mike called earlier and said his little baby had died and he had taken her to the coliseum. He wants to know if you can try to locate her body."

"Let Mike know I'm at the coliseum and I'll jump right on it. And Jenn, please give him my deepest sympathies."

+

Wayne stood watch while Jimmy Mack hauled the loot up into the attic at Jack's Auto Repair. He hadn't seen a single car pass since they pulled in. The two had absconded with an impressive inventory. Wayne lifted a small blanket bundled up like Santa's sack from the back of the van. He carefully untied the rope that held it together and surveyed the contents greedily.

"Don't be slippin' any of that out until we settle up now, you hear?" Jimmy Mack said.

"You know me better than that, now." Wayne feigned sincerity.

Jimmy Mack just grunted as he hauled the last television into the attic. "You sure this is a good place to stash this stuff?"

"Ain't nobody been up there for years. I can't think of no place better, can you?"

"My place comes to mind."

"Soon, my friend. Soon. Let it cool off first."

"That's the last of it. What now? This calls for a celebration!"

"Yeah, let's go kick back over at my house with a few cold ones. Whatcha think?"

"Hell, yeah! Lead the way."

The aroma of stale hops assaulted the two as they made their way through the fast food bags and pizza boxes that littered the floor of Wayne's apartment.

"Shit, man, don't you ever pick up around here?"

"Nah, just gets trashed again, ya know."

Wayne turned the local news on. The camera panned across the crisis center.

"Local officials have responded quickly to this emergency, Chris, setting up a…"

"Holy shit!" Jimmy Mack slung beer all over the avocado-green shag carpet.

"That's Latrice Rutherford! She works with my cousin Paris!"

Wayne leaned forward and studied the screen. "Hummm, not bad. She looks a little lonely, don't ya think?"

"You crazy? That bitch is so cold, man, she'd freeze your balls off."

Wayne reached over to a small side table and pulled out the drawer. He unconsciously looked around the room as he pulled out a small plastic baggie containing several chunks of what appeared to be white rock candy. Wayne grinned and looked over at Jimmy Mack.

"Whatcha say?" Wayne's eyebrows arched in a question mark.

"You crazy? I thought you didn't do that crap."

"I don't. Just sell it, but, hey, I got all this stuff just sittin' here with nobody to sell it to. Besides, this is a special occasion, right?"

"I don't suppose those Guard docs are gonna have time to fool with drug tests in the middle of all this craziness." Jimmy Mack glanced at the news on the television set. "A little hit might take my mind off all this death and dying, now wouldn't it."

They both chuckled.

"Well?" Wayne encouraged.

"What the hell. Why not."

Wayne reached under the sofa mining for an empty beer can. Wayne took a pocketknife from his jeans and cut a hole in the side of the aluminum can. He poured a few drops of leftover beer out of the bottom half onto the carpet and folded the blade back to return the knife to his pants pocket. Wayne held the baggie out to Jimmy Mack. "You wanna do the honors?"

"No man, you go ahead." Jimmy Mack didn't want to admit to his friend that he had no idea what to do next.

Wayne unzipped the bag, extracted one of the small crystal-like rocks, and placed it in the beer can. He took a small, lighter-sized torch from the drawer, lit it, and heated the bottom of the can for several seconds until a faint trail of gray smoke danced within the can. Wayne carefully lifted the cooler top half of the can to his face, opened his mouth and drew in the smoke through the hole in the side. He sucked the smoke deep into his lungs, not saying a word as he handed the makeshift pipe to Jimmy Mack.

Jimmy Mack accepted the offering. He felt his heartbeat speed up in anticipation of the rush to come as he heated the crystals and lifted the can to his mouth.

As the afternoon wore on, an orgasmic euphoria engulfed Jimmy Mack and Wayne as they recounted their evening's adventure and watched with detached delight the news of the global death and dying on television. Their crack-induced haven would soon dissipate, leaving them to awake in the hell of their own making.

+

Latrice placed the latest death toll data in a manila folder and headed over to the media area that had been set up in the far corner of the crisis center. "Okay y'all, here are the latest statistics for the middle Georgia area." She handed out copies of the report. "As bad as it is, it should help folks put things in perspective and quell the panic. We have to get the word out that catching this flu is not an automatic death sentence."

The young TV reporter scanned the information and shook his head slowly. "Holy shit! Quell it? This is the stuff panics are made of."

"You're going on TV to calm the nerves of the public? Maybe we need a new angle," Latrice offered kiddingly. "How about the Internet? Are folks really surfing the net in the middle of all this?"

"Oh, yeah," replied a young woman in charge of the newspaper's website, "especially when they find good up-to-date information like this. We're getting thousands of hits on our site and I can't keep up with the e-mail volume."

"Let's post these latest stats online. Unfortunately the numbers of fatalities are still climbing, so we haven't turned the corner yet." Latrice headed out. "Y'all keep up the good work. Strike a balance between calming the hysterics and flushing out anyone with his head in the sand. No sweat, right?"

She exited to a combination of moans and mumbles from the press people. One reporter followed Latrice down the aisle. "Ms. Rutherford? Can I speak to you?"

"Sure." Latrice stopped to face an attractive Asian girl in her twenties. "Call me Latrice. What's your name?"

"My name is Linh, and I have something that I need to report. I understand that you're the lady in charge."

"I am. What's happened?"

"One of the National guardsmen over there, a black man with 'Scott' on his badge, came up to me just a little while ago and demanded to see my ID. He and another soldier said they were patrolling the area to remove people like me that didn't belong in the crisis center. He said something to the effect that all this death was caused by people like me and that I was to get out. He said the Philippines was a backward country that tolerated terrorists and failed to appreciate all that America had done for them. He was carrying a weapon and wearing an MP badge. I don't know what would have happened if they hadn't gone away when someone walked up. Latrice, my parents are from Vietnam, not the Philippines, and I was born in Orlando, not in Asia. But even so, I can't believe this kind of behavior is allowed."

"Linh, I'm going to go straighten this out right now. You can expect a formal apology very soon. We don't tolerate that kind of behavior and I apologize to you on behalf of the community." Latrice excused herself and marched immediately over to the security post.

"Major Manus?"

"Hey, Latrice. What's up?" The officer and Latrice had spoken several times before.

"You and I need to talk to one of your MPs, please. An African-American soldier with the last name of Scott, I understand."

Within ten minutes the young Guardsman was interrogated, confessed that the woman's story was substantially correct, and sent searching for the young reporter to make an apology. Upon returning to his post, he was relieved of all responsibilities at the crisis center and sent home to await a hearing.

Afterwards, Linh found Latrice. "I wanted to thank you for resolving that situation. I hope you weren't too tough on Mr. Scott. I hate to judge people too harshly on one incident. Some people who say insensitive things are hateful, but more often they just don't know any better. Thanks so much."

Linh touched her hand gently and left.

Latrice watched her leave, her brow furrowed.

+

During those first couple of days at the center, no one would have accused Latrice of being an angel. A drill sergeant maybe, but certainly no angel. Even the military personnel had found her somewhat overbearing at first.

The situations at the crisis center called for steely directness and quick decision-making, but also for diplomacy. Many of the people at the center had already lost someone they loved to the pandemic, but they kept on helping others. Latrice quickly recognized the need to adapt her style for the volunteer workforce, finding ways to drive consensus with the unique personalities that ranged from pastors to colonels. After all, the majority of her crisis center workforce was volunteers and if they didn't buy in, they could simply ignore her. What was the penalty—not getting paid? Being sent home? And yet there was a huge need for someone to turn to, someone willing to step forward and take the risk to lead. Latrice was that someone.

Over time, Latrice found her reaction to others evolving, and varying based on the circumstances. Many of the emergency, public service, and military people at the center had never been around a woman directing their activities, much less a black woman. Many were "good-ol'-boy" types, traditional and narrow in their beliefs. Initially they didn't take her seriously and frequently asked to see the "man in charge." She could sense the hostility and assumed that they were murmuring about her behind her back.

But Latrice quickly won them over. With each of her decisive and insightful suggestions, the men grew to respect her and seek her advice. In turn they provided their technical expertise to create mutual successes. Guys she would have blown off as rednecks a week earlier were now crucial allies in a war against an unseen enemy.

+

The hour was late as Latrice sat alone at her makeshift crisis center desk. The hum around the center had died down and she used the quiet to sort the paperwork on her desk. One of the morbidity reports caught her eye and she casually scanned down the long list of names when one leapt from the page: Paris Hawkins, Jones County.

Latrice pressed her fingers silently to her lips. A lone tear rolled down her cheek as the painful reality invaded the protective cocoon of the center.

+

Around 6:00 A.M. on Friday morning, Mike awoke and immediately checked on each of the kids. Everyone was resting comfortably, still too sleepy to get up just yet. Never again would he take quiet breathing for granted.

Mike found Courtney in the nursery, sleeping fitfully on top of an old bedspread with a mattress cover for a sheet. Her forehead felt relatively cool, giving no clue of her broken disposition.

Mike went downstairs and out onto the back deck. He took the dog outside and started to go to the mailbox for the paper before he realized how futile it would be. No garbage collection this week either. No groceries, no gas, no baby, no nothing.

Back inside the house, Mike took inventory of the food in the refrigerator and on the shelves—some cereal, canned goods, and sundry items. Certainly not full shelves, but enough to last them a few days. The biggest problem was the lack of milk. He filled a glass full of tap water and studied it in the light. It looked clear and smelled clean. Then he caught himself, realizing that he hadn't seen the flu invade their bodies either. He poured the water into the sink.

The old Y2K supplies in the attic proved handy as Mike retrieved four ten-gallon plastic containers filled with water. The water might taste like plastic, but at least it wasn't contaminated. He found his emergency stash of candles and matches in a drawer. He also found two flashlights and some extra batteries, then gathered several rolls of toilet paper for safekeeping.

"Good morning Daddy." Amy was sitting on the steps, looking a little peaked, but smiling. "Am I going to school today?"

"No, baby, You won't be going to school for a few days, just like Christmas break. When your brother and Emily come down I have something to explain to the three of you." Mike drew Amy into his embrace, squeezing her in a bear hug.

"What do you mean three? You always say there's a six-pack of us Spikers!"

Mike just held her tightly, trying to find words to tell them about Beth.

+

Latrice called Mike first to make sure he had heard about Paris.

"I don't know how to tell you this, Mike, but Paris died of the flu," she reported sadly.

Mike said nothing.

"I just saw her name on a report. Says she died in Jones County. Must have been at her family property." She paused for a response. "Mike, you there?"

No answer. Latrice didn't know if the line went dead or if Mike was that upset. "Mike! Are you still on the line?"

After several moments of silence, Latrice heard Mike sobbing. She gave him a few moments to collect himself.

"I can't believe that Paris is gone, Mike. I'm downtown at the crisis center that the government has just started up. I'll tell you later how I—"

"My God, now Paris is gone. Courtney's a wreck. Beth died yesterday…" Mike broke down again. "I'll call you later, Latrice."

He hung up.

+

Next, Latrice called Dwight. "I'm sorry about Paris, but I lost a son and Claire's mother died from this friggin' plague. What're you doing calling me, Latrice?"

“Only trying to stay in touch. I’m sorry about your losses, Dwight. I just talked to Mike. He and Courtney lost their little baby. He was so upset and then I laid this news about Paris on him.”

“And now you’re doing the same to me,” Dwight said coldly.

“Sorry, Dwight, sorry about John, and about Claire’s mother.”

Dwight was silent on the other end.

“Well, goodbye. I’m going to call the others. Please, call me on my cell line if you need anything.”

After two horrible calls, Latrice was reluctant to call anyone else, but Jennifer turned out to be in fairly good spirits. They talked for several minutes about how lucky they both had been since Tuesday.

Jennifer was secretly encouraged about Latrice’s long-term commitment to the crisis center. With Latrice tied up, Mike would count primarily on Jennifer to get BLuR back on its feet.

“You focus on the crisis center, Latrice. I’ll help Mike get BLuR back on track,” Jennifer said solemnly.

Chapter 22

Stealing from the Thief

Monday, September 21

On the sixth day of the pandemic, Jay declared himself recovered sufficiently from the flu to join his thieving buddies. He helped Wayne transfer the stolen goods from the van to the attic of the auto shop and sort through the inventory. As much as they wanted to be out robbing people, they settled for hitting their targets after dark. Ironically, Jimmy Mack worked from 6:00 A.M. to 4:00 P.M. each day as a military policeman, maintaining order at a food distribution point in the parking lot of a grocery store, using the information he picked up to elude police and MPs during their night raids.

Up until this point, police efforts focused on enforcing curfews and maintaining order. Routine investigations ceased and petty crimes, mostly thefts of food and other necessities, seemed insignificant in light of the very real and immediate threat of death that faced the general population. Personal injuries from crimes were actually down, so the police didn't allocate any of their limited resources to the crimes that had been reported. But as the days continued, citizens lodged more and more reports of burglaries and looting, and public tolerance of crime declined. Slowly police resumed their investigations. Most of the crime activity appeared random and unorganized, except for one particular series of robberies with a common modus operandi.

Then on Saturday, the 911 dispatcher at the crisis center received a report that demanded attention. A woman was found dead in her bedroom in the upscale neighborhood of Shirley Hills. Her kid brother was a detective with the sheriff's office. She was found lying taped to the bedposts and all the jewelry, electronic equipment, and some food were missing. The police classified it as murder. They got what description they could from her children and immediately began investigating the burglary ring.

"Hey man, the county and military police are tracking us now," reported Jimmy Mack. "Some woman at one of the houses we hit ended up dying, and now they suspect the burglaries are part of some ring or shit. We ain't no ring, man."

"We didn't kill anyone, you know that, Bubba. Will they pin the whole friggin' plague on us, too?" Wayne tried to act unconcerned.

"You think we should call it quits?" Jimmy Mack offered it more as a proposal than a question.

"You're kidding me, right? We've barely scratched the surface."

"We've got a lot of good stuff. What do you say we hit a couple more and quit while we're ahead," Jimmy Mack argued.

"Tell you what. We'll keep going for a couple more days and you keep your ears open down at the Guard. They're still probably looking for two guys around Shirley Hills. We'll move on to the suburbs on the north end of town." Wayne said.

Just after nine that night, the pilfering threesome drove through the massive brick pillars at the entrance of Country Club Estates. Wayne had cruised the area earlier and selected several targets based on no alarm and a garage door out of view from the road.

"Slow up, Jimmy Mack. The first one's down here on the left."

"Let's drive around the block and check out the area first."

Wayne pulled out the panty hose and tossed one into the back of the van to Jay.

Jay pulled on his mask and Jimmy Mack checked his weapon.

"Looks like the coast is clear. Let's hit it."

Jimmy Mack nodded and turned the van around and headed back the other way.

"That's the one—with the brick mailbox and front porch light on there."

"Got it." Jimmy Mack pulled into the driveway and shut off the engine.

There were no lights on inside the house. They approached the back door quickly but cautiously. No lights could be seen, but they paused, holding their breath, listening. When they heard nothing, Jimmy Mack took out his glasscutter, but found the window was already broken. Jimmy reached through the hole in the window and found the dead bolt with the key in it. He opened the door.

The men immediately split up to survey the house. Wayne roused a belligerent teenager from bed, while Jimmy Mack rounded up the parents. Jay checked out the rest of the bedrooms. There was another bedroom that looked occupied but no one was present. With flashlights in one hand and automatic pistols in the other, they marched their hostages to the kitchen. Jimmy Mack stood guard while Wayne bound their hands and feet to kitchen chairs with duct tape.

As he bound the father to the chair, Wayne couldn't help but notice the guy's resemblance to his own old man. It must have been the contempt in his eyes or that white belly hanging over the top of his boxer shorts.

Once their victims were secured, the trio ransacked the house. Once the loot had been secured, including a nice new Dell laptop computer, the thieves returned to the kitchen.

Jimmy Mack ripped the tape from the old man's mouth as Jay and Wayne dumped the last load of stuff by the back door. "Where are the car keys?"

When he failed to answer immediately, Jimmy Mack backhanded the wife for effect. She let out a muffled scream.

"Okay, okay. The keys are on my bureau in the bedroom."

Wayne headed in that direction. A plump wallet rested under the keys. Wayne flipped it open to check for cash.

"Holy Shit! I'll be damned!" Wayne said slowly. He couldn't believe his eyes. He blinked repeatedly to make sure he read the name on the driver's license correctly: Dwight Williams.

He looked back and forth between the name and the picture. No wonder this guy resembled his old man. *Un-damn-believable! Of all the houses to hit, I pick my own damn brother.*

He pocketed the wallet and grabbed the car keys in the other hand.

Barely through the kitchen door, Wayne tossed the keys to Jay and instructed, "Get us the hell outta here. Fast."

Dwight's car was pulled out of the garage to allow them to load the loot into the van. Wayne shook his head as they moved to their next target.

+

After Dwight's place the trio hit three more houses in the posh subdivision. At the first house, they found an old man dead. They didn't get very much of value, and it only took a few minutes.

At the next home, lights were on, even though it was after midnight. When they knocked on the front door, a six-foot-five-inch, 250-pound man answered, and it sounded like the house was full of people. They apologized for their mistake and moved on. Clearly their work would become a bit more challenging as people recovered from the flu.

The final hit of the evening was easy enough with no one home, but it yielded little. Looking at the pictures, the place belonged to some old lady with a penchant for antiques. Not finding much that plugged in, they decided to call it a night.

Despite having left some things behind in Wayne's rush to leave, the loot that they had gotten from Dwight's home was one of their better heists. The PC looked valuable, but they had no idea of the secrets it contained or how to release them. Had they been a little more inquisitive and computer savvy, they could have blackmailed Dwight into cutting them in on part of the three million dollars.

+

The next morning Dwight's father Roy called. When no one answered, he drove over to the house using side streets to avoid the police. Roy came in through the open garage doors and found Dwight, Claire, and Charles struggling to escape their bindings. He promptly cut them loose. For once Dwight wasn't the least bit embarrassed that his father's old rusty Mercury with the peeling vinyl top was sitting out in the driveway. Even after the duct tape had been removed, Dwight sat quietly in the chair. The only thing on his mind was getting to a computer.

"Damn punks." Roy muttered as he cut through the last of the tape. "What kind of pitiful lowlife scumbags would stoop to thieving at a time like this?"

+

Tuesday afternoon.

"Hello?"

Jennifer smiled to herself at the familiar sound of Mike's voice on the other end of the phone. "It's good to hear your voice, Mike."

"Oh, hi, Jennifer. It's nice of you to call."

"I've been worried about you since I heard about your little girl. I can only imagine how hard you and Courtney must be taking it. How is everyone?"

"Courtney's asleep right now. She hasn't been the same since Beth died. Maybe there's something I could have done to wake Courtney sooner. Maybe there's something she could have done to keep Beth alive that I didn't. I just don't know..." Mike struggled to regain himself. "But what about you guys? How're R.T. and the kids?"

"They're all fine." Jennifer felt a twinge of guilt as the words escaped her mouth. "About to go stir crazy though, you know? I'm thinking about letting them go to work with R.T. tomorrow so I can go by and check on things at BLuR."

"Oh, Jennifer, you don't have to do that. This is really no time to be concerned about work. Give it a few more days."

"I know, Mike, but to tell you the truth, I am going a little stir crazy myself. I never have been much of the haus frau type."

"Right."

Jennifer could tell Mike was distracted.

"Tell you what, I'll give you a call tomorrow from the office and let you know what's going on, if anything, okay?"

"Well, alright. Actually, maybe you're right. Getting out and focusing on work may be just the ticket to get our minds off all this for a little while. Now that you mention it, I guess that I'm getting pretty antsy, too. Maybe I'll see you at the office tomorrow, just for a few minutes. Thanks, Jennifer. Thanks for calling."

Jennifer smiled again as they hung up.

Chapter 23

Bayonet the Wounded

Wednesday, September 23

Jennifer gave R.T. a peck on the cheek as she headed out the door the following morning. Just another Wednesday.

"Thanks, honey. I really appreciate your watching the kids!"

On the ride to work, Jennifer called Latrice's house to get an update on how people from BLuR were managing through the crisis. She had seen Latrice on TV and was glad to hear from her daughter that the rest of her family was doing fine.

With Latrice tied up at the center, the deaths of Paris, Mike's daughter, and Dwight's son, Jennifer would likely need to assume primary responsibility for getting the local operations back in order. She smiled.

There was no way of knowing how the rest of the BLuR network was functioning—whether Macon was creating a bottleneck or was down like the rest of the corporation. As she turned into the parking lot, it appeared from the sparsely scattered cars in the lot that she wasn't the only diehard coming to work.

As Jennifer walked down the largely empty halls, she couldn't help but chuckle cynically, thinking about the months of work that had gone into the company's contingency planning. A killer flu had never been a contingency considered.

The number of cars in the lot had been misleading. There was only a handful of people at work and none of them were on her technology team. The systems had been down since Thursday, and nothing had been received from the sister operations around the country since Friday. She called headquarters in Wilmington. No answer. She methodically called each of her IT team members at home and got a sense for when they thought they would report back to work. She called a couple of corporate IT folks she knew well enough to contact at their homes in Delaware and a couple of her IT peers at BLuR branches in other cities.

The situation was far worse than anything Jennifer could imagine. Nearly every BLuR Financial Center employee or a close family member was sick or recovering. Few, if any, had given work a thought in days. Many had died. Some tried to project when they might come back to work, but most didn't even try. No one had any intention of coming back in the midst of the current environment. Jennifer quickly grew weary of their whining. One or two were actually angered by her call.

Jennifer surveyed the office facility. The exterior doors and windows were all secure. Outside, the normally manicured lawn surrounding the facility was badly in need of cutting, and trash from the nearby neighborhood was blowing across the lawn. Inside, a handful of people worked in various departments. Some were at work to do what they could to get the business going again. Others had suffered tragic losses and simply had no idea where else to go or what to do. Coming to work felt comfortable and familiar.

Without long distance lines there was no customer contact. Without computers there was no processing and without mail there was no invoicing or cash received. The employees were just going through the motions. Jennifer considered sending everyone home, but decided against it. Being at work seemed better than sitting in front of the television listening to the death stats.

Instead she spoke briefly to each one and explained their primary responsibility for the next few days. She instructed them to assess what needed to be done in preparation for when things got back to normal. She stressed security and asked them all to travel in pairs when leaving the building. She even found herself looking over her shoulder as she moved through the facility. It had an eerie feeling when it was nearly empty, her footsteps echoing behind her as she walked.

Though she rationalized her own need to come to work as an escape, Jennifer was shocked to find Dwight among those who had returned. She tried to talk to him about the loss of John, but he wanted no part of her sympathy. He looked terrible—disheveled and unshaven. She expected a bear hug, but couldn't get him to even look up from his computer. He only discussed the need for Jennifer to get Internet access back up.

"I'm sorry about John and Helen, Dwight. And then to get robbed too, that really sucks. How are Claire and Charles?"

"When can you get me back online? I want to track this epidemic on the Internet," Dwight replied, not even acknowledging her last question.

"C'mon Dwight, go on home to Claire and Charles. We'll work on the network, but it's going to take a day or so."

Dwight said nothing, so she left him to deal with his tragedy in his own way. But as a favor to a man in need of help, Jennifer restored Internet access for Dwight.

Jennifer returned to her desk, thinking about how lucky she and her family were to be alive and healthy. At that thought she called R.T. at work to check on the kids. She had just hung up when Mike came around the corner of her cubicle.

"Hey there, Jennifer!"

"Mike, hello!" Jennifer stood and shook his hand with both of hers. "What a pleasant surprise. I didn't really expect to see you today."

He looked exhausted, dark rings encircled his eyes and his face lacked its usual expressiveness. He had shaved and his clothes looked clean, but not his usual pressed-with-light-starch look.

"Well, after we talked, I decided it might do me good to get out of the house for a little while."

"Good for you. Not much going on around here though. Pull up a chair."

Mike told her all about Beth's death. "Courtney is taking this very hard," Mike said. "I know losing a baby must be the hardest thing a mother can endure, but I feel like she's blaming me! Beth was my baby, too!"

"Courtney is just taking her own feelings of guilt out on you. It really has nothing to do with what you did or didn't do. It's a natural reaction. Just give her a little time to sort it out. How are the kids taking it?"

Mike sighed. "They're doing fine, great in fact. They probably don't really understand everything, but they're so resilient, they just go on. One thing's for sure, they don't like what's going on with their mom. It's got to be frightening for them. They need her desperately, but she wants little to do with them."

"It's been a nightmare for everyone. I still can't believe Paris is gone."

"Yeah, all of this has been so hard to take. I just don't get it." Mike rubbed his neck. "Maybe we could go out and visit Paris's gravesite."

"Uh, yeah. I guess we could do that. Why don't we plan on it tomorrow? I'll call Paris's daddy and clear it."

"Alright. I'll meet you here tomorrow at, say, eleven."

+

Thursday, September 24

Mike arrived at Jennifer's cubicle a few minutes later than promised.

"Good morning. Are you still planning to…go pay our respects to Paris?" Mike said tentatively, trying to decide between following through on the plan and facing up to more agony over the death of Paris.

"I suppose. I talked to Otis this morning to let him know we were coming. He said that would be fine." Jennifer noticed that Mike looked more like himself today, although the dark circles still framed his eyes.

They drove to the Hawkins property in Jones County. With very little traffic out on the roads, they arrived quickly. She pulled into the drive at Paris's house to find her father rocking slowly on the front porch. Otis's eyes were filled with grief.

"Not s'posed to be this way," he murmured as they approached. "Jest ain't right when a baby dies 'fore her daddy."

Mike stiffened and he clenched his jaw.

"Can I get y'all some tea?" asked Otis as they neared.

"No thank you Mr. Hawkins. We're sorry to bother you, but we just wanted to pay our respects to Paris." Jennifer had no plans on staying any longer than necessary.

"I am very sorry for your loss, Mr. Hawkins. I thought the world of your daughter…everyone at BLuR loved her. I know you were very proud of her."

Otis Hawkins nodded in acknowledgement as he rocked rhythmically, lost in his own world.

Relief flooded over both Jennifer and Mike as the screen door squeaked open, and Paris's young cousin walked over with a glass of tea for Otis. He took a slow sip.

"Ohhh, that baby o' mine, now she could make the best tea. Can't nobody's touch it." Otis sat forward in his rocker and put his head down.

The young girl patted the old man on the shoulder. Jennifer beckoned her silently with her index finger.

"Are you taking care of Otis? Is he okay?" asked Jennifer.

"You got to understand about Uncle Otis. He's not doing too well today. Jest found out his brother Horace died during the night. Not even the flu. Heart just stopped."

"Wasn't Paris working on some big family business with Horace?" Mike remembered Paris talking about her uncle and a cousin named Jimmy or Mack.

"Yes sir, she sure was. Uncle Otis is frettin' 'cause Uncle Horace never did sign some papers or something."

"Well, I'm Jennifer and this is Mike Spiker. We worked closely with Paris and wanted to pay our last respects. Otis told me this morning that she was buried near here. Could you point us in the direction of her grave?" Jennifer was anxious to move on.

"Sure. Paris wasn't the only one. So many died that they started a little graveyard up over the hill there on the right. You can't miss it. Don't look for big headstones, just some wooden crosses. Paris is…" The girl paused. "…is buried on the far right, close to the big oak."

"Thanks for your help. I'm sure that Paris would appreciate the way you're watching after her father…even if he doesn't appreciate your tea." Mike smiled at her and gave her a wink.

"Nice to see you, Mr. Hawkins." Jennifer said to the unresponsive old man. "We're going on up to the grave site now. You take care and we'll see you soon." Jennifer headed for the car.

Mike stood frozen for a brief moment, torn between going up on the porch or heading for the car. In his head he was telling Mr. Hawkins how he understood, that it wasn't right for a child to die before her father. He wanted to tell him that he too had lost a daughter, and he knew the vast emptiness it left.

Jennifer broke the spell. "You coming Mike?"

She led Mike by the arm.

Mike sat in the passenger seat and closed his eyes as Jennifer closed his door.

"Are you sure you want to do this Mike? Maybe this wasn't such a good idea. We can head back, you know." Jennifer reached over and covered his hand with her long tapered fingers.

"No, no. I'll be okay, really. After all, we're already here." He took a breath. "Let's go."

The gravesite was just a few hundred yards up the bumpy gravel lane. Jennifer pulled off to the side and put the car in park, but she left it running like a thief contemplating a quick getaway. She sat silently with her head cocked, looking over at Mike.

He continued to stare straight ahead.

Only when Mike made the first move to open the door did she turn off the ignition to follow him over to the fresh graves.

Neither one spoke. The thought of Paris lying lifeless beneath them was inconceivable. What would they do without the company cheerleader, the soul of the division?

"I wish she was here now to make us laugh. No one made us laugh like Paris," Mike said quietly.

"Few women can manage professional and funny, but she mastered both."

Jennifer's respect was unusually sincere.

"Remember that management retreat when we all went horseback riding in the mountains? The look of terror on her face?" Mike began laughing.

"And the times she played Santa at Christmas…with no padding!" recalled Jennifer, grinning as she shook her head.

The more they tried to concentrate on the fun times and great memories, the sharper the pain of the loss. Mike felt the blood rushing to his face. Images of Paris and Beth flooded his thoughts until they escaped in a torrent down his checks.

Jennifer reached out to touch his hand. His thoughts consumed by loss, Mike instinctively pulled her to him, desperately seeking relief from the grief that filled him. They stood in a silent embrace for several moments. Finally, he allowed her to slip from his arms.

Neither said a word as they walked back to the car side by side with their arms around each other.

They drove back to BLuR in silence and Jennifer dropped Mike off at his car. He paused beside the driver side window and put his hand on her shoulder.

"Look, uh, I don't know what came over me back there, but thanks. I guess I just needed a little support and I appreciate your being there."

"Sure, Mike," Jennifer nodded understandingly. "You've had a tough week. You're under a lot of pressure." She leaned toward Mike and slowly shifted in her seat, uncrossing her legs for a moment to adjust her skirt.

"I'll probably stop by work tomorrow," Mike said as he patted the car door. "See you then, if you're here."

Jennifer just smiled.

+

A cheer swept through the crisis center like a wave at an NFL game. Words like "vaccine" and "discovery" passed from worker to worker. The volunteers' weariness turned to jubilation at the prospect of an end to the nightmare of the past week.

Washington had sent word that researchers had developed a vaccine. Prototypes were being tested and the results were good so far. The lab that developed the vaccine was an NIH facility in Leesburg, Virginia that was created in 2001 to work on a small pox vaccine in the wake of terrorist threats following 9/11. The concentration of virology researchers and equipment in one center, ready to quickly identify and destroy any virus that came along, cut the research time by weeks.

The researchers didn't rest after developing a vaccine for the Manila Flu. They immediately began working on anti-viruses for possible future mutations.

The president had given FEMA permission to waive normal FDA approval procedures. Once released, the formula would be given to pharmaceutical companies all over the U.S. to rapidly produce the quantities needed. It would take many days before cities like Macon received any vaccine, but the prospect of the vaccine represented a psychological victory more than anything else—like convicting and executing a murderer. In reality, it appeared that the virus had run its course in the cities first hit by the plague.

The command team agreed to immediately announce the discovery to the public. A spokesman was needed. The team called the mayor to make the announcement, but his own bout with the virus had left him too weak to come out. Local FEMA director Zeke Jarrell was still at home with his family. Everyone quickly agreed on his stand-in.

Within minutes, Latrice stood at the podium in the press area of the crisis center. The lights, cameras, and microphones all focused on her. A FEMA cap disguised her unwashed hair and a borrowed navy blue blazer dressed up her T-shirt and shorts.

"On behalf of us all at the Macon-Bibb County crisis center, I am pleased to announce that a vaccine has been produced that will prevent the further spread of the Manila flu virus. It will be several days before supplies can be manufactured and delivered to our area, but again, a vaccine has been developed."

Even Latrice could not contain her elation, clasping her hands in front of her and bowing her shoulders forward in an almost giddy expression of joy. She paused for a moment to let the message sink in and the celebration in the hall quiet down. She felt like a political candidate declaring victory to a roomful of campaign-weary volunteers.

"This is a tremendous breakthrough," she continued, "but we have a lot of work yet to do. In the days and weeks that it will take to get the vaccines distributed to everyone, we ask y'all to please continue to check the website, watch television, and listen to the radio for more information. Please continue to give all law enforcement and medical officials your full support. We still need additional volunteers to help our city recover fully from the events of the past week. Stay tuned for details about where and how to volunteer. Together we will recover from this tragedy!"

Despite the determination in her eyes, a tear rolled down Latrice's cheek, as she finished her remarks. As soon as the bright lights dimmed, she shifted off autopilot and suddenly felt the full weight and cumulative stress of the role she had assumed. Reality washed over her like a wave and she looked out across the room full of the faces at the people who had become friends. For the first time in her life, Latrice didn't see men or women, black or white, redneck or professional, just a room full of caring people to whom she would forever feel connected. She stood silently, struggling not to cry.

She became awkwardly aware of the long silence after her remarks and quickly stepped down from the podium and returned to work, her hand dabbing at tears.

Chapter 24

Exterminate the Plague

Thursday night, September 24

The Spiker kids were getting cabin fever from being home so much with little to do. Without school and soccer and dance and Taekwondo sessions, they soon began picking at each other and even that got old after a while.

The kids didn't say much when Mike told them that their baby sister was gone, they just listened quietly. There were no tears, no anger. Having never been through this, Mike kept talking about the tragedy openly in the hopes that the kids would discuss it with him and that, over time, they would grow to understand what had happened.

Mike was heading into Amy's bedroom to check on her when he heard her mention Beth. Amy was of particular concern to Mike because she was the only one to have seen the dead baby. He hated to eavesdrop on his daughter, but it was his first insight into the soul of one of his children.

"You lie still, baby," Amy was saying to one of her dolls as she rocked it in her arms, "and God will come see you and take you to heaven. Then we will all be together again in heaven someday. We can have a tea party, so don't get your dress dirty."

Mike was taken by how the five-year-old was dealing with her sister's death. Amy had asked where Beth's body was, and he had told her that her spirit was in heaven, but her body was in the ground. Amy had asked what Beth was wearing, and Mike had fibbed about her wearing one of her Sunday best outfits.

Mike entered the room and sat on the floor near Amy. "You miss your little sister don't you, Amy?"

"I miss Beth a lot, Daddy, but I'm afraid that Beth is very lonely. I'll bet she misses us even more than we miss her. I think I hear her crying sometimes," Amy said. "When I get old and die and see Beth in heaven, will she still be a baby, or all grown up?"

"We're going to have to ask your momma on that one, baby. I don't know for sure, but I believe she will always be five years younger than you. Hey, how did you ever get so smart for a little kid?" Mike wrapped his arms around her and squeezed her.

"Daddy, why was Mommy so mad at you when Beth died?" Amy asked.

"Sometimes when people are real upset, they say things they don't mean. Your Mommy was so sad about Beth's going to heaven that she yelled at me and then she snapped at you. Your Mommy didn't really want to be mean to you or me, she just couldn't help it. It's going to take a while before she gets back to being as happy as she used to be, baby."

Amy sat quietly, caring for her doll.

"I love you, Amy," Mike said as he hugged her. "And I think Beth can somehow feel it when we hug each other. So let's agree to hug each other every day. And give your Mom some extra hugs because she needs them, too. Okay, baby?"

"It's a deal, Daddy!" Amy said in a muffled voice, smothered in the grasp of her father's embrace.

+

As the new cases of virus attacks subsided, area law enforcement redirected their attentions to another form of pestilence—a group now referred to as the Duct Tape Gang. The ring that appeared to consist of three males hit three to five homes in a neighborhood each night. One witness also reported that an official permit was affixed to the windshield of their white van. They wielded weapons, but had not yet used them. They were also the lead suspects in the death of one woman whose home they had burglarized earlier.

In the humid haze of the late evening, on a Thursday just before midnight, a police cruiser spotted a white van in a driveway in Covington, an affluent neighborhood on the north side of town. He called in the tag number. There was certainly no shortage of white vans around town and the police had been running tags all week, but the registration on this one was not current. The officer exited his patrol car to investigate further. A walk around the empty van revealed an official permit in the window. From what he could see, the back of the van was loaded down with electronics and televisions. He quickly jotted down the permit number on the back of his hand, and returned to the car to call it in. The crisis center referred the radio operator to the National Guard unit to which the permit had been issued. They reported it had not been properly logged out.

When the policeman called for backup, the crisis center dispatched a special Guard unit that spent their nights cruising the streets to preserve order during the crisis. The Humvee arrived in minutes along with a squad car manned by two county officers. The Guard unit parked down the street where they met with the other officers to plan their strategy. They had to assume that a hostage situation could develop. The first officer on the scene had pulled his patrol car out of sight and had watched as one of the suspects moved a car from the garage to the street, backed the van into the garage, and closed the doors. He briefed the reinforcements.

Approaching the house on foot, the two officers made their way around to the back of the house in order to attempt to assess the situation inside. Crawling along the back wall of the brick ranch house, the officer motioned for the second deputy to position himself underneath a window on the opposite end. They eased up to each window, their backs securely against the brick wall, carefully peering into the house. So far there were no victims in sight. A half-open window permitted them to overhear the voices inside.

"This shit just gets easier and easier," bragged Wayne.

"Whatcha expect, there's nobody home," Jay retorted from the next room.

The officers relayed what they had heard over the radio, maintaining their positions in the back of the house. Having confirmed that there were no civilians at risk, the enforcement team surrounded the house and abandoned all efforts to conceal their presence. Having heard the radio transmission, a third patrol car with one of the department's more seasoned ranking officers arrived on the scene. After quickly being brought up to speed, he barked instructions to the younger officers, positioning two in the back of the house with the original officer and the soldiers scattered around the front of the house. Once they were in position, the lieutenant pulled his radio microphone through his car window and flipped on the car's PA system.

"This is the police. The house is surrounded. Open the front door and throw out your weapons. I repeat. This is the police. You are under arrest." Lights from the Guard vehicle lit up the front yard like a baseball diamond.

Jay and Jimmy Mack froze in place, their eyes wide with terror. Wayne shut off the lights, dashed to the window, and looked out, trying to avoid being seen.

"Holy shit." Adrenaline rushed through Wayne's body. "Okay, just let me think."

Jay whimpered to himself, staring nervously at the flashing lights outside.

Jimmy Mack stooped on the floor and crawled closer to the window in order to see out. He felt his stomach flip as he recognized two of his fellow Guardsmen. Fear clouded his thoughts, but within moments he had arrived at his own course of action.

"You two do what the fuck you want, but I'm outta here. I didn't escape the flu to get blown away by those guys." Jimmy Mack motioned towards the Guardsmen. "I may be in the brig, but at least I'll be in one piece." He headed for the door, then stopped when Wayne spoke.

"Not me. Been there, done that, and I ain't going back. Jay, quit pissin' in your pants and get over here." Wayne tossed him the keys to the van. "You drive. I'll cover us." He turned to Jimmy Mack. "Give us two minutes, then head out the front door like they say. See ya, man." They clasped hands in high-five style.

Wayne pulled Jay by the sleeve out the door into the garage. He pulled a submachine gun from the back of the van to augment the pistol strapped to his hip. He tossed a rifle on the console and climbed in on the passenger side as Jay took the driver seat. Without windows in the overhead door, Wayne trusted his memory that there was enough room in the yard to swerve around a police car that blocked the end of the driveway.

The lieutenant loudly announced a third and final warning over a PA.

"This is the police. Throw your weapons out the front door and come out of the house with your hands on the top of your head. This is your last warning."

Jimmy Mack waited a long thirty seconds. He slowly opened the front door.

"Don't shoot! I'm coming out," he yelled from behind the door, tossing his pistol out onto the grass.

"Show me your hands and raise your arms above your head!" The lieutenant's voice bellowed from the top of the car.

On that cue, Wayne instructed Jay to start the engine.

The officers in the front of the house all focused on the front door. The sight of a familiar face momentarily disarmed the Guard members.

"Hey, I know that guy. That's—"

"Go!" Wayne slugged Jay in the arm as he shouted one final order.

Jay gripped the steering wheel for dear life and floored the accelerator.

As predicted, the vehicle tore the flimsy door from its track with ease. What they failed to anticipate was that the officer standing in the driveway on the other side of the door was directly in the path of the van.

Both men saw the startled soldier at the same time, but there was no where else to go. He dove for the grass, but his body made a loud thud as it bounced off the front of the van, and a sickening bump as the truck tires ran over his body. He lay motionless from the impact as the rear wheels rolled over his body. Shots immediately rang out from every direction. At first the officers aimed for the tires to stop the van, but their target shifted to Wayne and Jay the moment the van ran over the young soldier. Wayne immediately returned fire hanging out the window with his pistol.

The officers had taken cover behind the vehicles on the street to return fire at the van. They bobbed up and down like tin targets in a carnival shooting gallery, alternating shots as the van sped across the grass lawn.

The lieutenant continued to yell instructions to Jimmy Mack. "Get down. Get down on the ground."

At first Jimmy Mack did as he was told, pushing his face as hard as he could into the cool damp grass. One after another, the lights in the houses all around them came on. As he kissed the lawn, Jimmy

Mack contemplated the various options for getting out of the line of fire.

Simultaneously, the lieutenant and one of the Guardsmen increased the firepower. The guardsman squeezed off a steady stream of shots from an M-16 while the officer took careful aim with the Colt. He delivered the first shot to Wayne's left shoulder. The bullet traveled so cleanly through his body that Wayne failed to notice he had been hit.

Mistakenly sensing a momentary lull, Jimmy Mack decided to make a run for it. Midway across the yard, he intersected with a spray of rounds from Wayne's weapon.

One of the Guardsmen delivered a shot that entered Wayne's skull near his right eye. His head snapped back and then forward as his body fell against Jay, his mouth opened wide in a silent scream. Jay looked up from his friend just in time to swerve to miss a pine tree in his path. The van lost its grip on the ground and flipped onto its side before coming to a stop.

The shots ceased abruptly and everyone waited and watched for movement. Guns poised, the officers moved in.

+

Over the next several days, the police traced the van to Jack's Auto Repair and found the stolen goods in the attic. In sorting through the mountain of electronic gear, one item in particular stood out—a laptop computer. In looking through the system for information to identify the owner, the officer browsed through a file labeled "Investment Summary." The file revealed a spreadsheet with dozens of investment accounts, each with individual balances in the hundreds of thousands of dollars.

Chapter 25

Rendezvous

In the past, Mike had reacted to grief by submerging himself in some activity until he could re-establish his normal routines. When his father died, he decided to take some college courses; the long hours of class and study left little time to grieve. When his dog died, he decided to build a tree fort for the kids. It was backbreaking work, but by the time he was through with the project, he was ready for a new pup.

Try as he might, Mike could bring no normalcy to his relationship with his wife. Courtney was a mess—physically and emotionally. She wouldn't talk to Mike, her mother, or anyone; she offered only snap answers or grunted replies. She communicated with the kids only to the extent necessary to keep them clothed and fed. There were no story times, nature walks, or bouts of tickling. Just when the kids needed some help dealing with the death of their baby sister and other kids they knew, their Mom had become a recluse.

Mike tried to convince Courtney to attend one of the many counseling sessions available through the church. Local churches quickly developed counseling programs to help parents and children deal with the tragedies of the plague.

"I'll go with you, if you'll just give it a chance. Please, Courtney! There's a class this Friday with room for you and me. Come on," pleaded Mike. But Courtney shook her head. "I'm not ready."

+

Friday, September 25

Up promptly at dawn, Mike set out on a long run to burn off some emotional energy. It had been more than ten days since he had run. There were few cars out so he decided to try some roads that he didn't normally run. He had called Latrice the night before to see if she wanted to run with him, but she was still tied up at the crisis center.

"Mike, I am still working long hours trying to get all the public services back to normal. Sorry, I can't run tomorrow, but thanks for thinking of me."

"Don't you worry about BLuR for a while. The community needs an Empress more than BLuR does right now. We'll hold it together until you get back."

"I've been sitting at a desk so much trying to get other folks moving that I don't think I could jog around the block," Latrice replied.

Mike couldn't help noticing a change in her tone of voice—a smooth, confident humility, where there once was an edge.

"Well, we're proud of what you're doing at the crisis center, Latrice. Sounds like you've taken volunteerism to a new level. There'll be plenty of chances to run when you finish your work there."

The run helped Mike clear his head. He began to think of ways to get back in gear at work. After all, he was the boss, the one everyone counted on for direction.

Mike finished his run, and after a quick shower and shave, found Courtney slumped over the kitchen table, mindlessly stirring a cup of coffee.

Rationing the little bit of coffee they had left was supposed to make the coffee as light as tea, but hers looked full strength.

"You gonna put some cream and sugar in that or are you trying to melt the spoon?" Mike quipped, hoping for a response.

Courtney simply shrugged her shoulders and continued her vacant stare into the dark reaches of the swirling coffee.

"Are you going to be alright if I go to work for a little while and you stay here with the kids?"

Courtney managed to nod, but avoided eye contact with Mike. "Yeah, like you raised these kids," she grunted.

The kids came bounding into the kitchen in search of cereal. Mike put down his briefcase to help get the kids situated with breakfast.

"I want some Rice Krispies, Dad," said Mark.

"Yeah, I want to hear Snap Crap and Pop!" echoed Amy.

"It's Snap Crackle and Pop, baby. And we finished off those guys yesterday. The only cereal left is Shredded Wheat, and there's only a little bit of watered down milk left," Mike reported. "How about some toast?"

Bread and peanut butter were the kid's favorites of the foods being distributed by the military.

Mike finished getting breakfast for the children. Courtney had not said a word or moved a muscle.

"Bye, kids," Mike shouted as he swung out of the garage. "Take good care of Mommy today, okay?" There was more truth to that request than Mike cared to admit.

Driving to work, Mike had a hard time getting Courtney out of his mind. Without warning, she had taken the scissors and cut her own hair, which had become matted from frequent naps and negligence. Makeup had not graced her face since Beth's death. She only showered when reminded. Her eyes seemed permanently encircled with the dark shadows of grief, though she rarely let Mike see them directly.

Mike missed his bright and beautiful wife, but even more he missed his closest buddy. At a time when he needed to talk about what had happened, Courtney had shut him out.

Arriving in the office by 10:00 A.M., Mike toured the facility to see who was in and let them each know how much they were appreciated. The few people who were there were glad to see Mike, and each expressed their sincerest condolences about Beth's death. While Mike appreciated the thought, he found their expressions of sympathy something to be endured. He was a little embarrassed to have people feeling sorry for him.

As Mike passed Dwight Williams's work area, he was surprised to find him working. "Hi, Dwight," he said solemnly. "Buddy, I'm very sorry about John. I've been thinking about you and Claire. I do know how you feel."

"Hey, Mike," Dwight responded without much emotion. "Thanks, I appreciate that and I'm real sorry about your baby, too." Dwight was too busy working on something on his PC to more than glance up at Mike.

"Please let Claire know how very sorry we are about the death of her mother. And I heard that on top of all that, your house was broken into, too. It's been a tragic week."

"Yeah, they wiped me out," said Dwight without emotion, clearly not interested in carrying on a conversation.

"I know all this has been really tough on you. If there is anything—"

"I'm fine, if people would just leave me the hell alone."

Dwight's brusque reply caught Mike off guard. There was an uncomfortable silence as Mike searched for the right response.

"Go home, Dwight," Mike said firmly, approaching his CFO. "Go be with Claire and Charles. Anything here can wait."

"Why aren't you home with your family?" Dwight responded curtly.

Ignoring his angry tone, Mike continued. "What the hell are you working on that is so urgent, anyway?"

Dwight didn't even look up.

Mike stood there a moment staring at Dwight before he turned, shrugged his shoulders helplessly, and left.

Mike visited the IT area and found Jennifer busy at work. The cheery sound of her voice was like music to Mike's ears. She and a couple members of her team were working hard to re-establish the data network between as many BLuR locations as possible. Most of the BLuR operations in other cities had not yet reported back to work as the plague was still completing its path of destruction in other parts of the country.

Jennifer began to update Mike. In the middle of their conversation, Mike's stomach growled loudly.

"Guess I should have eaten breakfast this morning, huh?" He was more surprised than embarrassed. They laughed loudly together.

While some businesses were beginning to awaken, the restaurants remained locked up tight. Restaurants had no food to sell, no people to serve it, and no patrons willing to use their precious fuel to drive there. It was just as well because few people had any cash to spend anyway. Like the ATMs, vending machines at BLuR and everywhere had long since been emptied. Many of the employees had brought in a sandwich or an apple or a candy bar from their home rations, but Mike had not thought that far ahead.

"Are you hungry?" asked Jennifer.

"I'm famished. I haven't had anything but snacks and dry cereal for days," replied Mike.

"We have plenty of food at my house. Want to drive over?" said Jennifer.

"Sure, I'll drive. Let me go get my keys and I'll meet you at the front door."

Feeling awkward about how this one-on-one outing might look, Mike stopped on the way to his cube to ask Dwight if he wanted to go out for lunch.

"No thanks, I'm real busy."

Mike left it alone.

He pulled his car up to the curb outside the front lobby as Jennifer came out the door. Even in the current devastation, Jennifer had managed to stay stunning. On the way out she had stopped in the ladies room to pull her hair back in a tortoise shell clamp and apply a little lotion to her tan arms and legs exposed beneath a sleeveless top and skirt. She approached the car with a confident gait and smiled brightly when she saw Mike.

"How are the kids doing?" asked Mike as they drove towards town.

"They were bored at first, but now R.T. takes them to his office. He puts them to work and they really enjoy helping. They stay with him all day long."

Mike missed the implication. "What on earth does he have them do down there?"

"Oh, cleaning and little chores, mostly. I'm sure they spend most of their time in the playroom downstairs."

They arrived at her house and pulled into the carport. Mike held the screen door open as Jennifer unlocked the huge wooden back door. He couldn't help admiring how the contour above her narrow waist mirrored the contour of her hips. Jennifer led Mike through the house and offered him a seat at the kitchen table while she prepared a feast of canned ham sandwiches, pineapple slices, ginger snaps, and bottled water. They ate in silence, the house so quiet Mike could hear a clock ticking in the foyer.

"All these years working with you, Jennifer, I never knew you were such a gourmet chef!"

"You don't know me as well as you think you do," Jennifer said, smiling.

"I asked Dwight to join us," Mike said, "but he seemed very strange. I'm concerned about him."

"I am, too. I can't get him to say two words to me, sitting there pounding away on his PC. He was all worked up about getting Internet access as quickly as possible; I have no idea why. He hasn't even mentioned losing his son or Claire's mother or the burglary. He stays completely to himself. All very unlike Dwight."

"We don't know him as well as we think we do," Mike quipped.

"Well, how are you doing, Mike? What's really going on with you?"

"I'm ready for things to get back to some semblance of order. Beth is gone, but there's been no closure. We need some kind of service, some opportunity to formally say goodbye."

Mike stared at the floor as he continued. "I can't get the image of Beth out of my mind, the sight of her tiny body. God, I can't believe I just left her in that wooden chest at the coliseum. I didn't know what else to do." The ham sandwich stuck in Mike's throat. All the emotions of recent days rolled down his cheeks. He put his head in his hands, embarrassed at his loss of composure.

Jennifer walked over behind Mike and wrapped her long arms around his shoulders.

"God, Mike I am so sorry. You did everything you could. No matter what Courtney says, I know you did."

Mike sat there for a moment, clearing his throat and recovering his composure. He could feel the warmth of Jennifer's touch.

Turning in place as he stood up, Mike embraced Jennifer, taking in every ounce of tenderness and comfort that he could extract from the moment. Mike's face was wet and warm from the tears. She gently pushed off his chest and reached up to dry his cheeks. He responded without thinking, looking into her eyes, he kissed her firmly and tenderly. She responded without hesitation.

With his thoughts racing between excitement and shock, Mike tried not to think. In his neediness, the disciplines of a lifetime succumbed to the ecstasy of the moment. Mike turned off the inner voices.

The kisses and caressing increased in passion and tempo. More than once they stopped momentarily as if they were each giving the other the opportunity to break away, but neither did. At one point

Mike opened his eyes mid-kiss. Jennifer's eyes were also open, filled with a look of determination he had seen before—at work when she was succeeding at something difficult and important. Heat poured from Mike's body. He had not felt this way in years.

Mike began to explore her lips with his tongue. Her tongue met his. As if to torture him with delight, Jennifer ran her fingers down the front of his pants on the way to take his hand to lead him to the living room.

She pulled the sheers across the windows.

Without a word, she pulled him to her as she leaned against the arm of the sofa. He pushed her skirt out of the way and caressed her bare thighs, all the time kissing her. She trembled as he moved his fingers further up her leg. Jennifer felt Mike over his clothes. She slowly unbuckled his belt and unzipped his pants.

They shed the last bits of clothing and eagerly pressed skin to bare skin. Sinking back into the softness of the sofa, Mike continued to caress her breasts and eagerly moved his hand between her legs.

He spread her thighs and slipped his hips over hers. He entered her slowly and tenderly. Jennifer's neck arched sensuously as she wrapped her lean legs around Mike's body, writhing beneath him. Jennifer held still, trying to make sure that the moment would last.

With his first thrust, reality surfaced and Mike paused. His eyes opened wide and caught a glimpse of a family photo on the end table beside the sofa.

He paused. "Jennifer, we can't do this, I don't have protection."

She smiled provocatively. "I'll be right back," she said. She jumped up and went into the kitchen, totally uninhibited walking around without clothes. She came back into the room opening a condom.

But the moment had passed, the magic spell broken. Mike sat up on the sofa, shaking his head. He got up before Jennifer could return, went over to his clothes and began dressing.

"Are we going for the instant replay?" The razor shape edge of Jennifer's voice cut the awkward silence.

"I'm sorry, Jennifer. I can't go through with this." Mike reached for his shirt, but Jennifer made no move toward her clothes.

She sauntered toward him. "Come on Mike. The deed is done, why not finish it? You deserve some R&R. Don't you want to feel better? I know I do." Jennifer pressed her naked body against his and reached her hand over his shorts.

Mike knew he had to be very careful here. The gig was over, but he had to salvage what he could. He didn't want to upset his relationship with his top IT executive any more than he had. *There must be a soft landing for this*, he thought. If there was a clear path, it escaped him. He resumed getting dressed. The signal was crystal clear.

As he pulled on his pants, he replayed the events of the past few minutes in his mind. *Why had Jennifer gone to the kitchen instead of upstairs to the bedroom for a condom? It must have been in her purse.*

Jennifer looked like she was about to say something very hateful, but stopped. This was certainly a first for her. She walked over, snatched her clothes from a chair, and left the room quickly. She said something under her breath that Mike was glad he couldn't understand.

Mike decided to focus on damage control and try to find a graceful way out of the situation. He couldn't just leave; her car was at the office. He went back into the kitchen and opted to stay there and let Jennifer make the next move.

A few minutes later she came back into the kitchen, looking as stunning and together as the moment she entered the house an hour before. "I can get R.T. to take me back to BLuR to pick up my car. Go ahead and leave now, Mike."

"Jennifer, I feel really bad about this. I do appreciate your friendship and I want to make sure this doesn't damage our relationship."

"Fuck you, Mike, okay? You're still in control, boss. You satisfied?" Jennifer flailed her arms in anger. Taking a moment in an attempt to regain control, she continued. "How do you expect me to react? Thankful that you saved me? Impressed with your self control? Well, I'm not. You stopped about three minutes too late to save your precious honor, boss. As far as I'm concerned you can go fuck yourself.

"I should have known you'd quit in the middle." Jennifer stopped for a moment, then continued in an oh-by-the-way tone. "Tom Mumford told me that Courtney pulled the same prank on him one night when y'all were down in Nevis. Guess you Spikers can't even finish a little roll in the sack. You two must be a lot of fun together in bed!"

For Jennifer there was a sense of relief. She had gone way too far by involving Courtney in this mess, but it put her back on top with Mike.

Trying to comprehend what he had just heard, Mike could only sit there flabbergasted. "Courtney and my boss? In Nevis?"

Jennifer just nodded. "Yeah, Tom told me all about it. I know him pretty well. Better than you think," Jennifer said with a smirk. She couldn't help it, kicking Mr. Goody Two Shoes when he was down.

Mike's mind raced while his stomach sank. He remembered the way Courtney avoided talking about Nevis. It explained why Tom treated him so irrationally. But there was no use in continuing this conversation with Jennifer. She hadn't been there, that was certain. Knowing the way Tom Mumford thought he was God's gift to women, there was a good chance the story was untrue or highly exaggerated. But saying anything more to Jennifer could only make things worse. Mike tried to forget the whole affair and concentrate on Jennifer and the current crisis.

He thought about asking Jennifer if she always carried condoms with her, but decided he wasn't up to the battle or ready to deal with the likely responses. Had Jennifer slept with Tom Mumford?

"Look, let's drive back to the office. You need to cool off and we need to talk some more."

"Is that an order, boss?" Jennifer's face hardened as she spoke.

Mike felt as though he was looking at a different person than the one that he left the office with a short time ago. This classy lady had turned coarse and common. She had turned on him like a wounded animal.

"Yeah, I guess it is. Let's go, Jennifer." They got back into his car and drove back to BLuR.

As they drove, Jennifer stared straight ahead, not saying a word. Mike was the first to break the painful silence. "Jennifer, this is my fault and I want to explain myself."

"Sure, Mike." The ice appeared to be melting.

"You are one of the most attractive and brightest women I have ever met. I should have known what could happen today. I could say we got caught up in the moment, but I feel responsible for putting you in a bad spot. When I realized what was happening, I couldn't go through with it. You and I know all too well that it was wrong. You have a family and I do, too. I think it is in both our best interests to forget this ever happened."

"You're right, Mike. We let ourselves get in a compromising position. I'll get over it," Jennifer said tensely.

Mike was relieved that Jennifer's attitude had improved. This was about as good as he could expect, all things considered. Not knowing what to say, Mike once again opted for silence. They arrived at work and went their separate ways.

Mike tried to digest Jennifer's accusations about Courtney. He needed to talk with Courtney about Tom, but that would tie right back to Jennifer. Surely it was a lie, but he needed to hear the truth.

Chapter 26

Diversion to Theft

Wednesday, September 30

Dwight's world was collapsing. He almost wished that he had died of the flu.

His son was dead and his wife Claire teetered on the brink, consumed by the grief of losing both her son and her mother within a matter of hours. Hoodlums had broken into his house and stolen his computer. The plague had turned everything upside down.

Dwight was most distraught over his failing investment scheme—the temporary borrowing that had now turned into grand theft. If he had been caught before the flu had struck, he could have paid back the money. He might not have even been prosecuted. Now, with the suspension of trading on Wall Street and the huge nosedive stocks would probably take when trading resumed, he would be short hundreds of thousands of dollars.

All the meticulous details of his investments now lay in the hands of thieves. With his PC stolen, he had only bits and pieces of the information he needed to manage his portfolio. He could only remember a few web site sign-ons, passwords, and account numbers. And the prospect that the thieves, or worse the police, might discover the records increased his sense of vulnerability and compounded his fear.

Wall Street had resumed limited trading that morning, but the market showed no sign of recovering any time soon. The pandemic had caused economic loss that would take months to measure. Memories of how poorly the market responded to past tragedies filled his mind.

Finally, after a week with no newspapers or Internet access, Dwight was able to get back online and track some of his investments. As best as he could tell, his $3 million portfolio, that had grown to $3.6 million, was now worth somewhere between $1.4 and $1.8 million. He would give anything to return the $3 million to the company and forget the whole thing. He could only hope that his creative accounting maneuvers had not been found in the days that he had missed when the flu hit. With the curfew in effect, he couldn't pick up any correspondence or bank statements from his post office box.

From every indication at work, Dwight was still in the clear. No one was around to discover his scheme. Everyone remained preoccupied with the viral onslaught and the resulting emotional and economic devastation. As Dwight slipped back into the routine of work, his fears of being discovered subsided, at least until he started running the numbers.

With the debt recorded on the company's books, the interest would be paid in the normal course of business. Other funds had been borrowed to backfill for the three million dollars that never got to the company's accounts. But Dwight didn't like the idea of being a felon. He preferred to think of himself as a creative accountant seizing an opportunity, raising the level of his compensation to where it belonged in the first place.

Dwight had been surprised to see Jennifer and especially Mike back to work so soon. And they sure were asking a lot of questions. Dwight was on high alert about his conversations with Mike, searching every word for a hint that he had been discovered. Mike clearly represented the greatest threat to Dwight's plan and was already on to the fact that interest expenses were out of line.

+

The ongoing successes at the crisis center continued to both treat the wounds of the city and provide a healing touch on Latrice's outlook on life. In the aftermath of the death and havoc, a great paradoxical wellness immerged. For Latrice, every day brought major new challenges and sense of satisfaction from serving the community. The boundaries of race and class diminished and in their place relationships were forged.

The progress was not without sacrifice, for Latrice was spending so little time with her family and even less keeping in shape. As the crisis began to settle down, she started bringing Regina to work at the center on occasion.

On the last day of September, Latrice was asked to represent the Macon area at a conference hosted by the CDC in Atlanta. The military arranged transportation that allowed Regina to go along. Latrice wanted a close companion and missed her little girl.

On the way to Atlanta, Latrice was struck by the lack of traffic on I-75. At a roadblock near Griffin, the Humvee slowed down to weave through a single lane path among dozens of cars parked behind the military blockade.

"What's going on here?" Latrice asked the military driver.

"Makeshift camps like this have formed at each roadblock. These people are from different parts of the country and had nowhere else to go when the flu hit. They couldn't travel on the highway, so they hung out here and lived with the soldiers to take advantage of their protection and supplies," replied the Air Force lieutenant.

Latrice and Regina arrived in Atlanta proud to have been chosen to represent Macon. Each emissary was screened by CDC officials to be sure they had already been exposed to the flu, leaving delegates from a few cities that had not yet been invaded by influenza to listen in by phone.

The convention center buzzed with activity as the conference began Monday morning. Starved for information and answers, the ravenous delegates fed one another from their bag of limited information, actively exchanging ideas.

"Ladies and gentlemen, let's begin our meeting," began U.S. Secretary of State Shirley Hawes. A hush quickly swept the room. "Both the president and vice president send their regrets that they are unable to be with you here today, as they had hoped." The statement further fueled speculation that both men had been stricken with the virus. The secretary of state quickly proceeded with introductions, greetings and opening statements.

"Our first item of business is to bring you all up to date on the latest plan for distributing the vaccine. The major pharmaceutical companies are operating on twenty-four-hour schedules to mass produce the necessary serum. Once it is available in sufficient quantity, the first deliveries will go to major cities such as New York and Miami that are on the brink of widespread infection. Cities not yet impacted will follow. Areas such as Cincinnati, Los Angeles, and

Macon will be last, since the wave of virus has already run its course."

Latrice felt like jumping up and complaining, but she couldn't disagree that the plan made a lot of sense.

"Unofficially, the FBI will immediately ship small amounts of vaccine in military vehicles to be given to government workers and volunteers in all major cities. The shipments must be kept highly confidential to avoid any attempts to divert these supplies."

The secretary opened the floor to questions.

The delegate from Phoenix identified himself and spoke. "Madam Secretary, we can't wait any longer for the vaccine. We already have major civil unrest. Two days ago there was a riot at one of our public hospitals when a mob heard that some people were getting medicine before others. They rushed police and six people died in the incident. Ma'am, we have normal citizens going berserk in the streets."

Several similar reports followed from cities across the country. Parts of Chicago had erupted in looting. A group of doctors in Richmond were caught selling penicillin.

"I understand what you are saying. We are doing everything within our power to deliver the vaccine to all these areas as soon as humanly possible," responded Secretary Hawes. "In the meantime, your most important job is not so much to treat the flu, but to quell the panic that it evokes. We could lose even more lives if we're not careful."

Secretary Hawes then introduced a FEMA official who presented the vaccine distribution plan. "Beginning within the week, all the trucks from the U.S. Post Office, UPS, FedEx, and all the other major parcel delivery companies will be deployed to disperse the supplies as quickly as possible. Distribution to all U.S. cities should be complete within two to three weeks. Voting locations and records should be used to disperse vaccines in an orderly fashion, one vaccine per registered adult plus one for each child who accompanies them. This might cause some long lines and stress, but it's the most orderly and familiar routine we know. Hospitals, schools, and other public places will be set up later to inoculate people who weren't registered."

The official reached down for a sample kit, then continued. "A sealed package with a disposable syringe and vile of vaccine will be handed out. Let me emphasize, there is to be no charge for any of the vaccine or supplies and anyone who violates this policy by charging for shots is to be prosecuted. Parents should be shown how to inject their children. You must recruit nurses and medical personnel to assist those who feel unable to administer the vaccine themselves. Extra security around the polling areas will be critical."

After fielding questions related to the distribution plan, the group adjourned for lunch. Uniformed military officers served up canned rations and handed out bottled Coca-Colas supplied by the company's home office located a few blocks away. The conference attendees spent more time comparing notes than eating.

Following lunch, an official from the U.S. Treasury addressed the delegates on an entirely different issue—how to restart the economy.

"Our plan to jump start the economy has never been tried before. It is quite unique. We are going to act as if the period from September 15 through October 4 never existed. Companies will not pay their employees, and no one will owe any bills for those days. Interest will not be due for that period and any principal payments due will be added to the back of the note. No one has to pay rent. A council of CPAs and attorneys will be established in every U.S. House district to arbitrate specific situations."

"How can you pull this off?" blurted out one of the city representatives.

"Well, this plan is certainly bold, but we've worked through a bunch of scenarios, and we think it'll work. Bottom line is the plan will become Federal law."

Secretary Hawes took some more questions. A representative from Los Angeles asked a question that was on most people's minds: "Madam secretary, do you know yet if this outbreak was started by terrorists?"

"We have investigated this thoroughly. There is very little chance that terrorists could create a new strain of influenza. All indications are that this started naturally. Good question, though, and I think that's a good place to adjourn."

Latrice and Regina rode home in a Humvee full of medical supplies destined for Macon. They made it home quickly, but the ride was depressing, given the emptiness of the asphalt ribbon.

+

That Wednesday night, Latrice attended church at Mt. Olive Baptist for the first time in weeks. As the initial impact of the epidemic subsided, churches all over America overflowed. Families gathered to hold special memorial services for loved ones lost to the flu. The threats to their health, which so many had taken for granted, heightened the emphasis on spirituality. People attended church to re-establish contact with one another and heal the scars.

"Hey, Latrice!" Dr. Bagwell called from a distant pew. "You're a sight for sore eyes!"

"Doctor Bagwell, I felt so bad after you saved my daddy's life, and then you got sick. I am so glad to see you here!" replied Latrice, rushing over and putting one arm around the man. "I can't believe that Beverly died from the flu," Latrice said, referring to the lady she originally replaced.

"She was a wonderful lady," Dr. Bagwell said, looking down. "We're going to miss her greatly.

"But the thing that shines out of all the tragedy is the way you handled things at the crisis center. I'd see you on TV and puff up with pride. 'That's my Latrice,' I'd say to folks. 'She goes to my church!'"

Latrice blushed for the first time in years.

Chapter 27

New Priorities

Thursday, October 15

"Mike, you are not going to believe what just happened!" Latrice made no effort to conceal her child-like excitement. "The CNN camera crew just left after being here for an hour. They came to interview me! Can you believe it? I could be on CNN!"

Mike called his BLuR staff leaders to share the news. Latrice deserved the spotlight and the employees needed something upbeat to rally around.

When Mike called Dwight, the CFO thanked him for calling, but there was no emotion behind it. Jennifer was business-like and detached. Mike winced as he spotted Paris's name on his company call list.

A month had passed since the plague invaded their lives, and Mike was beginning to return to some sense of normalcy in his own daily routine. He usually worked full days, but occasionally came home early to play with the kids. Courtney managed to function at a minimal level, not doing much more than bathing the kids and throwing something quick together at mealtime.

Mike finished dinner, then tuned into CNN.

"Good evening and welcome to our continuing coverage of the Manila flu pandemic. Tonight we have several reports from cities throughout the US. First, with a report on the Federal government's efforts, here is Jack Gibson, live in Washington. Jack, what are the latest statistics on the total death toll in the US?"

"I'm standing in the lobby of the Federal Emergency Management Agency headquarters where officials are tracking the number of deaths related to the pandemic. There's some judgement in the numbers, but the agency reports that about 60 of the top 100 cities in the U.S. have been affected by the flu in some significant way. About 90 million people in the U.S. became sick from the flu. The agency is now estimating that a staggering 2.5 million Americans have died from flu-related causes.

"The death toll worldwide is projected to be 200 million. Areas with dense populations in Asia, South America, and Africa are expected to suffer much higher losses than the US. The vaccine couldn't be distributed in other countries as efficiently as it was here, and less sanitary conditions in some areas are leading to higher mortality rates.

"This is unlike anything the world has ever experienced and the full impact may not be fully understood for years." The broadcast returned to the studio.

"Thank you, Jack. Next, let's take a look at how the flu pandemic spread across America." A map of the world, then the US, highlighted the areas as the newscaster explained the path of the virus.

"Restrictions on public gatherings, blockades of highways, and improved health habits by the general population kept the disease out of several major U.S. cities altogether. Dallas, Houston, and San Antonio were for the most part spared. Very few people in Seattle and Portland have become ill. Denver, Boston, Minneapolis, and other cities have been impacted only lightly. The I-75 and I-95 corridors in the East were hit very hard, as was the I-5 corridor in California.

"For a closer look, we go to Trudy Johnson in Macon, Georgia, one of the cities hit hard and early by the virus. Trudy?"

"Good evening, I'm standing in front of the Macon City Auditorium where, for the last few weeks, officials and community leaders have set up a crisis center to work together in responding to the flu crisis.

"Mr. Zeke Jarrell has joined me now. He's the local FEMA director. Mr. Jarrell, what are the latest fatalities in the Macon area?"

"Well, there have been about 13,000 deaths in the Macon area related to the Manila flu. That's about four percent of the population. We understand that the only American city hit harder than Macon has been Cincinnati."

"That kind of death rate must put an extraordinary strain on a community," injected the reporter.

"Well, it certainly has. The good news is that Macon is now out of danger, as those few people who avoided exposure have now received vaccines."

"Thanks Zeke. Next, we have Latrice Rutherford who has become the unofficial volunteer leader of this crisis center over the past few weeks. Latrice, tell us about some of the challenges you faced here in Macon."

The image of Latrice filled the screen.

"While our doctors were treating the sick and the military was enforcing a curfew, those of us at the crisis center made sure that folks around Macon had enough food and water and adequate communications. The soldiers from Robins Air Force Base and our local National Guard unit helped hundreds of volunteers keep our telephones, Internet, and broadcast media in service. Sharing the latest news and providing some spiritual encouragement were crucial in avoiding panic and helping the community recover."

The reporter broke in. "And we understand that, despite the fact that Macon was one of the earliest and hardest hit cities, there was a lot less crime and civil unrest here than other areas of the country."

"That's right," replied Latrice. "We had a wonderful crisis team and a lot of cooperation from the Federal government, the military, local businesses, and the medical community."

"Latrice, it sounds like you have been very busy. What were the greatest challenges in Macon?"

"There were so many, it's hard to know where to start. The first thing we focused on was getting key decision makers together, then we tackled the problems one at a time. Trash and sanitation issues were overwhelming, as you can imagine. People ran out of supplies like soap and trash bags and began having problems with rats and other pests. Hundreds of volunteers and soldiers distributed supplies along with the food rations and assisted our local trash collectors. They worked constantly and within a few days had things back to normal.

"The most amazing thing is the way that people around here joined together. Thousands in this community worked shoulder to shoulder with an indomitable spirit."

"Thanks Latrice. From Macon, I'm Trudy Johnson reporting."

Mike turned the TV off and crawled over to where his kids were playing on the floor of the great room. "Did you see that? Wasn't Miss Latrice great? You know someone famous now!"

Mike played with the kids for a while, read to them, helped them brush their teeth, and put them to bed. Courtney had gone to bed long ago. Mike checked in on her before he returned downstairs, called Latrice to congratulate her, and went to bed.

+

Friday, October 16

Mike could hardly fathom that the field before him was actually a cemetery. It more resembled a farmer's freshly planted field with metal stakes growing in rows. Dozens of acres had been dug up, covered over, and seeded with grass. Gravel lanes divided the fields into a grid. Trees were left standing in occasional thin rows to prevent erosion and provide some shade.

Thanks to the help of R.T. Sanders, Mike had been able to locate the site where baby Beth was buried in the government cemetery a few miles across the county line. Nearly 9,500 flu victims were buried there in common graves, with detailed records kept on a website showing the exact location of every body. Temporary markers with the names had been placed there until they could be replaced with granite stones, if the families chose to do so. Beth's memorial was already on order.

The afternoon sun shone bright as Mike, Courtney, and the children gathered with a few friends for a graveside service. A pastor and friend performed the belated funeral.

"Hear the words of Paul in his letter to the Corinthians," the pastor read to the group. "Listen, I will tell you a mystery! We will not all die, but we will all be changed. For the trumpet will sound and the dead will be raised imperishable, and the mortal body will put on immortality. Death has been swallowed up in victory. Where, O death is your victory? Where, O death is your sting?"

I know that sting, Mike thought. *I know it well.*

He turned and looked at his family as the preacher's words continued.

He realized that there must indeed be something beyond what he understood about mortality. Beth had crossed over into something better than life as Mike understood it. Beth would be okay, suspended in a perfect immortality.

Mike watched his kids. They too would survive this tragedy; they had their whole lives in front of them. He must not let them feel defeated, and he must look death in the face and deny it victory.

There wasn't much to eulogize about the life of a six-month-old child, but the preacher reflected on the tragedy of the past few weeks and read scripture related to how the innocence of an infant assures them entry to God's kingdom. As the minister spoke, Mike stood behind Courtney, rubbing her shoulders.

Before Tim finished with a heartfelt prayer, Courtney's brother played his guitar and sang *Tears from Heaven*. The tears flowed silently and freely.

Staying at the gravesite long after everyone else had followed the preacher back to the cars, Mike looked down at the cold, metal marker.

"Beth," he prayed, "I know you probably can't understand what I'm about to say, but I need to make a commitment to you. I've done a couple foolish things over the last few weeks. I just want you to know that I'm going to do whatever it takes to make things right and help your mom get better. No matter what, I'm going to rebuild our marriage in honor of you. Goodbye, little Beth."

Mike could feel a kind of lightness, some relief in his burdens and renewed sense of hope in the future. Visions flooded into his mind and tortured his conscience—Beth, Courtney, Jennifer—each with its own unique torment. But as he thought about how things could be made right, he became filled with an excitement for the future.

After several minutes Mike returned to the others and R.T. drove the Spikers back to the house in his black stretch limousine. Mike made himself look R.T. in the eye. Maybe the preacher had a scripture to deal with how a man who had wronged another man could make things right.

+

After the service Amy asked Mike to push her on the swings in the backyard.

"Daddy, why does God let babies die? I thought God loves us."

"Are you sure you're only five years old? Amy, that's a great question that all of us have a hard time understanding. You just have to have faith that God has a plan. Maybe we will all be a closer family as a result of Beth's passing, I don't know. But we have to trust God."

"Is Beth up in the clouds?"

"Well, Amy, we don't know that much about heaven, but we know it is a good place. So if you think the clouds are a good place, then it's okay if you believe that's where God took Beth."

"I hope she doesn't fall. Those clouds are real high." Amy looked up at the sky.

"Don't you worry, the angels would catch her," Mike whispered, following his daughter's gaze heavenward. "Don't you worry."

+

Tuesday, October 20

Mike asked Courtney if he could accompany her to one of the grief recovery sessions at church. Her reaction was the typical shrug of the shoulders that Mike had become accustomed. Courtney had attended sporadically for the past couple of weeks.

On the ride to the church she stared stone-faced out the window.

Mike was one of only two men among the fifteen or so women who made up the group of mothers who had lost a husband or child. As they entered the room, Mike was taken aback by the gaiety of the gathering, women hugging each other and laughing. Courtney was pleasant but not nearly as animated as the others.

The facilitator, Dana, began and asked each participant to take a seat in the circle of chairs in the center of the room. They went around the room and introduced themselves and mentioned the name and relationship of the loved one they had lost.

"I want each of you to tell us how you are handling the clothing or toys or other personal possessions of your loved one." As Dana spoke, she made eye contact with each of the women in the circle. "Who's first?"

"I am probably going about this all wrong," one woman began, "but I closed the door to my son's room back in September and haven't been in there since. I have placed pictures of Conner everywhere."

"Becky, there is no right or wrong way to handle this," Dana responded. "Your reaction is probably one of the most common. How many others have closed the door to their loved one's space?"

"I would if I could, but the daughter I lost shared a bedroom with her sister," reported one mom, several others nodding.

"I'm just the opposite," another mom said. "I have cleared away every bit of Ronnie's things. My brother came over and we boxed everything up either to go to Goodwill or to be stored in my attic."

"Well, both closing the door or clearing everything out are forms of denial, aren't they? As we discussed, denial is a necessary and normal step in the road to recovery."

Another mother, Cathy, spoke up. "You know, I don't understand how any of you find the time or energy to deal with housekeeping chores like boxing stuff up or even closing the bedroom door. Since the day I lost my little boy, I haven't had the energy to get out of my own way. Listening to all of you each week makes me wonder if y'all even loved the ones you lost, or if I'm the one who has lost her mind.

"I hate myself. I can't even hug my other two kids I'm so mad at the world, at myself…" Cathy started to cry. "I don't know how all of you are so together so quickly. I keep thinking of killing myself…

"I think about taking my husband out with me. He's just like y'all, getting back to work, cutting up with his buddies, laughing as if nothing ever happened. I want to ask him if he ever really loved his son."

Cathy was standing now, crying, her fist clenched. "If little Sam didn't have ear infections and colds all the time I don't think he would have died of the flu. Why was he the only one of the five of us to die? If I had taken him to the ENT specialist like I said I would, maybe he wouldn't have died. But my husband says I always sweat the small stuff, and we couldn't really afford to pay what the insurance wouldn't cover, so I kept putting it off. I hate my husband for being so greedy, and I hate myself for not taking Sam to the doctor. Now my baby is dead and I can't look in a mirror without…"

Cathy broke down, her body shuddering. A couple of the women rushed over to console her. Dana went over to Cathy with a box of tissues and hugged her as she whispered comforting words in her ear.

Mike looked over at Courtney. Her chin was on her chest and she was sobbing. Mike put his arm around Courtney and she looked up into his eyes. Her body was hot and trembling. He kissed her on the forehead and she melted into his arms.

On the way home, Courtney reached over and put her hand on Mike's leg. "Cathy really let go tonight," she said quietly. "We had a lot of that in the early sessions, but I thought everyone who was going to let loose had done so already."

"Not everyone," returned Mike quietly.

Courtney squeezed Mike's leg.

+

A few weeks later, Courtney was beginning to show signs of improvement.

One night she took the time to fix herself up, complete with Mike's favorite perfume, and a sexy top and skirt that she hadn't worn in months. She looked Mike in the eyes.

"Hey, Running Man, what does it take for a woman to get a little attention around here?" she said in her best Mae West voice.

"You look fantastic!" Mike responded as Courtney came close. "And you smell great, too!" Their lips brushed as they held each other's hands. Mike pushed up against her torso and Courtney slowly tilted her head back as Mike tenderly kissed her neck.

They kissed slowly and longingly for several moments, but Mike was distracted by thoughts of his rendezvous with Jennifer and the accusations she raised about Courtney and Tom in Nevis.

"Hey baby, I don't know what's wrong with me. Maybe it's been too long, I forgot how to do this."

Courtney looked into his eyes, wondering. "Awe, I know how to take care of that!" Courtney let her hand roam seductively.

"No, I think this may be a good time to ask you something that's been bugging me for a while, since before the epidemic." He guided her to sit on the side of the bed.

Mike took a deep breath. "What happened between you and Tom in Nevis?"

Courtney was visibly taken aback. She looked away and then back.

"In a way, I'm almost relieved that you brought it up, but I wasn't expecting it here and now. It's something I should have told you months ago, but I never felt the timing was right." Courtney looked at him anxiously.

"Remember that last night in Nevis when we had the big beach party? You and your worn-out golfing buddies had gone to bed, but a group of us stayed up and kept on dancing. I had way too much to drink and probably egged him on, but Tom took it the wrong way. He offered to walk me home from the beach pavilion to our villa and I agreed. I didn't say no when he held my hand, and, this is the part that I really regret, I didn't pull away when he kissed me good night.

"Well, he must have figured that I wanted to go further because he got all fired up and started groping and pressing me to go off with him. I had no idea that he was such a pervert, but the way he kept bringing up that you worked for him was really disgusting."

"God, I'm sorry that happened to you" Mike tried to disguise his feelings of betrayal and anger. "Tom can be a real jerk. I'm surprised that he hasn't self destructed at BLuR. He comes off as real slick when you first meet him, but after you work with him for a while, you realize that he's really a conceited blowhard."

"Why did you bring Nevis up, Mike?" Courtney asked.

For a second, Mike considered spilling his guts about Jennifer. But as he faced her, he saw in her eyes a glimmer of hope, a chance for recovery that could be blown to pieces by telling her about his encounter with Jennifer.

"Oh, I just know how more than once you seemed upset by the mention of Nevis. And Tom made some reference to it a while back, so I thought this might be a good chance to get it out in the open." Mike put his arm around Courtney and held her, wondering if she would buy such a thin reason.

"It's nice to have you back, Courtney Spiker," said Mike.

Courtney met Mike's lips with hers and pulled him backward onto the bed.

Chapter 28

Uncovered

Thursday, October 22

Envelopes and packages spilled over the tops of the bins and carts at the main U.S. Post Office in Macon. So few postal employees had reported to work that all they could do was receive and sort letters. Mail had not been delivered to businesses or homes for weeks. Now that the government had lifted the restrictions on the use of highways, businesses and retailers such as grocery stores and gas stations began to reopen. Banks and other commercial enterprises began to slowly resume operations.

As the mail began moving again, the post office was so overwhelmed by the backlog that they called in the military to help sort. Veteran post office employees supervised the efforts of military personnel to sort the mountains of mail.

A young airman from Robins Air Force base was sorting those zip codes that were assigned to the larger companies in Macon such as BLuR Financial. In an effort to process the stacks as rapidly as possible, he looked only at the company name and ignored the address. Unknowingly, he placed a special bank statement that was addressed to a unique post office box in with the rest of BLuR Financial's mail.

The next day Ellen, a member of the BLuR accounting team, sorted the backlog of mail and spotted the unusual bank statement. She couldn't identify it as one of the accounts she worked with regularly and noticed the strange post office box number.

She opened the envelope to find a beginning balance of $102,824 that was brought forward without any activity except a credit for interest. *Funny, such a large balance and so little activity*, she thought. All of the regular BLuR accounts were zero balance, serving only as holding accounts until the funds were swept to the corporate accounts at headquarters every night. She had never seen one earn interest. At first she chalked it up to the general chaos of the past few weeks, but then decided to investigate.

Ellen dialed the bank's local number to find out more about the account. They forwarded her call to the research offices in Charlotte.

"Hello, this is Ellen Tucker. I'm an accountant with the Bio-Lab Research Financial Center in Macon, Georgia. I need some history on one of our accounts." She gave the bank representative the account number and balance.

"Well, about all I can tell you over the phone is that the account was opened on June 15 and the highest balance has been three million dollars."

"Three million even?"

"Yes, ma'am, that's correct."

"Thank you very much. I will be in touch if I need some more information." Ellen tried to keep the shock out of her voice.

Ellen took the statement to her team leader, Debbie. They decided it warranted further investigation, if for no other reason than to lay their curiosity to rest. Debbie called a good friend who worked at the bank locally and asked for the account history.

Debbie's friend at the bank called back a little while later. "Debbie, I've got your information. Dwight Williams opened the account. The three million dollars came in on June 15 by wire transfer from U.S. Commerce Bank in Atlanta. It was electronically transferred out in multiple increments over several days between June 15 and July 1. The fifteen withdrawals were in varying amounts ranging from $300,000 to $500,000. A balance of $96,000 remained in the account at June 30. There has been no activity except interest in the account since June 30. The signers on the account are Dwight Williams, Mike Spiker, and yourself."

Debbie thanked her friend and hung up. She sat back in her chair in shock. She knew that she had not signed any signature cards for this account. Someone had forged her signature. Who? It must have been Dwight. But why?

Could Dwight have stolen the money? Not Dwight! she thought.

Debbie shared the information with Ellen first. She hoped her colleague could see some reasonable explanation before she took it any further. They pondered the situation together, and reached the same conclusion: the statement had been delivered by mistake, and it smelled like fraud.

They both recognized U.S. Commerce Bank as a lender for the leasing portfolio, and found the three-million-dollar note recorded on the books on June 15. It all matched, except for the deposit into the special bank account. Where did all the transfers in late June go? Loans were never disbursed that way. Their suspicions grew with each new discovery.

Who opened the special post office box? The women decided to confide in Trip Lewis, an internal auditor on the financial staff in Macon. Trip tried to figure out a way to trace the electronic transfers from the suspicious bank account. There was no way without Dwight or Mike's authorization, so with Trip's concurrence, they took their findings to Mike early the next morning.

The shock and dismay on Mike's face was dramatic. Mike tried any angle that didn't point to Dwight, but there just weren't any. Debbie showed Mike the entries where Dwight recorded the debt on the company's books without depositing any cash. Creative as it was, the illogical accounting had clearly been intended to cover up a fraud—a three-million-dollar fraud. There were no other explanations.

After all the years they had worked together, he couldn't fathom why Dwight would do a thing like this. He searched his memory for any indications of major purchases or life style changes from Dwight over the past few months, but came up blank. The three million dollars was gone, but Dwight had shown no signs of spending any of it.

Mike thought about how, at the very least, Dwight's career would end, and at worst, he would spend several years in jail. Mike called the corporate lawyer in Wilmington. After more than an hour discussing strategy and legal implications, they arrived at a course of action. The attorney would contact the FBI for assistance. He asked Mike to make sure that no one gave Dwight any indication he had been discovered.

While Mike was on the phone, he had another call. The message on his voice mail was from the police. Mike immediately returned the call.

"Investigations. Daniel's speaking."

"Yes, sir. This is Mike Spiker with BLuR Financial Center."

"Yes, sir. We have a piece of stolen property that was recovered from a series of recent thefts. It's a computer that belongs to you or one of your employees, I believe. The PC contains records for a Dwight Williams, but the only phone number or address we could find was for your company. When I tried to reach Mr. Williams earlier this morning, he didn't answer, and a young lady by the name of Debbie took the message. She called back a few minutes later and said that this may be a matter of company security and that I should talk with you first."

Mike briefly explained the situation to the detective who confirmed that the PC contained information on a number of investment accounts. The officer indicated that they would gladly release the computer to the FBI.

In the several weeks that followed, Dwight had no idea that the company and the authorities were investigating his activities. Things were so disrupted by the flu epidemic that nothing seemed normal or routine.

The stock market began trading again and recovered from its lowest levels during the pandemic, but not nearly to the levels preceding the Manila flu outbreak. Dwight's investments were now up to $2.5 million. He considered returning some money to the company, but decided the risks were too great. More and more he regretted his scheme.

+

Latrice met Zeke Jarrell at the City Auditorium to pack away her files as they dismantled the crisis center.

"I know that the mayor and governor are planning to recognize your efforts, Latrice, but I want you to know how much I admire what you did," said Zeke, extending his hand. "I get paid to react to emergencies, but you did a better job than I could do."

"I got a lot more out of this than I contributed, Zeke. The experience was great, I made a lot of new friends, and my daddy's alive because I ran into Dr. Bagwell."

"I'm not supposed to tell this, but we almost had a second wave pandemic with a new strain of influenza. The military warned us that this could happen. Unbelievable isn't it? Can you imagine going through a second wave that could have been worse than what we went through? Thank God it turned out to be a harmless variety. We got lucky.

"I found out that the military was making plans to take over the crisis center and places like it in other cities if there were any screw ups in operations or if another bout of influenza hit us. Thank God you did such a good job and Mother Nature cooperated. We suffered enough loss without becoming a police state."

"Thank God is right!" Latrice said, shaking her head. "Thanks, Zeke. I hope that the next time I see you it's in an unofficial capacity."

Latrice hugged him, turned and left the building hoping that the next time she visited the Auditorium it was for a concert or graduation ceremony.

+

Dwight's family was slowly recovering from their losses. Time numbed the pain slightly as the family resumed some degree of normalcy. That was until two FBI agents knocked on the door at the Williams house at 7:30 A.M. on Friday October 30.

The agents were polite and professional. They were careful not to alarm Claire and Charles. Dwight successfully concealed his paranoia and feigned surprise. The agents asked to speak with Dwight alone in the living room.

The two agents proceeded to recount for Dwight his every action over the past five months. Their case was airtight. They explained about recovering his PC, how the bank statement went to the wrong address, and how the accountants at BLuR had diligently investigated the unusual account. The phony accounting entries had been discovered. Dwight was amazed at how his own staff had uncovered the fraud without his knowledge. In a twisted sense, he was proud of them.

Dwight had no choice but to reveal his actions to his wife and son. Claire wept. Charles shot him a look that Dwight knew all too well. He had given the same look of disdain to his own father more times than he cared to recall.

The agents accompanied Dwight up to his bedroom to allow him to pack some personal items. They read him his rights. Dwight knew better than to say anything or resist them in any way. At the local FBI offices in the federal building, the agents showed Dwight the evidence. They had copies of bank statements and accounting records. They had seized control of his special post office box and screened all activity without Dwight knowing. They even had pictures of Dwight picking up his mail at the post office a few days earlier.

The FBI interrogated Dwight about the web of investment accounts he had created. They wanted to make sure they had identified everything so that the funds could be returned to BLuR. Under the threat of prosecution and a likely prison sentence, Dwight fully explained the structure of his investments. Ultimately, he submitted a formal confession stating that he had acted alone.

The U.S. Attorney's office had limited resources to devote to white collar crimes such as this case. The pandemic had further increased their caseload and reduced their resources, so they reluctantly agreed to help BLuR bring Dwight to justice in an out-of-court settlement.

Corporate counsel and Mike visited Dwight the next day at the federal courthouse. The lawyer had drafted a settlement for Dwight to sign. Dwight, who had spent the evening in the county jail, was passive but cooperative. The judge had set bail at one million dollars and Claire was so distraught that she hadn't even tried to meet it.

Mike was relieved that the net loss to the company was less than a million dollars in lost capital plus interest. Dwight had only spent about $65,000 of the principal and earnings. If it weren't for the crash in the stock market, the funds would be intact.

Usually soft spoken when under pressure, Mike made no effort to conceal his anger when he was finally given the opportunity to confront Dwight. "I trusted you and you spit in my face. You had people who loved and respected you and you let them down—both at work and within your family. After all the things we've all been dealing with, you have betrayed your friends and family."

"I never meant to steal the money. I intended to—"

"Don't Dwight. I can't listen to your excuses," Mike retorted.

Fury boiled up within Dwight as he stared at the tabletop.

"You're lucky we don't file criminal charges, Dwight. Consider that your retirement gift from BLuR."

Mike and the lawyer left.

+

Mike expected to be criticized by his corporate leaders for not spotting the disappearance of three million dollars. He had missed a chance to unravel the whole thing when he noticed that interest expense was out of sync weeks before, but again, he had misjudged the tip of an iceberg as a harmless block of ice. On the other hand, Mike's team had saved the corporation from a huge loss with great instincts and follow through.

The company had bigger issues to worry about than people like Dwight. Ever since Tom Mumford and a couple other higher-ups at headquarters had died from the flu, the corporate execs were thankful to have leaders in the field like Mike, and more than happy to let them run their operations with even more local discretion.

The settlement required Dwight to repay the money over time, but with interest accumulating on the debt, and with little likelihood that Dwight would get a good job anytime soon, the hole Dwight had dug for himself looked more and more like a grave.

+

Dwight returned home later that afternoon. The house had been a wreck since Claire had taken Charles and moved in with her sister across town.

"I've got some bad news, son," his father called to say.

"Shit, things can't get any worse," replied Dwight, not caring if his father knew about how he lost his job at BLuR.

"Your brother Wayne is dead. The police shot him. They caught him robbing a house, he was part of that Duct Tape Gang that was all over the news."

"Chip off the old block," Dwight said under his breath and hung up the phone.

Dwight's helplessness and anger left him silent. He could almost hear his father laughing, could almost feel the dead puppies in his hands.

Chapter 29

Healing

Friday, November 6

Mike called a meeting of all the BLuR employees on the first Friday in November. It had been six weeks since the flu had struck Macon, and most of the people that were coming back to work were present.

It was the first meeting without Paris and the void lingered like a damp fog. Her favorite music played over the sound system, but missing were the exaggerated laughter, the spontaneous boogey in the aisles, and that look of amazement with mouth and bottomless brown eyes wide open. She was so good at motivating and keeping a meeting on track. Dwight was also good at leading a meeting, but now both were gone. The mood was somber and uneasy.

Mike stood in the front of the room greeting people as they entered. He took a sip of water and glanced over his notes one last time.

The music faded. The lights were dimmed as Mike asked for everyone's attention. He had previously arranged to have a few key people, all comfortable with speaking in public, join him at the front of the big room. Mike also asked his minister to join them.

Mike picked up the microphone. "Good afternoon! I want to officially welcome everyone back to work. We have suffered losses both individually and as a team. We have survived the biggest disaster in modern times and I am truly grateful for each of you. We have all had a lesson in setting priorities in recent weeks as we focused on families and our health, lessons I hope we all carry with us as we rebuild.

"We cannot spend the rest of our lives dwelling on the losses we have suffered. You all know that my family and I are working through the death of my baby daughter, Beth. It is…ah…very difficult." Mike paused a moment. "We cannot become paralyzed by the grief of past losses or the fear of future ones. But it is also important that we pay our respects to those we have lost and recognize the debt of gratitude we owe to those who contributed to the welfare of their fellow citizens." Mike's voice fell off its rising pitch. "Then we must move on. And that is what I want to do this afternoon as a community of coworkers.

"We lost a total of twenty-three BLuR team members over the past weeks. They were friends that will all be sorely missed. This time is devoted to each of them. Please join me in prayer and reflection as we recognize our fallen friends." The four employees who stood on the platform in front of the room began to slowly read each of the names of coworkers who had died. During the several seconds of silence after each name was read, they lit a candle on the table for each individual. "...Lynn Chadwick..." Occasional sobs interrupted the silence. "...Marc Jackson..." Each time the mourners were supported with hugs and whispers. "....Sonya Kaplan..."

After all the names had been read, Mike introduced his minister. The candles flickered as he led the group in prayer.

"Such loss cannot be comforted by my words alone, so let us each go to our Lord in prayer." After a moment of silence, the pastor continued.

"Lord of us all, our grief will be healed only through time and faith in a God that offers hope and light even in our darkest time. With each passing day, the pain of loss will be replaced with the joy of our memories, but until then, we need the love and support and encouragement of one another. Father, as I look around this room this afternoon, I know that You will help us be there for one another. We ask that You guide us through the dark hours and help us reach for Your light. Amen."

Mike concluded the tribute with an announcement. "As we stand together here in this place, twenty-three oak trees are now being planted in the grassy area on the east side of our office facility. Soon a granite marker inscribed with the names of each of our co-workers who died in the pandemic will be erected in this new memorial garden. We have granite benches coming to put under the trees. This Saturday I'd like all of us to help fix up this area. The construction crew will do the heavy work, but I think we would all like to have a hand in fixing up this park in honor of our friends."

Mike paused a moment before beginning the next part of the program. The candles were extinguished and the lights made a little brighter.

"Now it is time to thank those of you who helped others in our community during the crisis. I would like to begin by thanking all of you who stayed at work after the crisis hit and all of you who came back to work before the rest of us could return. We don't have a list with each of your names, but to each of you, please know that we are all greatly indebted. However, we should single out one of you for a special new award.

"I know you would all agree that Paris Hawkins was a very special part of this company. She was here from the beginning, and played a big part in hiring each of you. She helped us all prosper and grow. She served as a role model and mentor, and her spirit lives on today in each of us. She is no longer here in body, but our lives will forever be enriched for the time we spent with her.

"In honor of Paris, we will begin to annually recognize a single employee who displays those same qualities and ideals that Paris practiced and inspired in others.

"The first recipient of this highest award is a lady who has worked side by side with Paris since the early days of this operation. She is an expert. She is a great leader and teacher. She exemplifies the values that make us a special and unique work place.

"When people first started dying of the flu in Macon, there was chaos and despair. This lady found a way to serve the entire Middle Georgia community. She volunteered her days and nights to lead us out of the crisis. Just like she does around here, she not only performed with extraordinary energy, but she provided brilliant leadership. Her actions saved lives, maybe some dear to those of us present here. And she is indeed the only person I have ever met who has been featured on CNN." The crowd chuckled.

"It is my pleasure to announce that the first winner of the Paris Hawkins award is the one we lovingly call the Empress of BLuR, Latrice Rutherford."

Loud applause erupted.

Latrice made her way to the platform from the middle of the floor, through the hugs and cheers of her coworkers.

"Thank you, Mike. Thank you all. This is the best recognition a person can get, from the people that I love and respect as much as my family." Her words were deliberate and her voice quivered as she spoke. "It also means so much to receive an award named for my good friend Paris." Latrice wiped away the tears running down her cheeks and took a moment to gather herself.

"When the flu hit, I did what I had to, things that each of you would have done if you had been in the same situation. I was fortunate to be in a position to help and the community has been generous in thanking me. But getting this award from you is the best." She paused and pressed on.

"I have had some awesome experiences in the past few weeks. I have observed a lot of things and had some time to reflect on how people deal with one another, especially when the chips are down and the world is turned upside down. I want to share a couple thoughts with you if you would indulge me for just a moment.

"The plague taught us just how precious and short life can be. We must use our time wisely. We have to stop worrying about little things that really don't matter and to stop trying to impose our values on others. Everyone has hidden talents—and shortcomings. We have too little time to dwell on differences when the truth is that we all have so much in common.

"Over the last few months, I realize that I allowed skin color to influence how I dealt with people. I had a cause, I was on a mission, but I was focusing on differences. I was causing division and distrust in our work community. Looking back, this was one of the things that Paris tried to teach me, but I wasn't ready to listen.

"I tell you this simply to say that I look forward to working with *all* of you, my brothers and sisters, as we rebuild together for the future and take this organization to a level higher than even we thought possible. Thank you, Mike. Thank you all."

Latrice held up the plaque and looked out into the crowd as the tears streamed down her cheeks.

+

As the room emptied, Jennifer walked up to Mike. Up until now, they had avoided one another except to cooperate on the unavoidable issues.

"That was brilliant, Mike." she said, shaking his hand. "It was moving. Just what the doctor ordered, I think. You're quite a leader."

"Thank you, Jennifer." Mike stared into her eyes, knowing she had more to say.

"I wanted to tell you this as soon as everything became final." She continued nonchalantly, "I'm leaving the company. In January, I'll start working as a consultant for a software firm in Atlanta. It's challenging work and I can commute from Macon. I think we both know that it is time for me to move on.

"R.T. doesn't understand why I would leave BLuR right now," Jennifer continued, "so you might be ready to field his questions next time you see him. I'm sure he'll ask you about it."

Mike shouldn't have been surprised, but he was. He took it as a personal defeat, regretting that the company would pay for his bad judgment.

"I'm sorry, Jennifer. BLuR is really going to miss you. You have the respect and admiration of everyone around here." Mike struggled to find an appropriate response. As a boss, he felt compelled to try to change her mind, yet he knew that to do so was not in either of their best interests.

The silence became awkward.

"You'll have my resignation on your desk before I leave today."

She turned and headed for the door.

Mike watched Jennifer leave the room. He stared with one part disbelief, and another part fascination. He fought at the hope—or was it desire—that this would not be the last time he would see her. But at the same time, he had a tremendous sense of relief.

+

Mike went to Latrice's cubicle and plopped down in the seat across from her.

"Gotcha!" Mike said as if he had just won a big competition.

"Oh, you got me, you certainly did! But you know, payback is hell, baby!" Latrice returned. "Honestly, Mike, I'll never be able to thank you for the honor. That's one of those moments that will replay in my mind for the rest of my life."

"Well, you sure deserved it!" Then Mike looked down, soberly. "Jennifer just told me that she was leaving to go work for a firm in Atlanta. I don't think there's any way to talk her out of it."

"Oh no, that's terrible," Latrice said, wondering if she should ask Mike for a reason, as if she really needed one. "But I'm not too surprised. She's been a different person since we got back and I've seen a big change in the way you two treat each other." Latrice paused for a moment, weighing Mike's reaction. "If you ever want to talk about…anything, you just let me know."

Mike looked at Latrice, then down at his hands. "Paris, Dwight, soon Jennifer…all gone. Can we pull this off, Empress?"

Latrice was not fooled by the way Mike dodged the subject, but she let it ride. "You know it boss! We have others to fill their shoes, people who may even take us to new heights."

"Funny how this epidemic has taken us to a new place so quickly," Mike said reflectively. "It's as if we traveled several years in a few weeks." Mike toyed with a small polished rock that Amy had given him recently for good luck. "People like Dwight self-destruct, people like me muddle through, but people like you seize the opportunity."

Latrice came around her desk and hugged Mike. She put her arm around his shoulder and turned him toward the hallway. "There have been some positive things that have come out of this dark time. Thanks again for the recognition, Mike. Hey, what do you say we take this show on the road? Did you bring your running gear?"

Chapter 30

What Doesn't Kill You…

Dawn, Saturday, November 21

The course that he ran was the same as a few short months before, but the world upon which Mike gazed seemed entirely different somehow. The romantic Southern landscape had lost its idyllic charm. The Southern grasses were brown, the trees had lost their leaves, and even the kudzu had withered back into the ground.

Mike's legs seemed much heavier and his breath shorter than he could remember. He knew that this first long run in months might not go more than a few miles at a slower pace. Instead of the fantasy that he was outrunning death, he now plodded along in hopes of putting some distance between himself and the nightmarish recent past.

Less than three miles from home, Mike's strength gave out and he broke his cardinal rule to never quit running. Bent over, with his hands braced against his knees, he struggled for breath as tears streamed down his face. The physical and emotional pain had built up past the breaking point. All of a sudden he dropped to his knees and wept aloud. Cries of regret and prayers for forgiveness erupted from somewhere deep within him.

It may have been Mike's first real prayer in his life. Slowly the lament gave way to deep shudders as the cold ground beneath him registered against his sweaty body. After a few moments he wiped his eyes with both hands.

Placing his hand on one knee, Mike pushed himself to a standing position. As he raised his head, his eyes fixed on the old wooden cross that stood in front of his family's church. They called it the church at the crossroads.

There was a sign in the church lawn listing the times of services that had a little saying each week for passersby. Mike read the words: *When hope in man ends, faith in God begins*." He stared at the words as he stood there for what seemed an eternity before a passing car stirred him to turn toward home.

Mike walked for almost a mile before resuming a slow jog. By the time he turned the corner onto Rivoli Drive, he had recovered sufficiently to reflect on what had just happened. He had neither words nor previous experience upon which to base the events in front of the church, except that it reminded him somewhat of the times he heard chants at the Indian Mounds. And no one would ever hear about this latest experience either.

As he pounded away the last couple of miles, an old freight train sounded its approach in the distance. The roar of its engine and the clatter of the wheels on the well-worn tracks drowned out the rumbling of an old pickup truck that passed by him in the opposite direction.

+

Dwight's life had unraveled following the humiliation and loss of getting arrested for embezzling. He severed all contact with his father. His son and wife did the same with him. Claire filed for divorce. Claire had even put their house up for sale.

All hope for employment had been destroyed as news of the fraud circulated. Once the gossip hit the north Macon community, it spread like wildfire. Any semblance of dignity that Dwight had enjoyed as an executive of BLuR had now been extinguished. He was back to being irrelevant, the good-for-nothing son of a no-count redneck.

The latest drinking binge had started four days, a case of beer, and two fifths of sour mash earlier. Somewhere along day three Dwight had rummaged through his household furnishings, those few things left that his brother hadn't stolen or his wife hadn't taken, for things to pawn for a few dollars.

Driving around through the night in his pickup truck without any particular destination in mind, Dwight drove past the Waffle House and could almost smell the coffee and bacon from the car. But without any cash, he decided not to stop.

Continuing his old route, the ex-CFO pulled into BLuR, where he parked at the far end of the lot to finish his beer. It was just after 6:30 A.M. At first he imagined that the past few months had never happened, smiling at the thought of exchanging playful banter with Jennifer at the next weekly meeting. Then his thoughts moved to

Mike and the smile vanished. Mike was the undeserving fair-haired boy that got everything he wanted, including credit for all of Dwight's long efforts.

A worker's car pulled into the BLuR parking lot and Dwight drove out the back exit to avoid being seen.

Driving aimlessly, he soon found himself at the entrance of Mike Spiker's neighborhood. He circled the block a couple of times, rehearsing his final confrontation with Mike, hoping to unload his anger and pain. But in the end, he stayed in his truck, his reaction limited to gunning the engine of the old truck in front of Mike's house as he drove off, back to Rivoli Drive.

Elbow out the window despite the cold weather, Dwight began to accelerate along the road when he spotted a runner in his lane a few hundred feet in the distance. *Dumb ass jogger*, he thought. *Why don't you run at the gym, you stupid queer. The streets are for trucks and cars!*

As Dwight approached the jogger, he realized that it was none other than Mike Spiker. *I ought to just run the prick over.*

Mike was looking down to avoid being blinded by the headlamps.

Dwight went around the next curve and pulled into a driveway. He sat there, thinking about whether to turn around. *This is my chance. Without Spiker at BLuR, maybe the next CEO would rehire me.*

Turning back onto Rivoli Drive, Dwight was now headed in the same direction as Mike, but in the other lane and about a half-mile behind him. He locked his elbows and gripped the wheel as he stomped on the gas pedal. Dwight didn't even look at the speedometer as it continued to climb. *Time to get yours, Spiker.*

Mike looked back over his shoulder, trying to figure out what kind of wreck was making all that noise on the road behind him. The train had moved on now, barely audible in the distance.

He didn't realize what was happening until the last few seconds. The noise from the truck was quite loud, as if the driver was standing on the accelerator. Mike turned around to see what the truck was up to when he thought he recognized the old beat up Chevy pickup.

Dwight? Could it be Dwight?

The headlamps were coming right for him, though the pickup was still in its own lane. But something wasn't right—the truck continued to accelerate where most drivers would let off the gas as they approached the curve. Mike wanted to play it cool, but he glanced down at the ground to see whether he should leap right or left if the need arose.

The truck crossed the centerline and headed straight for him. At the last moment, Mike decided to jump from the road and out of Dwight's path. With a running leap, he jumped over a drainage ditch and landed on some grass. He turned to see Dwight's look of panic as he tried to get control of the pickup as it swerved sharply right, then left until it disappeared down the road.

"He's going to kill someone in his own self destruction," Mike said shaking his head, and hoping that he had just witnessed a stupid drunken prank and not attempted murder.

+

As Mike's jog ended near his house, he considered what he would tell Courtney about his morning. He decided to simply explain his delay and disheveled appearance as a result of being way out of shape. *Embrace the precious present,* he thought.

Mike walked up the deck steps and in the back door. He could hear the children laughing and playing in the next room. Courtney was in the kitchen fixing breakfast for the kids. Sporting a new haircut and glimpses of a new outlook, she looked terrific.

"Have a good run?" Courtney asked as Mike entered the house.

"Oh yeah, a memorable run," Mike said with a tired grin, figuring that he might later tell her about running into God and nearly getting run over by Dwight.

"You don't look so good there, Running Man. A bit out of shape, eh?"

"You want to go race?" Mike said, giving Courtney a flirtatious squeeze out of sight from the kids.

"Leave me alone," Courtney said, playfully swatting at Mike. "I have a lot of things to get done around here. You'll get yours later, lover boy."

Mike raised his eyebrows at the prospect. "I'm going to go take a shower. Wonder what it would take to get three eggs over easy around here?"

Epilogue: Twenty Years Later

...Makes You Stronger

Mike's legs wobbled and he panted as if on one of his long runs twenty years earlier, but all he was doing was traveling the few feet from the bathroom back to his bed. Instinctively he looked at the digits on his wrist monitor to check his heartbeat, a measure of which he had become so powerfully aware, but on which he could no longer depend. One hundred and forty beats, elevated but not high enough to adjust his medication.

Years earlier the doctor had diagnosed him with cardiomyopathy. The disease had weakened the muscles in the heart. Over the decades, medical science had perfected valve and vessel replacement, but replacing the entire heart muscle still didn't assure someone in Mike's condition of a full, long life.

His latest attack had struck months earlier and earned him a couple nights at the Medical Center. He came close to death before the doctors stabilized his condition, but the attack left his heart badly damaged. He had been given only a matter of months before another such attack would probably kill him. Courtney arranged for a hospital bed in the first floor master bedroom of their house near a large window.

Fully aware of what was going on around him, Mike was in control when he was awake, but he slept often and for long periods. He stayed in bed except for an occasional trip to the bathroom, the oxygen tubes limiting his mobility.

Emily spent many hours every week helping her mother take care of her dad, and Amy came down from Atlanta about every other weekend. Mike cherished every minute he spent with his family for he knew his time was near.

It's strange how life prepares you for death, Mike thought. *The quality of life declines to the point that death seems almost a blessing, an end to the pain and misery.*

Compared to the way his dad had died suddenly of a massive heart attack, Mike's slow deterioration gave him plenty of time to put his affairs in order, even if the belabored farewells did become painful.

"Are you sure you feel like company today, dear?" asked Courtney, nudging him out of his nap.

"Absolutely," Mike replied with all the enthusiasm he could muster, but his voice was weak. "Just let me rest a few minutes before she gets here."

Mike sat up in his bed and stared out the window. He still insisted on getting dressed every morning in the same basic khakis and button-down shirts that had been his mainstay for as long as he could remember. He had reluctantly retired five years earlier, only after the doctors insisted, but now just getting dressed wore him out.

He watched the rays of sun as they penetrated the glass and warmed the room. He stayed cold most of the time, the effects of increasingly poor circulation. Closing his eyes, he drifted between consciousness and slumber, a zone where he often found his favorite fantasy: running again with long powerful strides, his feet barely touching the pavement. The fantasy was complete with the requisite sights and sounds—dogs barking, cars passing, Yoshino cherry blossoms in full bloom, and the roar of the train in the distance.

"Mike?"

The voice was familiar, and he opened his eyes to a welcome sight, a friend he hadn't seen in months.

"Latrice, it's so good to see you! Come here and give me a hug, girl. Now don't you look great? You must still be running."

Latrice tilted her head down and cocked one eye in his direction. "Only running I do these days is around that company of yours."

"My company? It's been yours for years now. When are you going to let me retire in peace?"

"It will always be your operation to me, Mike." Her voice softened. "You know you left some mighty big shoes for this gal to fill."

"Oh, quit being so humble, Empress. You've taken it to a new level, especially the way you've expanded. I've known since the very beginning that you would run BLuR Financial one day."

"It never would have happened without you, you know. Well, you and Paris."

Her name lingered in the air like heavy perfume. Neither had heard Paris's name in years.

"Boy that brings back some memories, doesn't it?"

Latrice shuddered, "Yeah, ones I have spent twenty years trying to let rest. But then you always told me that that which doesn't kill you makes you stronger. I guess, for once, it turns out you were right. Now, let's talk about you. What are the doctors saying? There must be something they can do. Hell, you aren't that old!"

"I agree with you Latrice, but unfortunately my heart isn't paying one bit of attention. It's just a matter of time I'm afraid. The old ticker is giving out little by little every day. Ironic isn't it? After all those years of trying to stay fit, and I find out there's a muscle that I can't exercise back into shape."

"If you don't mind me saying it, you sound surprisingly calm about it all."

"Well, I guess it's called coming to terms with the inevitable. A sturdy dose of faith helps some, too, you know?"

"Yes, I've known that for some time. I'm glad you finally figured it out, too."

The silence lasted a little too long. They made small talk about Regina and the people at work.

"Well, Mike, I guess I had better get back to work."

"Why? You're the boss now."

They laughed weakly.

"Yeah, and thanks to you I have to set the example instead of enjoying the privileges of the position!" She paused before continuing. "Mike, I know I screwed up a lot in the earlier years."

"Latrice, you don't have to—"

Latrice interrupted. "Let me finish, will you? Jeez, just like old times." She smiled and reached out for his hand. "I know that there were folks out for my head in the days before the whole flu fiasco. And frankly looking back, I can see why. But you never gave up on me. I owe you."

"Latrice, you don't owe me a thing. Except maybe to continue to prove me right and keep growing. You ought to be running the whole corporation; they ought to move headquarters down here for you to run. There is nothing you can't do! Nothing." Mike's breath gave out at the end, and the words escaped on a mere whisper.

"That's why I can only visit with you for short times." Latrice's kidded. "You always have to dangle stars in front of me. Never content. Now I have to try to take control of the whole damn corporation. I was perfectly happy struggling with the position I have."

Mike's tired smile was a clear sign that he was already exhausted.

"But, boss or not, I really need to go. You take care, old friend. I'll see you soon." She leaned down and gave Mike a big, long hug.

"I know that we coworkers aren't supposed to cross the line, but I really got to say something, boss man. I do love you…" her voiced faded and she turned to leave before she cried.

By the time she reached the door, Mike had returned to his beautiful daydream of streets lined with magnolias and kudzu topiaries.

+

Amy Spiker woke to the chirp of the alarm.

"Alarm, off," she said and sprang up from the bed.

"Display daily planner" she commanded, and turned to the large wall monitor to check her day's schedule. She had thought that she and her boyfriend Bill had agreed to ride bikes this morning, but there was no entry on her schedule. "Display mailbox," she ordered. "Open mail from Bill." Bill's smiling face appeared on the screen, stamped with "12:15 A.M. February 19, 2023."

"Good morning, beautiful! I had a great time at the concert last night! I know we talked about riding bikes in the morning, but then I remembered that I have to lead a Sunday school class at nine. Hope we can have dinner tonight. Let me know! Love you!" The picture faded.

She smiled, touched with how lucky she was to have found a guy like Bill. He even enjoyed accompanying her on frequent trips to see her family in Macon. Secretly expecting a marriage proposal any day now from Bill, her reply would be delayed for effect, but a definite yes.

Amy fixed some cereal and coffee, thinking of a creative way to respond to Bill. It wasn't long before her thoughts switched from Bill to her Dad, and her broad grin slowly slipped away. She stared out into space while her hand guided the spoonfuls of cereal into her mouth like a robot. She wondered how he was doing today. They had spent long hours visiting and talking over the phone in the past few months, and their time together had become both urgent and priceless.

"Amy, you know why I don't want to be buried in a graveyard with a headstone?" Mike had asked Amy in one of their recent conversations. "It's because I don't want my whole life reduced to a dash, you know that little line between the date you were born and the date you die. All those years full of love and pain and adventure, all reduced to a half-inch line. If you're going to remember me, it won't be because of a headstone. Just save the money and space, give my organs to medicine and cremate me."

Beyond the obligatory fatherly lectures, the best part of their talks were when Mike told stories about the times when the family was young and what Mike was thinking as they were growing up.

"Do you remember when you were a kid and I used to tell you the rules of life for the Spiker children?" Mike asked Amy on another occasion.

"How could we forget them, you drilled them into our heads every week for years! Finish college, get a good job, get married and then have a family—in that order!"

"See, it worked! And once you start working for BLuR in Atlanta, and marry Bill, then you can have a bunch of kids." Mike smiled as he spoke, but they both knew he was quite serious. "You and Emily have years before you need to start a family."

Amy wished there could be more years, but she knew it was a matter of months, maybe weeks, before her dad would be gone. He would never get to see her children.

+

Amy worked as a graduate student at Georgia Tech's biomedical research facility in Atlanta. Her passion was antiviral medicine. She loved the challenge of identifying microorganisms that would attack infectious agents and eliminate them without damaging the host cells. She and her research team were studying the long-term effects of viral infections. It was becoming increasingly clear that outbreaks such as the Manila flu pandemic had a significant, latent impact on major organs. People may have survived attacks of viruses, but the ordeal would leave their heart, liver, or other organs in poor condition. It wasn't until years later that the impact became apparent.

The entire bioengineering field had exploded following the chemical and biological terrorist threats after 9/11 and the subsequent Manila flu pandemic. Biotechnology was changing the way people lived, raising their confidence that surprise attacks by man or nature would never again kill millions or limit the freedoms of society.

At the same time researchers were rapidly introducing natural agents to counter many harmful effects on the environment, such as algae that ate pollution in rivers, and bacteria that kept insects off crops. Two big local successes in Georgia were the introduction of a caterpillar that ate kudzu and a hybrid wasp that feasted on fire ants.

Amy had grown into a beautiful woman, blessed with her mom's dark complexion and great looks. Her big brother Mark lived in Houston, raising a young family. His work on transmitting solar energy back to earth was so demanding that he seldom had a chance to visit his family back in Georgia. Emily Spiker, now twenty-three, was living at home while attending the medical school at Mercer University. If excellent grades and a passion for the job mattered for success, she was certain to become a world-class surgeon.

+

Amy finished her breakfast. She went to the refrigerator for some juice when she saw the picture of her and Mike at the Indian Mounds stuck on the fridge. The corners were curled and the color had faded. Touching the image of her father gently, she marveled at how incredibly young and handsome he was.

The loud ring of the phone startled Amy from her thoughts. She expected it to be Bill calling before he went to church. It was her Mom.

"Amy, dear, please come home as quickly as you can. The ambulance just picked your Dad up again. It doesn't look good."

"Oh no, Momma! Oh, God! Oh…I'm on my way…Tell Daddy I love him." Amy hung up sobbing. She ran into the bedroom, her hands stretched open above her head, looking up to heaven, "Oh God, please no!"

Packing for a few days in Macon, Amy searched through the clothes hanging in her closet. She broke down and wept when she came to her long, black funeral dress. She had no choice but to pack it. She called Bill to see if he could join her in Macon. He would meet her at the train station.

On the way to Macon, Amy sat in Bill's arms and cried. What would she do without her daddy?

"Oh Daddy, please don't die," Amy whispered to herself. "You did so much for everyone else, and now when you need us, there's nothing we can do. Come on, Daddy, hang in there."

Bill held her close.

Suddenly, Amy felt as if there was a huge crash in her chest. The internal explosion lasted only an instant, but she could feel the percussion. An invisible flash accompanied the boom, but it seemed to reverberate within her. Amy had never felt or experienced anything like it, but intuitively she knew exactly what it meant. Her Daddy's suffering had ended.

Amy arrived at the hospital within an hour to find her mom and a few friends huddled and mourning. Latrice held Courtney and talked to her gently. As Amy approached, Latrice held out a hand, welcoming her into the embrace. "Oh, baby, I'm so sorry." Amy put her arms around her mother and Latrice, their sobs threatening to topple them all.

+

There wasn't much to discuss in the way of funeral arrangements. In typical Mike Spiker fashion, he left detailed instructions regarding his wishes. The memorial service was held at the Methodist church and the music was decidedly upbeat. Hundreds of people filled the church, many of them old timers from BLuR.

R.T. Sanders handled all the memorial service arrangements himself. Though he had long since retired and passed the business on to his son, he insisted on handling everything himself. R.T. and Jennifer came to the Spiker house after the service. Courtney insisted that they help eat the mountain of hams, casseroles, and cakes that everyone had sent over. Jennifer seemed particularly distraught and gave Courtney a long loving hug.

"Mike was a great man, Courtney. He helped so many people live rich, meaningful lives. And what a beautiful family you and Mike have raised."

R.T. handed Amy a simple bronze urn. "These are the ashes of your daddy, Amy. He said that you would know what to do with them."

At first, the instruction puzzled Amy, but soon she grinned through her tears with the satisfaction that she did indeed know exactly what to do. "Thank you, Mr. Sanders."

+

The morning after the memorial service Amy got up at dawn. Her mom was sitting at the kitchen table, drinking a cup of coffee, looking out the window.

Amy hugged her tenderly. "I love you, Momma. We know how much you miss Daddy. We all miss him very much. Mark and his crew will be arriving soon and we're going to have a wonderful family reunion, just the way Daddy would want it. But first, I have something I must do. When I get back we're going to eat 'til we burst. Now you rest up and I'll be back in an hour."

Amy took the urn that R.T. had handed her and sat it carefully on the passenger seat. As she drove across town, she found herself humming her Dad's favorite tunes—Orbison, the Beatles, the Stones.

The gate to the park didn't open until nine, so she parked at the entrance and headed down the path on foot, carefully cradling the urn in her gloved hands.

She stopped first at the Earthlodge mound, standing still to listen for the chants that her father had always said he could hear. But instead, all Amy heard was the voice of her Daddy spinning tales about the Indians and telling her stories about all the things he did when he was her age.

Continuing along the trail, Amy listened to the quiet, reminiscing of happier times. As the sun lit up the morning and warmed the air, she made the long climb to the top of the Great Temple Mound with Mike's words accompanying her all the way.

"Watch your step. Let me hold your hand, baby."

"And over there is the Funeral Mound. That's where all the Indians were buried…it's been so long their bones have probably returned to dust."

The wind was calm and a peaceful silence filled the air. All seemed just as it was when she came here as a child. Amy carefully opened the container full of ashes. She said a silent prayer as she prepared to set her father free. Just as Amy tilted the urn, an ever so gentle breeze came up from behind her and caught the ashes on its wing.

As the dust scattered across the sacred space, Amy could hear her father's voice once again saying, "And over there is the hospital where you were born…"

Amy closed her eyes and drifted back to when she was a little girl. Her Daddy would pick her up and dance with her cheek to cheek, her feet dangling off the ground as he sang softly:

Close your eyes and I'll kiss you
Tomorrow I'll miss you
Remember I'll always be true
And then while I'm away, I'll write home everyday
And I'll send all my loving to you.

Amy looked to heaven, blew her Dad a kiss and turned toward home.

THE END

...earth to earth, ashes to ashes, dust to dust.

Burial Rite from the English *Book of Common Prayer,* taken from Genesis 3:19: "for dust thou art, and unto dust shalt thou return."

Acknowledgements

Half the credit for this book goes to...

My partner Beth Dunwody who wove a story out of a series of write-ups, and put depth and feeling into a mob of facts and sequences. According to our deal I'm the author, but Beth deserves an equal share of credit.

Special thanks to...

All the people who read early drafts and offered suggestions: Sherry Weiss, Trudy Maier, Clarence Violet, Shirley Broadwater, Bill Kaminski, Jay and Julie Maier, Jordy Johnson, George Sledge, Chapin Henley, Danny Highsmith, Peggy Ellington, Jimmy Snyder, Gene Dunwody, Betty Karnay, Elliott Dunwody, Allen Fletcher, Mike and Bonnie Maier, Ad Hudler, Cynthia Glance, Pete Anderson, Gina Fry, Jack Hoeft, Jennie Foulkes, Ed Grisamore, George Mettler (both Ed and George gave me invaluable advice on the manuscript and on getting published), Ed Bond, Jessie Maier, and Debbie McMahon.

And to the employees at IKON Office Solutions in the 1990s who inspired me so much, especially Nancy Sheppard, Nancy Deile, Susan Morrow, Gisele Harris, Lisa Bryant, Shirley Scott Smith, and Rosa Hawes.

Once the initial writing was done, many thanks to...

Kevin Manus for editing, Mary Frances Burt for designing the cover, Debbie McMahon for the drawings, Steve Schroeder for the photo, Nanette Jaynes for editing and Chris Rennie for his help in publishing.

-RM